HIS ANGEL 1

# His ANGEL



## H.L. PACKER

# READER NOTE

Please note, The Sect and Her Devil should be read ahead of this story. The Sect is available for free here: https://dl.bookfunnel.com/t4aqupbw3, and Her Devil is on all retailers: https://books2read.com/HerDevil

# RECAP, TIME!

So, for those of you that aren't following straight on from the last book and have had a little gap in between, I figured that a recap might be helpful. If not, feel free to skip straight to chapter one.

In 'The Sect' we met our four heros; Nick and Jacob Barrett—the twins—Leo Windsor, and Wyatt Chambers. We meet them at their induction to The Sect, where they have to fight for their position, and fight they do.

The opening for Her Devil introduces Ivy, our heroine. Here she has a fall out with her father when he demands that she puts her dreams on hold and attends Pendleton Prep for a year. She's not happy about it, but for the first time, she sees the cracks in his façade, the masks he wears.

Luckily, she gets to take her bestie with her, and her and Tamsin set about their trip to Pendleton Prep. On arrival they find out they're not in regular accommodation, but some kind of pool house behind a huge stone building.

The two of them meet some hot guys, get an invitation to a party, and Tamsin gets hot and heavy with one of them at the Pendleton Prep mixer. Ivy's ex makes an appearance, and he warns her away from Leo.

She finds out that Nick and Jacob are twins, enjoying a kiss with Nick who drives her completely crazy, and not always in a good way, before some dresses arrive at the house ahead of the party. When they're picked up and taken to an abandoned church, shit gets weird.

Ivy ends up paired with Nick and Wyatt, Truth and

Dare, Devil style, being the event of the evening, before she shares a kiss with Wyatt on the way home. The boys are checked up on by The Sect, the noose tightening around them all.

Ivy finds Nick beaten up on the way back from an ice-cream trip, and that ends up with them getting sexy in the woods, the adrenaline doing a number on both their inhibitions, but when she realises what she's done, she tries to push him away. Easier said than done.

When the girls are pulled into their new job for The Sect—the Big Sister project—things start to get really busy, and not just because the girl she's paired with seems to hate her. George is removed from the competition, and someone is watching them, and a few days later, they find out someone has targeted Stephanie.

Oliver, not being one to take these things laying down, rallies the Devils and makes an example of him. The Angels are not to be messed with. And Wyatt and Nick formulate a plan to keep Ivy safe.

# ONE

## Ivy

I don't know if it's the shakes, or the racket, that wakes me from the emptiest sleep I've ever known. It's not deep in that vivid dream kind of way, it's just void of anything, and as I slide my phone off the nightstand and look at the harsh numbers that flash back at me, I can't believe it's been so long.

"What the…" I start, the words echoing around my head causing me to wince, only exacerbating the tremble in my extremities.

Curling back up under the covers with my phone is the only option as I will the contents of my stomach to stay put, not sure I could make it to the bathroom if I had to. *What the hell is going on?* The rest of the girls laugh outside the room, a million miles away, and yet it's loud enough for me to hear over the sound of blood rushing around my body.

What the hell is this? I didn't even drink, did I?

Attempting to rack my brain through what happened the night before gets me nowhere.

A party, with Tamsin. I think.

Turning over stops the shivering momentarily, until it starts back up again, the noise in my head easing slightly as

I try to focus my mind.

The party with Tamsin.

The moment with Leo.

*"I don't want to take anything. I want it to be given, freely and willingly."*

Heat rushes through my veins, his tone practically reverberating through my body as I try to push further through my memory. *I came home.* Or as far home as this place has come to be. But I didn't stay here.

The memory hits me like a freight train, the message from Tamsin, the panic as I rushed from the house and into the night. Quickly, I flick to my messages, checking the chain with Tamsin, but it's not there. The last message reads:

**T: Staying with Taylor, see you tomorrow x**

There's no mention of me turning up afterwards, nothing of the panicked message that had me rushing there in the first place.

Oh, God.

The shorts. Leo's face. And then… the masks.

Shooting up out of the covers, my stomach rolls but holds, the shakes almost gone and the blinding headache finally receding. It's not a hangover, I'm one hundred per cent sure I didn't drink, so this must be the after-effects of whatever *they* gave me.

I look around the room, attempting to work out what's different, what's moved, but everything looks the same. And as I physically check over myself, all my fingers, toes, arms and legs are attached. I'm still alive.

The rush of relief is unexplainable.

Surely, if I'd been somehow maimed, or killed, I'd have realised it before now? Unless I was dead, I suppose. Fuck, clearly my head is more messed up than I gave it credit for.

The familiar scent of my favourite dark roast finally registers, and before I fully realise it, I'm rolling myself out of bed and dragging on the closest dressing gown, heading to the bathroom. The room wobbles slightly as I get up, using the edge of the doorway and the counter to catch my balance.

I use the toilet and wash my hands, and that's when I notice it; sleek black leather wrapping around my wrist. *Where did that come from?* There's no buckle, no stud to pop open, and as I push it, it won't fit over the curve of my hand.

The coffee just a few steps away is completely forgotten as I run my fingers over the logo, the crest familiar, the lions on either side distinctive, as is the gold rivulet that runs around the band. The Devils.

My stomach rolls again as memories flash infront of my eyes.

The car sliding to a stop, the black figure outlined against the darkness of the night.

The glass.

The black mask. The gold slash running left to right.

*"You're mine now, sugar."*

There's only one person that calls me that.

Only one person that would be cocky enough to stand infront of a moving vehicle knowing it would stop.

*That absolute wanker.*

Who the hell does he think he is and how the fuck can

I get this off?

Twisting and turning it gets me nowhere, and as I attempt to slide it over my hand, I'm met with a more than frustrating amount of resistance. My hand bangs on the side of the counter, the bracelet still in place as that frustration burns into anger.

The door slams into the stop as I force my way back into the bedroom, finding leggings and a top and throwing them on as quickly as I can manage, all thoughts of the after-effects long gone, thank God.

I know one place I'll be able to get answers, and it's not here.

"Nice of you to join us," Stephanie comments from the dinning table, looking up from her laptop, but her smile and cheery attitude sit frozen on her face as she absorbs the fury rolling off me.

It's with stunned silence they sit there, watching me throw my trainers on and stalk out the front door, slamming it closed behind me. I'm sure they'll all be scrabbling to get their shoes on and find out what the hell is wrong with me as I pass Penelope's car—parked perfectly, with not a scratch, dent, or broken window in sight.

Of course.

With a growl, I stomp down the driveway to the obnoxiously large wooden doors.

Ringing the doorbell is not nearly satisfying enough as I hammer my fist against the door, willing someone to come and open it quicker.

"Woah, girl. What's got you so twisted up?" Oliver asks as he peels the door back.

"Where is he?" I growl.

"So lovely to see you, Ivy. Why don't you come in?" he asks innocuously as I barge past him.

"Where is he?" I repeat.

"And who exactly are you looking for?" he asks, a mischievous smile on his face. "Wyatt and Jake are downstairs, and Leo's in the den, I think." Holding up my wrist is the only answer I can manage as he grins before calling out loudly, "Nick, you've got company."

"You knew," I hiss, narrowing my eyes at him. *It's not an accusation when it's the truth.*

"Sure thing, princess. That shit got me so fucking hard."

"You're disgusting," I dismiss, heading past him and into the entranceway proper. *Where the fuck is he?* "Nick," I call loudly, hoping he'll hear and finally come my way.

He's always so irritatingly there when I don't want him to be, but now that I'm looking for him, he's nowhere to be seen, and it's not his broad shoulders that pop out of the den at the sound of my voice, it's Leo's, his crystal blue eyes looking me over with concern.

"He's in the gym with Jacob and Wyatt, what's up?" he asks, seemingly attempting to find a physical reason for my agitation as he looks me up and down, searching for damage.

"Gym, what gym?" I ask, stomping around the small space.

It's not tiny by any stretch of the imagination, but way too small to hold in all the anger coursing through my veins right now.

"Downstairs, I'll take you."

Concern lines his eyes as he heads towards the changing room, pushing open a door I didn't notice last time we were here.

"Do you have to?" I clip out at Oliver, who's practically walking on the back of my heels.

"Oh, I'm not missing this one, sweet cheeks."

It's just my luck that the doorbell goes, probably the rest of the girls finally catching up with me, but at least he hurries away, Leo and I heading down the stairs to a huge and fully-equipped gym.

Nick and Jacob don't even look up, too busy hitting each other to notice anyone else even exists as I storm across the room to their stupid ring.

"What the hell is this?" I yell, holding my wrist up.

It takes a minute for either of them to acknowledge the words, or the fact I'm even here, Leo taking hold of my arm and looking over the offending item, irritation flicking over his features as we wait.

"Well, who wants to explain?" I demand.

"It's not as bad as it looked," Wyatt starts, appearing around the side of the ring as the twins finally give it up, unstrapping their gloves and coming our way.

"You were in on this?" Leo asks, his disbelief as clear as mine. "*Him* I can believe this of, but you?"

The accusation is clear, the threat less so, but there's no mistaking it's there.

"What the fuck is this?" I seethe, more than ready for the answers nobody is giving me as I look at Nick and Jacob for an explanation.

"It's security," Nick replies, keeping the safety of the

ropes between us. "Things are getting tricky around here and we wanted to know you'd be safe."

"We?"

"I suggested that claiming you would be a good way to ensure you're not a target for The Sect, or the rest of the guys here," Wyatt admits. His hand reaches for me, but as I pin him with a thunderous glare, he retreats. "The execution of that… was not my doing."

Leo raises an eyebrow.

"Things got a little out of hand," Jacob admits, just as the stairwell fills with chatter, Oliver and the girls finally catching up with us. Not that I care.

"Out of hand?" I screech, jumping up and climbing through the ropes, slapping him in the chest. "Someone pulled me from the car by my hair. By. My. Hair."

The hissed intake of breath from the stairs would be funny if it weren't drowned out by the rumble of disapproval from Leo, and it placates the rage coursing through me in a way that I can't even describe, Jacob ducking through the ropes to intervene as Leo draws ever closer to Wyatt, a beast stalking his prey.

"It wasn't supposed to go down that way," Nick attempts to explain, holding his hands out placatingly. "You were the one that locked the car doors, so what were they supposed to do?"

"I nearly hit you with a car, in the middle of the night and it was pitch black. What did you think I was going to do, jump out and check you over in your creepy fucking mask? You must be out of your goddamn mind."

"Got you safe though, didn't it?" he replies smugly.

I barely even register doing it, but the sound of skin hitting skin echoes around the shocked silence of the room, my hand smarting as his face reddens, the imprint of my palm crystal clear on his skin.

Someone whistles behind us.

All I see is the quickening of his breath and the darkening of his eyes, fear quickly replacing the anger that rushed through me barely seconds ago as he replies, "You're fucking welcome."

He brushes past me, stepping out of the ring silently with his head held high. *And I thought Spencer was an infuriating pompous ass.*

"This was your idea, you deal with her," he clips out at Wyatt, shoulder-checking him as he stalks across the room.

"You fucking—" I can't even manage words as I lunge after him, ready to do as much damage as I can until Leo picks me up as I attempt to get past him, "Woah there, angel," tumbling from him.

Infuriatingly, Nick doesn't even look back as he grabs a shirt from the side and pushes past everyone else to make his way back upstairs.

I'm still kicking and attempting to break free when Leo's words finally make their way through. "Angel, you've got an audience."

"Who cares?" I snap. "You lot have made us all a target by taping our pictures all over campus, and now I've got a bullseye on my damn wrist. And *he* didn't even have the decency to talk to me about it. I just wake up with the thing. No recollection. No explanation. Full body shakes and a headache like I've never had in my life."

The fight falls out of me as I rant, Jacob getting rid of our captive audience as the adrenaline wears off and I crumble, not even acknowledging the silent conversations happening over and around me.

"If Jacob and Wyatt did this, there's a good reason, angel," Leo says quietly, placing me back down as he rests against the edge of the ring. "We just need to allow them to explain."

He pulls me back against his chest and wraps his arms around me, the security blanket I didn't realise I needed.

"It wasn't supposed to go like that, and you can rest assured Jasper got what was coming his way for handling you like that," Jacobs says. "I'm sorry you got hurt."

"You think I'm pissed off because I got hurt?" I huff out a disbelieving laugh. "I was terrified. I thought you all came to kill me." The admission falls from my lips in a whisper, Leo's security tightening around me.

"We would never," Wyatt says soothingly, reaching out for me once again. "We would never hurt you. You have to believe that. Nick might be hard-headed, but he cares more about you than you give him credit for."

"Fucking looks like it," I clip, my breath shuddering in and out as I push back the fear and panic clawing at the back of my throat.

His gentle hands come to my forearms, carefully drawing me from the security of Leo's embrace to face the truths that he has to offer.

"How do I get it off? Take it back. I don't want this."

The admission is bitter on my tongue, because part of me does want it. I do want to be cared for and protected. I do want whatever this magnetism is between Nick and me. But I don't want it to be chosen for me.

"Nick claimed you in front of two of The Devils, there is no taking this back. Your life is now intertwined with his," Wyatt explains softly. "Can I take you somewhere, show you something?"

I eye him warily through my lashes, not sure who or what in this absurd game I can believe or trust.

"Please?"

Acquiescing, I take a step towards him.

"I'm coming too," Leo demands from behind me, his protective heat a balm I didn't realise I needed.

I trust Wyatt.

He's kind, sweet, and he makes me laugh.

He's broken the tension and soothed my pain unintentionally and without looking for anything in return on more than one occasion.

And then, there's this.

It might have been Nick bathing in my fear and blossoming under its weight, but it was Wyatt that set it all in motion, Leo willing to protect the pieces left at the end of the day.

Mostly, I want to curl up and hide in my bed, hoping that a new day will bring a whole new perspective, new thoughts and new ideas that will make this okay, but without this explanation and understanding, how can that ever come?

"It's fine, I'll go," I agree with a deep breath.

"Why don't you stay with me?" Jacob asks, looking at Leo hopefully. "I can explain…"

The flare of Leo's agitation certainly doesn't have Jacob

shrinking back, though. If anything, he stands taller, his confidence bigger than the genteel placating tone his words come out with, until he says, "Or you could tag along with them like the left-out lovesick puppy you're acting right now."

I can almost imagine him flicking his hair over his shoulder and storming out, much like his brother just did, but jealousy is an interesting look on him.

My amusement falls out on a laugh as I step towards Wyatt, not quite ready to take his hand but feeling more prepared for the explanation I know is almost here.

"Get my number from Tamsin and text me, I'll let you know I make it back safely," I say to Leo. "And hear him out. If I'm going to, then you should too." I squeeze Leo's arm reassuringly, with a smile that doesn't meet my eyes, before making my way to the stairs, Wyatt hot on my heels.

"Hey, what did I miss?" Tamsin asks as I make my way back through the entrance way. "Apparently, even best friend status doesn't get you access to whatever's going on down there."

She steps out of one of the rooms, her dark hair sleep mussed despite her flawless makeup. Taylor can't be far away. It hits me like a sledgehammer that he used her last night, to get to me, and she doesn't even know—clearly doesn't remember.

There's no point in bringing it all up now though, starting an argument between them really isn't fair. I know misery likes company, but it's too far for me.

"I'm fine, it's nothing important." I sigh, exhaustion coming over me. "Wyatt's just taking me for some fresh air,

I'll fill you in later."

Wyatt appears behind me, a bottle of orange juice in one hand and a couple of waters in the other before he ducks through a doorway.

"Are you sure you're okay?" she asks, seemingly picking up on the tension. "I can give you a hand with that paper if you need it?" *The out she thinks I need.*

"It's not the paper, but thanks. I'll catch you in a bit." I follow the direction Wyatt went, through the doorway and into a garage, catching the flicking of the lights on his Alpha Romeo before climbing in.

# TWO

## Nick

The door slamming does nothing to ease the rage that courses through me, and neither does touching the heated skin of my cheek.

She hit me.

And she fucking meant it.

Sure, I didn't leave flowers and a welcome card on her nightstand, but I was sure she'd see the good in what I did. *Maybe I should have let Wyatt be the one to do it after all.*

Yeah, that was never going to happen.

She's mine.

I know it.

She knows it.

Everyone else knows it.

And now, so will The Sect.

I am not going to be one of the guys disappearing without a trace. Not now, not ever. Linking her with me will keep her safe, and stop her from ending up in an unmarked grave one day.

But no, she doesn't care about that.

She only cares about the fact that I didn't wine her and dine her before making her mine. *Like she'd even let me if I tried*. I'm not here to get in her pants at any and every given opportunity, and I thought I'd proven that already.

She'll forgive me when she realises, won't she?

It wasn't supposed to happen that way, but once it did, how could I not take advantage of her vulnerability? It was like a drug I couldn't get enough of. My heart pounded as she fought back, or tried to, and as her tears fell, I needed a taste, craved it, and when her breathing evened out and she collapsed into my chest, I was done for.

There was no way anyone else was going to end up anywhere near her. Wyatt and Oliver helped me to get the wristband safely secured and get her home without disturbing any of her housemates, while the guys got the car taken care of.

She wasn't under any longer than she needed to be, and I spent way more time than I should have watching her on the camera to make sure she was okay. Yes, I'm aware that's a complete invasion of her privacy, but watching her sleep from the side of the bed was not an option.

The stress ball is in my hand and flying towards the empty bed before I even consider that I left Jacob downstairs with Ivy, and Wyatt hasn't come back up yet. *Where is everyone?*

With a sigh, I grab the ball, placing it in the basket on the bedside table before heading to the shower. As much as I'd love to jack off to the thought of Ivy here and excited about being mine, all my mind can conjure up is the hurt look on her face as she demanded answers from me. Giving up, I get clean and dry, heading back into the bedroom, and yet there's still no sign of Wyatt.

A search around downstairs doesn't show him, only providing more questions from the girls now taking residence in the den. At least I find out Wyatt's taken her out, to show her what we were trying to do, as I seek out Jacob. He'll have answers. Or he'll be able to do something about the anxiety that swarms through my stomach, and yet, he's nowhere to be found either.

Heading back upstairs, I knock on his bedroom door twice before calling out to let him know it's me. The door opens, his hair mussed as I push past him, my frustration finally spilling over.

"Do you think this was a mistake?" The question is out before I can even consider it as a thought.

"Yes," not being the answer I expected, although, as I turn and take in Leo's comfortable laze on my brother's bed, I guess I should have.

Wow.

He was supposed to be interested in Ivy. Someone else chomping at the bit to get near her, to take her away, and yet here he is, way too comfortable in my brother's space. Whilst part of the plan was always to get him away from Ivy, I never really considered how that would look when he moved on to my brother.

Interestingly, Jacob gives him some kind of look that I can't decipher, sighing heavily.

"Well, that didn't take you long, did it?" I clip out, dismissing him.

"I wouldn't have stood by you if I didn't think it was needed," Jacob says, attempting to intervene. "But I don't like how it went down."

"I—"

"And I know it wasn't your intention," he continues, cutting me off. "But I can see why Ivy's upset, and so can you. That's why you're pacing like a caged animal."

"I am not," I say, before realising he's right and pulling the chair out from his desk.

He gestures to Leo for one of the balls on the bedside table, and he grabs one, giving it a testing squeeze before launching it in my direction.

"Hey, what was that for?" I ask, throwing it back.

"You didn't even apologise to her," Leo says from the bed.

I cut a glare in his direction, waiting for Jacob.

Why doesn't he just get rid of him? This is nothing to do with him anyway.

"He's right," Jacob admits, sending the ball back my way. "You can't just keep pushing like this all the time."

"Where's Wyatt?" I ask, deciding I'm not going to get the support I was looking for with Leo here puppeteering my brother.

"He's taken Ivy to the church," Jacob replies.

"Right." I nod, knowing there's nothing else I can do now. I just have to wait. I throw the ball back to him. "Guess I'll leave you guys to it then."

"Stay," Jacob says as Leo huffs an unimpressed noise out.

Both Jacob and I glower in his direction, but his only response is to roll his eyes. *Wanker.*

"I'm already interrupting," I counter, getting up. "Catch you in a bit."

I leave the two of them to it, a strange mix of disappointment and irritation tumbling around my system as I throw my trainers on and head out for a run.

I could head back downstairs and pummel the miles out on the treadmill, but there's a reasonable chance someone would come and try to make conversation. Then again, Wyatt is out with Ivy, Leo and Jacob are holed up in his room, and with two already gone and the girls to entertain, how many does that leave to interrupt?

The crisp afternoon air makes the decision easy for me. I might not make it as far, but there's something about being alone, your brain pushing through what ails you as your body heats against the cold, placing one foot in front of the other with no goal or destination in mind.

# THREE

"**I** don't know how you put up with him."

"Give over," Jacob replies with a weary smile, putting the chair back as I rest against the headboard. "You're just pissed off he beat you to it."

He settles over my thighs, worrying the edge of my shirt in his fingers.

"That's not fair, and you know it."

Yes, I want Ivy, but she's not the only one I'm interested in, and he damn well knows it.

"Really?"

His hazel brown gaze connects with mine, the green outline as stunning in the late afternoon sun as I'm sure it would be in the mid-summer heat, although I'd have an excuse for peeling the clothes off him in the latter.

"I don't like people making decisions for others," I argue. "There's no need for it. Why not just give her the choice and let her choose him? Because he knows there's a chance she won't. She'd pick Wyatt, or me, or you, or just about anyone else."

"But she didn't—"

"No, because she didn't get a choice."

"Leo," he says with a sigh. "If she really wanted to cut it off, do you think anyone could stop her?"

I shrug my shoulders, avoiding his gaze and the logic he's trying to ply me with. "Can we talk about something else?" I grumble.

I'm so sick of talking about his brother and the beyond stupid thing he's done. Not only has he hurt someone I care about, but he's also taking the limelight right now, and I'm not here for that. No, I'm here for Jacob and the softness I've never found before.

"What did you have in mind?" he asks, his eyelids fluttering as I grip his hip points, grinding him against me.

"You didn't tell him," I say quietly, a vulnerability to the words that I wasn't expecting.

I never thought he would say anything, not ot because he's ashamed of who he is, but because he knows deep down exactly how Nick feels about me, how he'd feel about us together. His broad shoulders loom over me, blocking out any thoughts other than the man in my hands.

"I will," he promises, rocking against me, his cock rubbing up against mine in a delicious agony that forces a rumble from my chest.

"I thought that was supposed to be a one-off, one and only, never to-be repeated performance?"

The memory of his lips against mine flashes before me, the heat of the fire at our side as the night blankets us in a secrecy we don't need to confirm with words. Just a taste, just a touch, just making good on the promises we've made silently for weeks.

"Yeah, well…" He shrugs, the cutest blush I've ever seen creeping across his cheeks.

Leaving his hips, I trail one hand along his jaw, the other coming to the front of his shirt to drag him down against me, a surprised gasp escaping him. His fingers push the fabric of my shirt up, toying with a nipple whilst tracing patterns across my chest.

"God, you make me feel like a kid again," I admit as his mouth hovers just inches from mine.

"Are you going to kiss me or what?" he goads.

"Maybe I'm still mad at you, maybe you've got some making up to do."

He kisses the corner of my mouth, placing closed-mouth kisses along my jaw before his wet tongue lathes a path to my ear, dragging the lobe with his teeth. A shiver of arousal ripples over my body and goosebumps erupt in its wake. His shirt disappears next, and mine follows swiftly after.

"What did you have in mind?" he rasps, the promise in his words worth taking him up on.

My hand slides through the hair at the back of his neck, gripping it firmly and pulling him back down to me, forcing his lips against mine. He opens eagerly, his tongue exploring my mouth as he braces his hands against my chest, finding him as hard as I am when I trace the length of him through his jeans.

Dragging him off takes more control than I thought I had, his eyes fluttering open in confusion. "Don't you dare leave me out of this shit again, brother or not. You'd be lucky to sit for a week once I'm finished with you."

His eyes flare, far too much excitement in them for the

punishment I'm promising. Voices echo from the corridor, someone else coming or going. Tapping his hip, he climbs off me, grabbing our shirts from the floor.

"Come on."

He intertwines our fingers, shoving his phone in his back pocket before following me out and down the hall. Luckily, we don't cross paths with anyone else in the time it takes us to change rooms and lock the door. I'm so sick of watching and waiting, trying to tiptoe around everyone else.

Even if this is just another one-off for him, I'm going to drag out every last second of pleasure that I can from his body. Unfastening my belt, I gesture to his pants and rumble, "Take them off."

He's quick to follow instructions, and I can't help but stare at the myriad of artwork along his chest. It doesn't extend further down his body, save for the lone design on his left thigh, and he smiles as I drag my belt free and wrap it around his wrists, walking him back over to the bed and dropping the loop over the central knot of the metal headboard.

"God, you're beautiful," I comment as his muscles strain with the angle.

His arms bulge, his abs contract, and his dick twitches behind the constraint of his boxers. *There's more than one way to guarantee he does exactly what he's told.*

Sliding my shirt off, I pause, my gaze flicking up to his through my lashes. "Do you trust me?"

His breath hitches and his feet flex nervously. I'm not sure how far this is going to go, but I can't go any further without his permission—I won't.

"Yes," he replies on an exhale.

"Safe word?"

"Watermelon."

I nod.

Odd, but I guess you're never going to say that in error. Nobody ever screamed *'oh, watermelon'* in ecstasy.

"Your brother is being a selfish prick."

Unfastening my top button draws his attention exactly where I want it, and when my jeans land on the floor, my hard cock jutting out, his eyebrow raises as if to say, *That's what you want to talk about right now?*

"Get's you hard though, doesn't it?" he asks with a quirk of an eyebrow.

Squeezing around the base and pulling my way to the tip doesn't ease any of the pent-up energy I'm currently holding back. Weeks, months, I've been waiting for a way to get my hands on him, longing glances and secret touches aside. This game we've been playing has been a tease of epic proportions, but he's here and offering an apology, one I'm more than happy to take.

"Absolutely not. But you do."

They might be identical twins, but there's nothing the same about them, aside from the looks, and whilst that look is hot as sin, one I'd kill and one I'd fuck.

"Shuffle down and open your mouth."

I was more than happy to get to my knees for him, to apologise for attempting to protect him when it wasn't needed. I know he's more than capable of doing that, and he made it oh-so very clear after the fact, but now, I get to enjoy him instead.

He awkwardly shuffles down the bed, the leather pulling tight around his wrists as I climb over him, swiping a lazy tongue over his nipple before straddling his chest and resting my dick against his tongue. He laps and lathes, his hot mouth wrapping around my length as he sucks me deep before pulling back and repeating the maddening motion.

He could pop the belt off its hook if he wanted to, untwist his hands and be free in nothing more than a matter of seconds, but he doesn't. He relinquishes control over to me so beautifully that I can't help the praise that falls from me.

My fingers slide through the length of his hair, holding him in place while I pump my hips, his watery hazel eyes looking up at me through thick dark lashes. It takes me back to the very first time I saw him, the same pleading look he gave me at the fight, and this is what I'd wanted then, what I'm finally getting now.

This tangled tease we've been playing for months is coming to an end, we're both getting what we couldn't admit to each other we wanted, and it feels good, so fucking good. My spine tingles, my balls drawing up, as I come hard down his throat.

"I should leave you like that," I say with panted breaths as I collapse back onto his thighs, his cock rigid behind the strained material of his underwear. "That would teach you a lesson about doing this shit without me."

His chest bounds almost as rapidly as mine does as he waits to see where I'll go next and if I'll really leave him this turned on with no satisfaction.

"I could have left you too," he comments quietly.

"When you pushed me aside like a defenceless child."

"I apologised for that."

"And I apologised for this."

He's right, and holding onto this would be unfair.

Sliding back off his chest, I settle between his thighs, running the tips of my fingers down his chest and grazing my nails over his nipples. His hissed intake of breath proves just how sensitive they are right now, and I can't help the smile that tugs at the corner of my mouth.

His cock springs free as I slide his underwear down, opening his thighs to sink my teeth into the firm skin on the inside as he groans, the sound tingling deep in my belly. He tenses and relaxes, a groan slipping free as I wrap my hand around his length and pump him hard before slipping him into the heat of my mouth.

Being tied up and tangled in my ministrations has him wound up and well on the way to satisfaction, and as I pull back, rolling his balls in my other hand as I jerk him harder and faster, he stutters and bucks, spilling over us both.

Licking the tip, I clamber off the bed, grabbing a towel from the bathroom before wiping my hands and bringing one for him, expecting to find him sated and comfortable on the bed, only to find him busy unfastening the belt with a smug smile.

"Have you calmed down now?" he asks, accepting the towel as I gather up his clothes for him, sliding my jeans back on.

I could lay down with him, slide our sweat-slicked skin together as the two of us cuddle up, but that's only going to end up with us going further and I'm not sure he's ready for that, not yet.

I watch him put one item of clothing on after another, the tattoos disappearing one by one as he waits for an answer.

I ponder my words carefully.

I'm here to win this, there's no other choice. And Jacob would arguably be a much better partner for me than Ivy, on a personal level. There's understanding there that she'll never completely get, as well as the fact that he's hot as fuck. But she was right last night, there's something between us too.

Is there a way I can have them both?

# FOUR

## Ivy

Liselle's SUV blocks the entrance, Wyatt's tyres crunching along the gravel as he pulls up in front of it.

"I guess that means I'm late," I say with a sigh.

I'm tired, fucking exhausted really.

Shitty sleep, the after-effects of whatever they used to subdue me, and the complete emotional overhaul. The whole thing has me feeling completely fucked.

Numb.

Empty.

Vacuous.

"I'm sorry we didn't make better time," Wyatt replies, his hand coming to my thigh.

I didn't realise just how cold I was feeling until the heat of his touch spreads warmth across a tiny patch, a circle of life blossoming in what feels like my cold and empty soul.

"Ivy," he says, calling me from a million miles away. "Ivy, I know it's a lot to take in, but you need to get it together right now."

His tone catches me off guard, the gentle soothing

sound traded for something sharper, more demanding. My gaze comes to his, but it doesn't focus, words are coming from him, but they never register.

*"It's a garden of remembrance, of sorts," he explains. "I'm told the wildflowers are beautiful in the Spring."*

*The dead patch of dirt doesn't look beautiful right now, and a chill creeps over my spine that I can't control. It looks dead, empty, and vacuous.*

"I'm going to be sick."

My stomach twists, a cold sweat breaking out as I open the door to his car and heave the contents of my stomach onto the stones beneath. Any benefit from the juice and water has long disappeared, and the reality is that I've found myself in a completely new life and I'm struggling to reconcile the two.

Wyatt rubs circles on my back, pulling my hair back over my shoulder as I fall back into the seat, closing the door again. He hands me a bottle of water, the tepid liquid soothing the burn at the back of my throat.

"I know it's a lot to take in," he repeats. *No shit.* "But those women in there need the security you now have. This puts you ahead. Nick isn't at risk as far as we know, not yet, and if anyone is going to get themselves entrenched in this game, it's him." *Or Leo.* "He's your best bet for security here."

"Good job you all decided that then, isn't it?"

He accepts the water, stashing it in the door bin without reply. I guess being angry is better than being empty.

"I better get in there."

"He cares about you, we both do, and I'm reasonably

sure we aren't the only ones watching your back right now. You've bewitched us all, but just watch yourself in there," he warns. "I know Tamsin is your friend and you've built relationships with these other women, but at the end of this year, where do you want to be?"

In the house, or the ground?

Those are the words he doesn't say, but that's what he means.

"It's time to put on your game face, babe. You can be scared, upset, angry—"

"Empty," I add.

"Empty," he repeats softly. "You can feel however you need to with us; with Nick, me, and to some extent Jake and Leo. You know we're all here for you, but right now, I need you to pull those big girl pants up and get your game face on."

Closing my eyes, I take a deep breath, pushing everything down as I exhale slowly.

"What is it that Nick and Jacob say, no retreat and no surrender?" he asks.

"No retreat and no surrender," I repeat.

"You've got this, and I'll have my phone to hand whenever you need me," he adds.

"Thank you."

Not for being the one to suggest this course of action, or for ultimately being the one who brought this on me. That's going to take more than a trip down memory lane, no matter how bad it is, but for being the one to try and explain the reasoning, for attempting to include me in this merry band of bastards that we've become.

With one final, deep breath, I smile. Still empty. Still vacuous. But ready.

They've tipped my entire world over, again, and now it's time for me to piece it together.

"And text Leo," he adds, my hand on the handle. "I'll let him know I'm back, but he'll want to hear it from you."

"Will do." I nod, climbing from the car.

I don't look back—I can't.

I know there's only pain there for me right now.

Once I've calmed down, once I've processed, then I'll be able to face him, to deal with the decisions they've made. Until then, they'll wait. They'll have to.

"Sorry I'm late," I call, closing the front door behind me and locking it, forcing more cheer than I thought I could manage into my voice.

"Congratulations," Liselle sings, her excitement a stone in my stomach as I force the smile onto my face.

"Thanks, I guess," I say, joining them all in the living area and dropping onto the floor in front of Tamsin. *At least this way I don't have to face them all.*

"I was just explaining to everyone the logistics of your situation. I'm assuming you'll be moving into the big house now that you and…"

"Nick," I reply.

"Yes, now that you and Nicholas have claimed each other."

"Well, it's not quite like that," I hedge.

"Oh?"

"He claimed her," Tamsin interrupts. "It's not been reciprocated, yet." Her hand on my shoulder is a comfort I appreciate more than words can say as I try to keep a cap on the emotions tumbling around my head.

"I see," Liselle says, surprised but otherwise unphased. "Well, it still stands. The two of you are mirrored now, so if you want to move there or he wants to move here, accommodations can be made."

I nod, not trusting my mouth if I open it. I can already imagine the thoughts swarming around my head spewing out unfiltered.

*Accommodations can be made.* Ha.

There isn't room for him here, we're already a full house. So, what? They're going to *make* space? Get rid of someone? It wouldn't surprise me if they did. And if I go to their house, what happens to Wyatt? Nothing by my hand, that's for certain.

"So, just to recap. Request in writing, the address is on the fridge, and it must be witnessed by two or more of The Devils. Ladies, be sure about your choice, because there's no going back."

*Great.*

Confirmation of how fucked I am is exactly what I was looking for right now.

"And in situations like Ivy's, what's the system there?" Charlotte asks.

She's not the person I thought would have me in mind, and it takes me by surprise. My gaze flicks to hers to see the sadness she's been carrying for the past few weeks. Clearly, there was more to her relationship with George than we knew or saw.

"That's a touch more complicated," she ponders.

"You're tied to him regardless, but you also get a choice here. There's no need to decide right away, but I wouldn't wait too long to make a decision. Someone else may make it for you."

She looks from one of us to the next, and suddenly it feels more like a competition than it ever has. What if one of them thinks strategically and picks Leo, or Jacob, or Wyatt? What if these Angels take *their* choices away, like mine have been, and mirror themselves with someone they want but it isn't reciprocated, or worse, that they have no interest in?

Not that Nick has no interest in me, he's made it more than clear he does. And there's chemistry there, no matter how much I'd like to deny it. I have a physical reaction when he walks in a room—there's sure as hell something between us.

"Right, someone had better find me a pen," Tamsin declares, making me jump and pulling me out of my thoughts. "I know exactly who I want to be mirrored with."

"Take your time," Liselle repeats. "And be sure. Because once you're linked, there's no way back. Not everyone in that house will make it through to the end, so this is not something to jump into without consideration, okay?"

"Great," Penelope says with a sigh. "Pick the right guy, get to the end, dream big. Got it."

"Something like that," Liselle replies with a grin. "Oh, and have fun!"

She's up and out before the wine glasses have been topped up, her usual security following dutifully behind her without so much as a word.

"Tequila?" Aimee asks as the silence stretches out, the moment turning awkward. "You can celebrate, or commiserate, with tequila. It's the perfect drink."

"I'm in," I agree, and so does everyone else.

It might only be the middle of the afternoon, but this has been the longest day of my entire life. I'm more than ready for something that will end all the chaos rushing around my brain.

Stephanie lines shot glasses up on the table as Aimee thunders down the stairs, apparently grabbing a secret bottle from her room before pouring and handing them out.

"Toast?" Penelope asks.

"I'm not sure there's anything we can all really get behind," I reply, huffing out a laugh.

"How about, to us?" Stephanie offers. "Six women, guessing our way through this shit show and hoping for the best."

"To us," Tamsin agrees, raising her glass.

We all toast and drink, slamming the glasses back onto the table in a line. Two more go down quickly, and the stress of the day finally feels like it's sliding off my shoulders.

"What a fucking day."

"Hey, I'm excited," Tamsin says, filling up the glasses again. "You should be flattered."

She doesn't know all the details, and I guess it'll have to stay that way for now.

"Sure. I should probably make a start on this assignment." I sigh. She doesn't get it.

Looking around, I'm grateful the onslaught of questions hasn't materialised yet. I know they have questions. Lots of questions. And yet, as I slink off into the bedroom, the bombardment never comes.

Tamsin, however, slides in behind me, and I know she's not going to take no for an answer.

"I came to your party like we agreed, and now I have work to do," I say, attempting to cut her off at the pass.

I have less than no motivation to get this work started, never mind finished, but I have to do something other than sit here and stew the mess my life has become.

"So, I got the low-down from Oliver," she says quietly, dropping onto the end of my bed as I prop myself up against the headboard.

It feels like a lifetime since I curled up in this bed, feeling as if I was dying whilst attempting to put the pieces of my memory back together. It's hard to imagine it was nothing more than a few hours ago.

"Are you okay?" she asks.

"Yes. No. I honestly have no idea," I admit. "It's been… a day."

"I can imagine."

*No, she can't.*

"You seem to have recovered pretty well," I comment, attempting to change the direction of the conversation to safer waters. "No hangover in sight."

"Taylor made sure I took painkillers and drank plenty of water before we went to bed, and then the same again this morning. He and Leo have been making sure I eat and whatever, looking after me and everyone else."

I nod.

At least they're looking out for her. Not that I'd expect

anything different from Leo.

"I can see why you like him," she continues. "Leo. Apart from those eyes, with that dark hair… yeah, he's gorgeous, but he's nice too."

He is, but there's something else going on with him too. Something darker. Something more illicit.

"He is," I agree. "He makes me feel safe, protected. All the things I could have done with during the early hours of this morning."

Intentional.

It was all so intentional.

She rubs her hand comfortingly along the top of my foot, the gesture meaning more than she can imagine as I close my eyes.

"Did you get what you needed from Wyatt this afternoon?"

Good question. Did I?

I got an explanation all right. Not one that I like, but I've got one.

"I think so."

"Good." She nods, the tension in the room awkward in a way it never has been before. A divide there.

"Do you know that Taylor was in on it?"

She nods, sighing heavily.

"I don't trust him," I admit.

She's my best friend, I can't lie to her. And I know she wants him as her partner in this game, I'm just not sure that's in *her* best interests. An awkward silence stretches out in the room between us, something foreign sneaking in.

"Do you trust *me*?" she asks.

"Of course."

Whilst these last few months have changed me in some of the weirdest ways, it doesn't seem to have done the same to her, she's still the same vivacious woman I've known for the majority of my life.

"Then trust I've got this. He's the one for me."

"Are you sure?" I ask with a raise of an eyebrow.

It's her choice, not mine. I can't and won't attempt to tell her how to live her life. If she says this is it, then this is it.

"One hundred per cent."

"Fine." I roll my eyes at the huge smile on her face, as if I was going to say anything else.

"Good, now you can help me plan our ceremony so that it's something special." *Not what I had.*

She pulls out a notebook, ferreting around in the drawers for a pack of pens as we huddle on my bed and make plans.

# FIVE

## Nick

The door opens unbelievably slowly as Tamsin comes into view, looking both past and around me before commenting, "You came alone. That's brave."

"Is she here?" I ask as she blocks the doorway.

"Who, Penelope? No, she's gone to the library with Aimee and Jasper." She grins.

"Yeah, I'm not playing these games, honey."

She's tiny, and there's nothing to the girl as I slide my hands around her waist and pick her up, placing her carefully to the side before barging through the hallway and striding down the corridor.

Two of the girls are in the living room as I pass through, one flicking through the channels, the other tapping away on a keyboard at the table as I head straight for Ivy's bedroom, Tamsin shouting a warning from the doorway.

The background music in their bedroom covers it as I open the door and slide in, quickly closing it behind me.

"Tell me you managed to get rid of him," Ivy says over her shoulder, her face stuffed in a book.

The overhead light reflects off the gold in her wristlet,

and I can't help the satisfaction that settles in my stomach.

"I'm afraid not," I reply with a smile.

Her head drops to her chest with a sigh, her muttered words lost under the music as she places her book on the table and I close the distance between us, picking her up and throwing her over my shoulder.

She's had two days to bitch and moan about me.

I tried texting and attempting to talk to her, and now I'm done being the nice guy.

"What the hell are you doing?" she screeches as I pick up her phone, stuffing it in my back pocket before striding back out of her bedroom and down the corridor.

Luckily, Tamsin is still standing in the doorway, mouth agape, as I swat Ivy on the ass, her tiny fists doing nothing but irritating me as they pound against my back.

"Text your boyfriend if you want," I clip. "He's not going to do anything. I'll have her back in an hour, if she's good."

Ivy hurls abuse at me, not stopping her annoying tiny fists as I head straight for my car and drop her unceremoniously into the passenger seat, clipping her in and locking the door. By the time I've rounded the car, she's unclipped the seatbelt and is attempting to get out. *Shocker.*

"You'd better knock it off. One way or another, you're coming with me." She can continue this as long as she likes. I'm getting an hour of her time whether she likes it or not.

"Like hell I am," she yells back, pushing against the door again.

I can wait her out, I've got nowhere to be, but as Jacob comes into view, I realise I don't have to.

"I'm going to unlock this car and get in. You're coming with me for a drive and you'll be returned safely to your little bestie in an hour. Got it?"

"No."

"Your hour is getting longer and longer," I comment, conscious of the audience gathering in the doorway.

Tamsin now has her phone to the side of her head, no doubt bitching me out to Taylor. *Oh, I already pre-empted that one.* And the other two girls are only here for the show as they watch along, their amusement clear.

Jacob moves from the side of their house, the secret garden path no longer a secret as he leans against the passenger door. Ivy's gaze is thunderous as she yells about his terrible traitor characteristics whilst I climb in, starting the engine and getting us the hell out of there. *I'll be sure to thank him for that later.*

"I can't believe you just kidnapped me like that," she huffs, looking out of the window.

She can, and if she's surprised by this, she better hold on, because I'm sure there's a hell of a lot more shit to come our way before this year is out.

The tension gets awkward in the enclosed space, her fury rolling off her in waves, the silence palpable, but music floods the car as I turn the radio on, the unexpected sound making her jump. She scowls at me before resuming staring out the window.

If she wants to silently fume, no problem, but it won't last when we get there. Luckily we're only a short ride from our destination, and as I pull down the stone driveway, her attention perks up.

"It looks different in the daylight," she comments.

"Didn't you come the other day with Wyatt?"

"Yes, but it was raining."

I shrug. It's not exactly mid-summer sunshine now but whatever.

Security is on the door, waiting, as I slide on my mask, climb from the car and go around to her side. Ivy does nothing when I open the door, keeping her eyes straight ahead and refusing to acknowledge me.

"I'm totally up for carrying you in there, ass to the world, but I thought you might prefer more dignity than that," I say.

"I have no shoes on," she replies as I look down at her feet.

Fuck.

I was so intent on getting in the house and getting her out that I never thought about the practicalities of what she'd be wearing. I guess it's lucky she wasn't sitting there in her pyjamas or something else stupidly revealing, considering the temperature out here.

"I'll carry you, don't worry, it'll be fine."

I'm sure the look she gives me is supposed to wither lesser humans into dust, but all it does is make me smile. It's probably for the best that she can't see it behind the mask.

"I won't tell if you don't." I wink.

"Maybe I'll just wait my hour out here in the car."

"Sure." I shrug, grabbing her around the waist and hauling her back over my shoulder.

The security knows better than to comment as I stride up the stone steps, opening the heavy wooden doors without so much as a word, the creak echoing around the empty room as they close it behind us with an ominous thud.

"You can't just keep doing that," she yells, amongst other things, as I cross the room and place her on the one scrap of carpet. God knows how clean or not it is in here. Sure, the blood stains from our fight night are gone, but I'm not sure how much that means anymore.

I nod, grabbing an ancient chair from the side and dragging it over.

"I don't know who the hell you think you are," she continues. "You don't own me."

"No, but you're still mine."

If I thought she was pissed off before, I was wrong.

A growl rumbles from her before she flies at me, again, her tiny fists raining down anywhere she can land them as she pummels my chest and arms, but it only takes a couple of seconds to wrangle her hands together and get sat on the chair, pulling her into my lap.

She's not impressed with that either as she wiggles around, attempting to get free. I manage to get her legs trapped between my thighs, her hands held down against the firm arm of the seat as she huffs and puffs, clearly less than impressed with me right now.

"Stop treating me like a commodity," she grits out between clenched teeth, her chest bounding like she's gone two rounds in the ring.

"That's not what I'm doing."

"You manipulated me onto that road, made a decision for me, and then you manhandle me—on more than one occasion—demanding time and attention like a fucking toddler not getting his way."

"Don't hold back now, sugar. This is your opportunity to get it all out. Go on, give me it. How do you really feel?" I add as much snark into the comment as I can manage, knowing that's what pushes her, what triggers a reaction.

She might think I'm just another dick guy trying to control her life, but that's not the intention. I'd give her the world, if she'd only give me an inch.

She wriggles and grunts, attempting to break free of my grasp. Even if she did, where would she go? The doors are locked and guarded. If she thinks she's getting past The Sect, she's mistaken. But then, finally, the gates open and all her frustrations tumble out.

She screams, yells, and flails in my arms.

It's not just her lack of autonomy when it came to me claiming her, but being here, her accommodation, her classes, and her place in The Sect. Her entire life has been selected for her and scripted by someone else.

All of it tumbles from her lips unguarded.

Sure, Jacob and I haven't exactly lived fast and free, but it's never been as prescribed as hers has. And whilst the two of us might not have known all the small details about what we were getting ourselves into, we at least had a clue, an inkling of what we were walking into and the outcome of that. Ivy's never been given that courtesy.

"I'm sorry, sugar," I admit as she finally stills, all the anger and frustration finally zapped out of her. "I'm sorry about everything."

But I wouldn't change it.

If I could comfort her better, I would, but all I've got is

the space to accept her anger and her frustrations, to allow her the opportunity to release them and process them, to acknowledge that they're real and valid and explain that she doesn't have to walk that road alone.

But without her father dictating her time here, we never would have crossed paths. Without The Sect and the rules therein, we wouldn't have found ourselves tied together. Sure, we met in an elevator, and we have a class together, there's a chance that things might have happened between us naturally, but not if I was part of The Sect and she wasn't.

Releasing her hands, she slumps forward in defeat. "I can't tell Tamsin about all of this," she says. "It's too much. The challenges… the graveyard…" Calmly, I wait as she processes, clearly able to see better now the anger and hurt have been released. "She's with Taylor now, he's got her, right? This is real for him, they're a thing?" she asks, her panicked gaze finally coming to mine.

"It's real," I agree with a nod.

"But… the party, the message?"

"It was a favour to us. One I'm sure he'll call in eventually," I admit.

She releases all the air from her lungs through pursed lips, her head dropping back as her hair grazes across the backs of my knuckles, her eyes closed. Her heat in my lap anchors us both in the moment, even as the wind rattles the windows, an eerie sound I'm reasonably sure she doesn't even hear right now.

She's beautiful.

Even in the face of this moment.

When her rage has subsided and her peace is finally

settling back on her shoulders.

It's not quite forgiveness, but maybe acceptance?

She sighs, turning back to face me, resignation on her face. "You've got me, but you don't own me or my decisions."

"Fine."

She's the one putting that meaning to those words, not me.

The moment stretches on, the seconds ticking by tensely as she anchors us both in the moment, her heat in my lap, my hands on her skin until she blurts out, "What am I going to do about Ruby?"

"Who's Ruby?" I whisper, confused by the change of conversation.

"Another problem I'm struggling to solve. She's my Little Sister in this mentor programme we've been enrolled on. I guess if you don't know what I'm talking about, you're not having to do something similar." She huffs out a half laugh. "Misogynistic or what?"

"I think I'd take looking after some girl over what we'll have to do," I comment with a chuckle, the tension finally seeping from the air.

She shrugs, knowing I'm probably right.

Not that I'd want her cleaning up the campus in the middle of the night, or any of the other things we're going to have to do…

"So, what's the issue?" I ask, attempting to keep my mind on task.

"The Little Sisters have all volunteered for this, they were cute and chatty, excited to be there and to meet us, but the girl I was paired with, Ruby, she couldn't care less. She spent more time staring a hole through her phone than attempting to make conversation with me."

"You've never had someone not falling at your feet for your attention, huh?" I ask with a smirk. The glare she throws my way is cute but ineffective. "Do you have to meet somewhere neutral, or could you invite her to the pool house?"

"I'm not sure, why?"

"Perhaps, if you show her that you're just another human being, with human things, thoughts, feelings and whatever, that'll encourage her to treat you like one. To involve you a little more."

"Insightful."

"I'm more than just a pretty face, you know?"

"Debateable."

I give her the moment, thoughts and feelings flickering across her face unfiltered. It's the most interesting thing I've watched in a while.

"She's not going to invite you into her space for you to get to know her better without meeting on some kind of common ground," I suggest again.

Give her a little and then she'll give you a little back, it's how friendship works, how everything works really, I guess.

"Any ideas?"

"What about a pamper session? You like that sort of thing, and there's the sauna and steam room outside if it's too cold to use the pool."

Thoughts of the temperature, or lack thereof, flitter

through her mind, goosebumps breaking out on her exposed arms. She always looks perfect as far as I'm concerned, but I know that's not just luck of the draw, it's intentional. She cares about how she looks, and how people perceive her, and that's not vanity, not on her part, it's care and consideration for herself.

She's not primped, primed and plastic; fake. No, she's always her genuine self, regardless of whether that's dressed to the nines and dropped in the middle of an abandoned church, or parading through my house in borrowed leggings and a jumper that doesn't even fit properly.

"I don't think that's her scene," she ponders, tapping her nails in thought against my leg. "She's more grungy than girly, but I don't suppose the two things have to be separate entities."

"And it's about her getting to know *you* before she can open up," I add. "This isn't about finding what she likes though, this is about showing her yourself, and hoping she'll share a little of herself too."

"I'm still mad at you," she says, but the words hold none of the mirth they did half an hour ago.

"If that's what you need to get through the day."

"And stop calling me yours." She side-eyes me before folding her fingers together in her lap. "We're mirrors, partners, and that means we work together and trust each other. We do not make decisions for each other." I nod. "And I'm not moving in."

"I never said you were…"

Didn't know that was an option, in all honesty.

"And you're not moving in with us either," she adds.

"There isn't enough space for you or your ego."

Ouch.

"I'm not going anywhere without Jacob, so that's not happening."

It's hard enough having him in another room across a corridor, although we've been used to that for a long time at home, being here and being in danger is different.

"You've been avoiding me."

"Don't be self-absorbed," she admonishes, once again refusing to give me her eyes.

"You think you're done with me, sugar?" I ask as she adjusts in my lap. Not moving away, but not exactly settling in either. "You think you got what you needed in the woods and are ready to drop it and walk away?"

She swallows, her tongue darting out to wet her lips quickly, nervously, as the vein in her neck pumps, the air between us crackling.

Oh, what I'd give to sink my teeth on either side of it, to feel her life force thundering beneath my tongue as I mark her. Obviously, that would be ten million times better with my dick buried in her sweet pussy whilst she rides me to oblivion and back, but that might have to wait. At this point, I'd just take the admission she still wants me as badly as I want her.

"What if I am?" she asks on panted breaths, her head finally turning to pin me with those sea-green eyes.

But I see the truth she's not willing to admit. The lust that twinkles in those very same eyes.

"You're a liar." I whisper the words, waiting for a response. "You can't walk away from this any more than

I can."

"Well, I can't now." She throws the words back in my face, and finally, I snap.

I'm done with her pettiness and her griping. I brought her here to get it all out, to divulge her soul into the air without anyone else interrupting, to savour every last confession that fell from her lips, and I will not return to that house with us anything less than united.

We're tied together now, whatever that means and whatever that entails. She's mine and she's damm well going to get over it. Gripping her by the back of her neck, I hold her leather-clad wrist in my hand before she even waves the proverbial red flag at the bull.

"Stop hiding behind that as a fucking excuse," I hiss. "You're better than that."

Her nostrils flare as she sucks in a breath, my dick already hard and pressed against the side of her thigh. If she notices, she doesn't comment, too tied up with the war of emotions that flutter across her beautiful features.

"You're fucking stuck with me, stop pretending you're unhappy about it."

It's a good job I've got hold of her hand, because for the longest moment, I can imagine the crack of her skin against my face, the heat that bloomed after, and the way the sound would echo in this huge empty building. The wind howls outside as we stay there, my fingers digging in either side of her neck as her gaze bores through me, her irritation once again simmering,

"I'm not leaving here until you've said everything you need to say. You can't walk around holding this in."

*"I can, and I will."*

She doesn't say it, but I can practically hear the words rolling from her tongue, her venom hissing in my face. But the words never come, and instead, she continues to glare at me as if she can create actual bodily harm just by thinking about it.

"If it's not me then who is it?" I ask.

If she doesn't want to be with me then she must want someone else, surely? *It's me.*

"You're so fucking pent up I can feel it." The attraction that buzzes in the air. "Only, Leo was happily cosied up with my brother when I left… and Wyatt? Well, sure, he'd kiss you and tell you all sorts of sweet things, but, sugar, he sure as shit isn't getting dirty for you."

*Oh no, he called me in for that one.*

Her silence is pronounced, her glare only slightly less, since she clearly knows I'm right.

"Come play in the mud with me," I say, leaning closer to her ear and whispering, "You might like it."

"Whatever," she clips, rolling her eyes, her anger still simmering beneath the surface, but there's something more beneath it, a desire that she's not willing to admit to.

"You were the one talking about mirrors and partners and trust. How can we have any of that with you holding shit in all the time?"

"Because clearly, you're mister up front." She scoffs, attempting to turn her head away but is unable to do so.

"I told you, sugar, that's been and done. I can't change it. You've got the reasoning, you've got the apology, now you're the one who's got to let it go."

"And I thought I was the one training in psychology."

"I don't need to know how your brain works for this one," I reply, gently squeezing either side of her neck.

Her eyes flutter inadvertently. A movement I'm sure she wasn't planning on doing as a shiver of anticipation ripples over her body, her nipples peaking between us. I wasn't looking, not intentionally, but how could I miss them?

She can deny this all she wants, but her body doesn't lie.

Two bangs echo through the room, someone's fist on the door.

"That's our five-minute warning." *Maybe I'm not going to get that admission after all.*

Releasing her, she shuffles back, climbing off my lap like that never even happened. The loss of her heat, her weight pressing against me, is a tangible thing, and I'm not sure why, but disappointment settles in my stomach.

I gave her what she needed, she just isn't ready to accept it.

"Just because I'm attracted to you doesn't mean that I want to be stuck with you," she replies, rubbing her wrist. "But I guess that means I'm nearly free," she says, attempting a smile but failing.

"Yeah," I agree, standing. "Do you want a lift back to the car?" I ask. "What with the lack of footwear and everything."

"Yeah, sure, that would be great," she admits.

I tap the chair, holding my hand out for her to step up before turning and letting her wrap her legs around me, her front at my back, piggyback style. Holding her in my arms and cradling her against my chest feels too twee, too sweet.

It's not me, and it's certainly not where we are right now.

No, right now she needs me to be the bad guy, at least for a little while. But there's comfort in the fact that she gets it, that she understands, that I've given her the apology she needed, even if she didn't accept it completely yet. It's not quite what I hoped for, but it's a start, and as we leave this place and head back to the house, I know we're in a better place. Aren't we?

# SIX

## Ivy

"**W**ill you just sit down already?" Penelope clips out, the room going silent as her exasperation finally shows through. "You're wearing a hole in the floor."

"This was a mistake," I say, the dread sitting in my stomach finally falling from my lips as I straighten the cushion for the twelve thousandth time. "We shouldn't have invited them here."

"Them coming here is a perfectly reasonable idea," she replies. "If you'll just sit down and chill the fuck out, that would be awesome. You're stressing everyone out."

"Let the girl stress if she wants to." The nail tech laughs, pulling out the last of her equipment and lining it up on the desk. "It passes the time."

What's more annoying is that I don't even know why I'm stressing out over this. It was a good idea; Nick's good idea, but still… it made sense—*makes* sense.

"So, our girl is feeling a little bit out of her depth here. Give her a minute, will you?" Tamsin appears from the kitchen, two glasses dangling from her fingers and a bottle of her favourite red in the other hand. I take the glasses and she fills them as we sit down silently.

The rest of the room continues their conversations, everything picking back up after my panicked interruption. *What if this doesn't work? What if she still doesn't open up? What happens if I fail?*

The questions circle incessantly, fear and panic clawing at the back of my throat even as I try to quash them with the wine.

Tamsin doesn't add anything further, watching me freak out without passing as much as a rogue comment on it. It's unusual, but I'll take it. She knows how much this whole thing is stressing me out, just not the gory details.

The drive back with Nick was awkward, at best. He did all the right things, carried me to the car and made light of the whole situation, pretending it didn't even happen, almost. Like I didn't just spill six months of anxiety all over his lap.

But what choice did I have?

The guy literally pushed me until the dam broke, and no matter how much I'd have preferred to keep that information to myself, there was no way I could stop once the words started tumbling from me. It was cathartic, in a way, but also, a whole lot of ammunition for him to use against me if he wanted to.

No matter the how and why of my situation, I need to suck it up and push forward to keep going. These guys have way more information than we do, and if what I need to do to survive is to follow their lead, then I guess that's what I'll do, dragging Tamsin along with me whether she likes it or not. That's what friends do after all, isn't it?

At least she's got a guy that's in it for her and not just for the prize at the end.

Do I sound jealous? Yeah, I know.

But I can't help it.

Nick is in this to win it, that's why Wyatt suggested mirroring me with him in the first place, because he knows that's the best way to keep me safe. And it's not like the guy is unattractive, far from it, or that we don't have some kind of crazy magnetism. Even in the face of my rage he still managed to turn me on, the bastard.

Yet, he's so self-absorbed and single-minded that he drives me to distraction. Honestly, who kidnaps a girl and then goads her into a hate-filled meltdown? No one with good intentions, that's for sure.

And then there's Leo… who's blowing hot and cold worse than Nick and Jacob were before I realised they were two separate people. I just don't think he knows what he wants, or who. If I mirror myself with Leo, where does that leave Jacob? He's a good guy, nice, sweet, as far as I know, and there's obviously something going on between them. The looks, the sizzle of attraction whenever they're in the same vicinity. Yeah, there's more than just friendship going on between the two of them.

I also haven't forgotten the warning from Spencer, or the way he now avoids so much as looking in our direction in class. That's weird, right? That Spencer was so hell-bent on warning me away from the guy one minute, and then the next he can't even look at me.

Maybe there is more to Leo than meets the eye. He was

quick to jump out of the pool when I saw whatever it was that I saw, and he's evasive. I'm not sure I've ever gotten a straight answer from him, always turning a question back towards me instead.

He's an enigma.

Interesting, exciting, but ultimately… probably not the best idea.

Wyatt, on the other hand, is much more like Jacob. He's sweet and kind, he knows how to break the tension and make me laugh, even in the moments I want to murder someone—namely Nick—but he doesn't have that same sense of presence, that magnetism, those shoulders. Where Nick is broad and dominating, Leo and Wyatt are lean and solid, their muscles less in your face, but no less appealing.

*That pool was such a good idea. Any excuse to get them half naked is good with me.*

The way the water slicked over the slopes of Leo's ass as he climbed out of the pool, Nick's huge hands holding me safely on his shoulders, or the devilish twinkle in Wyatt's eyes as he emerged silently from the water beside us. Fuck, these guys are something else, and they've got me all tangled up.

Maybe there's another option…

*"It's okay to want what you want, it doesn't need to fit into anyone else's box of propriety, just remember that."*

Leos' words come back to haunt me.

A proposition, but not.

A seed he's planted, that I'm apparently growing.

Aimee grabs a glass and joins us, breaking me from my reverie with a start as she tops up the glass in my hand, but she's barely taken her first sip when the door goes. And I don't mean that someone knocks or rings the bell, oh no, it bangs back against the wall, the sound of people laughing and talking filling the room before they even enter the space.

Liselle and Amy are unsurprisingly the first ones through the entranceway, their animated conversation stopping to thank us all for the 'delightful invitation'.

"And you started without us," Liselle comments, gesturing to the wine glasses. "I'll take a vodka tonic if someone's mixing."

I didn't even notice her security in the mass of bodies hustling through the doorway until one of them steps through the throng, heading straight to the kitchen and making himself at home. He doesn't spare a thought for anyone else, no offer of a top-up here before he strides towards Liselle and hands it over with a nod.

"Perfect," she declares, dropping into one of the armchairs as Amy pulls a dining chair over to join her, Tamsin moving to make space for Ruby as she shuffles our way. I watch her and Mercedes tumble onto the other sofa, hugging and smiling. *Yes, I'm totally jealous.*

The nerves kick back in as Ruby joins me, throwing an oversized heather grey sweater over the back of the sofa before turning to face me, her legs tucked together as she cuddles into the soft fabric. Her arms cross over her chest, a contradiction to her open body language.

"So, hey, Ruby, nice to see you," I start nervously.

Her gaze flicks to Liselle and Amy over my shoulder, her eyes narrowing before she plasters a fake smile on her face and nods over-enthusiastically.

"So, this is our place. I share a room with Tamsin," I explain, awkwardly pointing at my best friend. "And it happens to be just in there. Can I give you the tour?"

I don't know why, but the way she looks over my shoulder once again solidifies the strange need to get her out of that room. She's almost as nervous as I am, a change to the disinterested way she acted while we were out in public.

She shrugs, flicking another look at Amy as I stand, grabbing the glass of wine and heading to the bedroom as she follows sullenly behind me. Ruby closes the door behind us, her gaze flicking over everything as I head straight to the chairs by the window, the sunshine finally warming the room through nicely.

"So, I take it this is your friend's side," she comments, gesturing to Tamsin's organised but overflowing makeup collection. "No offence, but you don't seem like the fifteen lipstick options kinda girl."

"No offence taken," I reply, taking a sip as she sits. "You're right, my stuff is over there. And Tamsin just likes to have options, that's all. She always has."

It's one of the reasons I have concerns over her and Taylor and their longevity, although Nick confirming that Taylor is in this with her properly went a long way to ease that. I'm still conscious that she gets bored easily and this thing that we're in has life-changing consequences, both positive and negative.

*Cold.*

*Empty.*

*Vacuous.*

*The rain frizzles against the umbrella, not strong*

*enough to hammer it, nothing more than a gentle tip-tap, tap-tip against the fabric. The sky is a grey blanket covering as far as the eye can see. The old church building looms ominously, the memory of masked men and confusing expectations causing a shiver to ripple across my body.*

"So, you've been friends for a while then, huh?" she asks, snapping me out of the memory.

"With Tamsin?"

She nods, pulling her phone from her pocket before checking it and holding it in her lap. I purposefully wait until she looks at me before I answer.

"Yes, since we were six years old. Do you have any friends you've known a long time?" I ask.

She's in high school, chances are she'll have friends from the last five or six years there. It's not quite the same, but it's a start, some kind of common ground we can meet on.

Reluctantly, she nods. "Yeah, but it's not like with you guys."

"How's that?"

She knows absolutely nothing about my relationship with Tamsin, so how she can determine her relationship is different, I don't know, but I'd like to.

"You guys are just girl friends… it's, I dunno, it's just different with him."

*Him.*

That catches my attention, and I raise an eyebrow, hoping for more, happy to wait out the silence, but it looks like she is too as she checks her phone again.

"Expecting a call?"

She shakes her head.

"Checking the time?"

She shakes her head again.

And we're back to getting blood from a stone.

Great.

"Isn't this supposed to be some kind of girly afternoon or something?" she asks. "Nails and whatever…"

"Yes," I say, jumping up. "And I forgot to turn on the sauna. Are you okay here for two minutes? I'll be right back."

She nods, checking her phone again as I slide across the room and out the door, escaping through the glass doors in the living room with nothing more than a smile to Liselle and Amy. They notice my escape, raising an eyebrow as I mouth an apology. *I just hope Ruby is still there when I get back.*

Following the path past the pool, it snakes around the brush and brings me out by the sauna and steam room, someone or something banging and clattering nearby.

Someone was here before, hiding, watching, waiting. Nick and Leo might have brushed it off as my overactive imagination, but what if it wasn't? What if there's someone else out here right now?

Cautiously, I hang back, waiting to see if it continues, if they, or it, know I'm here. As suddenly as it started, it stops, a voice carrying through the silence. *There* is *someone here.* I step back, my heart pounding. I was right, someone is watching us, and I'm here, alone, without so much as my damm phone. *Fucking idiot.*

The voice gets closer and I square my shoulders, taking

a deep breath before shouting, "Hey, who's there?"

Hopefully, it's enough to have whoever it is running away. Hopefully, they haven't been waiting around for a random girl to turn up out here and I'm walking right into whatever trap they have set up.

The muttering continues, getting closer but not responding as I call again, "You should know I'm not alone. Who's there?"

What an absolute liar. I have no way to protect myself from whoever should come around that corner in nothing more than seconds, clearly not giving a shit about the fact that they've been caught.

Maybe they know I'm alone. Maybe they don't care. What if that's what they were hoping for all along? The Angels pottering around outside just waiting to be taken and *disappearing* just like George. *Fuck.*

I take a step back, my nerves faltering, the bravado I was holding onto crumbling as someone rounds the corner and walks right into me.

I scream.

Like a big fucking girl, scrabbling to get away from the hands that hold me up when I would have otherwise fallen flat on my ass.

"Woah, woah, woah," Wyatt says. "What the hell's going on?"

His voice cuts through the panic after the longest second of my entire life. I swear I see stars, gardens, my expansive home, me and Tamsin laughing as kids, half my life flashes before my eyes before the words register and I stop flailing around, planting my feet on the ground and looking up into the concern lining his dark eyes.

"What's up?" he asks, one hand leaving my arm to pull his headphones down.

"I thought you were… fuck." I pant the words out between shallow breaths, my heart rate once again sky-high. "I didn't know it was you. I called, but nobody answered. I thought… I thought it was something bad."

"Breathe," he placates, taking a deep breath himself and looking me over. "You're okay, it's just me. I'm sorry, I didn't hear you," he says, tapping the headphones. "Podcast." He shrugs.

I scared the shit out of myself for a fucking podcast.

"Fuck. My. Life."

"You good?" he asks, stroking his hands down my arms now I'm stable enough to stand unaided.

"I'm good," I reply with a relieved sigh. "Are you sure there wasn't anyone else around there?" I clarify, peeking around him. "I need to get the steam room and sauna going, I forgot, but it's not worth my life if there is"

"Yeah, I'm sure. It was just me." He shrugs. "I'm sorry to disappoint, or not, I guess. Do you want a hand?"

"Yes, please," I agree, pushing the panic way back down as he turns, the two of us making our way around the corner to the wooden building and the supposed relaxation inside. "So, yeah, that's why I'm out here alone, apparently scaring myself half to death unintentionally. What on earth are you doing out here anyway?"

"Emptying the bins," he says, gesturing around the side of the building as we stop at the double entrance.

"Of course." I sigh.

He talks me through the instructions, doing it as he goes, and before I realise it, the job is done.

"Give it half an hour and you'll be ready to go."

"You're amazing," I reply, my relief evident. After all the drama of getting to it, setting the steam room and sauna going is reasonably straightforward, even if the instructions are pure rubbish. Next time, I'll just ask him to do it for me and save on the drama of crossing paths with people alone and away from the house.

What an idiot.

"Thank you for all your help," I continue. "Now I just need to get Ruby on board with the whole thing." I sigh despondently.

"That's your Little Sister, right?" he confirms, his hand on the small of my back, butterflies swarming in my stomach as we head down the path towards the pool.

"I'm beginning to think there's more to her than the grumpy persona she's been putting forward," I admit.

Maybe it's just the adrenaline rush from thinking someone was attacking me and him being my saviour, so to speak, but I can't help but notice the sparks flying between us, there's more to  the kindness he's shown me this afternoon.

"Always," he agrees with an easy smile, a twinkle to his eyes that takes me back to that night after the masquerade party, the night where he kissed me. "Do you want some backup?"

"In the sauna?" I confirm, my mind going to one place and one place only. "Are you trying to suggest that half-naked men are the ultimate distraction to your woes?" I ask, thinking of us all squashed together in the steam room, sweat slicking over his glistening skin.

His eyes hold none of the concern they did just five minutes ago, heat kicking up between us despite the slight chill in the air.

"Well, I'm fully dressed right now, but I guess that could be accommodated…" He smiles, and it sucks all the air out of the nearby vicinity.

My mouth going dry.

"It's supposed to be a girls' afternoon," I say, attempting to convince myself as well as him that this isn't a good idea, but what could be bad about him and the rest of the guys joining us for a sweaty half an hour?

"What brings girls together better than hot guys at your beck and call?" He grins, knowing he's won this round as we stop by the side of the pool.

"So true," I agree, expecting him to be joking. *He's joking, right?* ""So, I'll take three shirtless butlers, pronto!" Ireply playfully..

"Only three, huh?" he ponders, his hand rubbing along the scruff on his square jaw. "Okay, I'll see what I can do. You'd better get your ass back in there," he says, gesturing through the bushes to the pool house. "I'm sure they're missing you by now."

"Yeah, probably," I agree, eying the path warily. Sure, those panicked butterflies took flight for an entirely different reason once I realised it was Wyatt and not some pseudo stalker-killer, but heading back through the bushes alone feels like a step too far right now. Crossing paths with him in the way I did raised more panic than I thought it had, and it's hard to push back down.

"How about I walk you back?" he asks, way more intuitive than I expect. "That was I can make sure you'll be home when your waiters arrive."

"Sounds good," I say with a small smile, his hand coming to my waist as we walk the short distance back to the pool house, the sound of the water splashing the only noise, until I slide the doors open, laughter spilling out into the peace.

"Once again, thank you for your help," I say, my hand resting gently against the heat of his forearm, attraction sizzling between us.

"Any time." He winks. "And keep an eye out for those waiters, I'm sure there'll be some hot ones loitering around."

"Sure." I laugh.

He always knows just how to de-stress me, to bring the tension down. I don't know how he manages it. Wyatt smiles before disappearing back into the bushes and down the path towards the main house, and, as I turn, it's obvious we had the attention of more than one person in the room, all eyes trained on me.

"Sorry, I forgot to turn on the steam room," I explain badly, turning to my room, only to find Ruby sitting on the sofa looking unimpressed. "It should be ready in half an hour."

The two of us disappear again, closing the rest of them out, along with any comments they might have had.

"So nice of you to join me," Ruby says, dropping back into her seat. Her usually cheery demeanour is nowhere to be seen, but, oh, wait… no, it's just more of the same sarcasm.

Adjusting my wristlet, I join her, taking a large drink of the deep red wine. After all that, it's more than needed. I should have brought the bottle.

"That doesn't look like your style," she comments, gesturing to the wristlet.

"It's not. It was a gift." It's not quite the whole truth, but what am I going to say?

"But not from Tamsin," she deduces. "She'd have got you something that matches your tastes and style."

She's not wrong, but it's curious that she's picked out this item and is finally asking questions, taking an interest.

"No, it's not from Tamsin."

I'm not quite sure why I don't just tell her, but this particular item is already out of the ordinary, and for her to have picked up on that and be running with it has me on alert.

"So, it's from a guy…"

"Yes," I agree. "Nick."

"That's your boyfriend?"

"Not quite. It's complicated."

Isn't that what everyone says when they don't have an answer to give? *It's complicated.* Cliché as it might be, it's not wrong.

"I bet it is." She hums, pondering.

Before she has time to delve any further, someone knocks on the door twice, opening it and striding in. The relief I feel is likely unwarranted, it's not exactly an interrogation, but still… it's something.

It's the first time she's shown any interest whatsoever in

something, especially me.

"Uh, it looks like you have some visitors… or assistants? I'm not really sure how to explain them…" Aimee says, wide-eyed from the doorway. "Perhaps you should come and see."

"Visitors?" I mumble, leaving my glass of wine yet again as Ruby and I follow her back into the living room. "What the hell?"

Glistening abs, dark hair, cheeky grins, and a set of twinkling eyes that are enjoying the attention way too much.

Wyatt, Leo, Jasper and Emmerson, stand there shirtless with hand towels thrown over their left arms. Their amazing bodies are completely on display, their smiles front and centre with the huge amount of attention they're currently receiving.

If I thought it was busy with the six of us living in here, then adding six Little Sisters, two chaperones, and four half-naked hot-as-hell men makes it a million times worse.

"Is it hot in here?" I ask.

"Your wish is my command," Wyatt says, ignoring my comment as I not so subtly fan myself. He's beaming as he closes the distance between us, placing a chaste kiss on my cheek, those devilish butterflies doing their thing once again.

"I didn't think you were being serious," I reply quietly before barking out a laugh.

"Now, I know we said no boys upstairs, but surely we can make an exception for this," Aimee says loudly, eyeing them up with interest. "Otherwise, it's going to get *really* busy down here."

"Hey, these are the best, most, only available right now, partially clothed people I could find," Wyatt says with a smile. "They're for looking at… no touching!"

"Shame," someone grumbles loudly from behind me, more than one chuckle following.

"So, two upstairs and two downstairs?" I offer, looking at Liselle and Amy for some guidance.

"There are a lot more of us down here than upstairs," Penelope says, crossing her arms over her chest. "I think we should have three."

"Sure," Liselle says with a barely interested shrug of her shoulders. I thought she'd have a lot more to say about this, but apparently not.

"I'll go upstairs," Jasper volunteers quickly. Too quickly if the way he looks at Aimee is anything to go by.

"The rest of those clothes stay on," Liselle adds as the two of them make it to the bottom of the stairs. "Please try and remember you're not alone here."

"Sure thing," Aimee replies over her shoulder, her Little Sister tagging along behind them as Charlotte and her Little Sister chatter away with their nail technician, following.

The guys head into the kitchen, in search of drinks or something, I'm sure, as the rest of us head back to what we were doing before. One of the techs follows Ruby and me into my room, leaving the door open as she sets everything up on the table. Grabbing the wine, I get comfortable on Tamsin's bed, Ruby sitting awkwardly at the table.

Ruby looks nervous as she follows the movements of the tech, who introduces herself as Eileen, one of Stephanie's usual nail support assistants. How often the girl breaks a nail and needs an emergency appointment, I have no idea, but a *team* seems like a bit much, in my opinion.

Eileen makes a start, soaking Ruby's hands in bubbly warm water, nothing but the sound of her bangles clicking together and breaking the silence. She pats her hands dry, sorting out the cuticles before attempting small talk with her. Unsurprisingly, it falls flat on its face.

I manage to stifle a smile, glad that it's not just my attempts to get her to open up that are failing. Until…

"So, that's the guy, is it?" Ruby asks, her gaze locked on whatever it is that Eileen is doing to her nails.

"Which guy?"

"Your bracelet, complicated, boyfriend not-a-boyfriend, Nick."

*So she was paying attention, interesting.*

"Oh, no. That's Wyatt. He's Nick's roommate. He helped me out with getting the sauna up and running. Completely coincidental timing."

"Obviously." She rolls her eyes.

"Top up?" Leo offers, red wine in hand as his head pops around the open doorway.

"Yes," I agree, much quicker than I expected. The three glasses of wine and crazy adrenaline from my brush with death, or Wyatt's headphones, clearly affected me more than usual.

His abs ripple as he crosses the room, and I can't help the action as I run my tongue along my lower lip. His scent envelops me as he draws ever nearer, his gaze darkening as he notices the movement, his heat way too close as he refills my glass.

He looks good. He smells good. And he sure as hell hasn't thrown me around anywhere. Not yet, anyway.

"Are you okay?" he asks quietly, sparing a glance across the room before training that intense blue gaze back on me. "Wyatt mentioned what happened earlier on, that's all."

"Oh, yeah, that. I'm okay," I brush off awkwardly. "Just a total misunderstanding, that's all. Completely my fault."

"Well, you know I'm here for whatever you need," he says, his proximity only getting closer. "Even if it's just for getting rid of the monsters under your bed," he replies with a wink.

"From what I hear, you could be the monster under my bed."

Oops. Where the hell did that come from? *Maybe I should slow down on the wine after all.*

"Only if you ask nicely," he rumbles quietly, a vibration I feel to my toes, the toes that curl involuntarily at the sound.

*Jacob.*

*Think about Jacob.*

They're together, right?

Either way, he's interested in Leo, and he's my… what is he? My not-a-boyfriend's brother… that should come before any kind of whatever the hell this is between us, shouldn't it?

"Can I get you ladies anything?" Leo asks, turning to Eileen and Ruby, clearly seeing how tongue-tied I am right now. "I have red wine…"

"Red would be great," Eileen agrees with a nod, looking up from Ruby's nail with a grin. "But there's no rush."

I suddenly realise how close we are, how intimate this

must look, and how quick his heartbeat is under my palm. When on earth did I place that on his chest? Shit.

"Sorry," I apologise, removing it and wrapping both hands around the glass. At least they're safe, wrapped around the wine glass.

"Don't worry about it," he replies with a wink, taking a half step away. "You know how I feel about propriety anyway."

With that, he strides away, need curling in my stomach. I pay way more attention to his ass than I should as he fills up Eileen's glass, Ruby declining with a shake of her head and a dip of her shoulders. It's almost as if she's avoiding him… interesting.

"Girl, that boy is into you," Eileen calls with a wave of her hand, Leo's fine ass barely out of the door.

"No, I don't think so," I argue. She's not seen the way he looks at Jacob. It's not a fair comparison.

"So, he's not the one that gave you that gift either?" Ruby asks, looking at my wrist.

"Leo? Nope."

"Well, if him strutting around like that for you isn't a gift, I don't know what is," Eileen counters. "That boy is hot."

"They all are," I add.

"Wait, there's more of them wandering around here?" She's half out of her seat and attempting to peer around the doorway within seconds, laughter bubbling up inside me. "Does this happen often?"

"Sorry to disappoint you but the guys live in the house you passed on the way in, just the other side of the pool," I explain.

"How many are there and when can I move in? Shit, that's one seriously good place to be. He is *hawt*."

"You've already said," I reply, watching her get seated properly again and taking Ruby's hand in hers. Apparently, that came out more possessive than I planned, if the way Ruby's eyebrows raise is anything to go by. "Anyway, there are eight of them, at the minute. Nick and Jacob, they're twins, Oliver, Taylor, and the four who came this afternoon; Wyatt, Leo, Jasper and Emmerson."

"So, Nick, your boyfriend—"

"He's not my boyfriend," I interrupt.

"Whatever." Ruby rolls her eyes. "He's a twin, and even hotter than these guys? That just doesn't seem to be possible."

Fishing, fishing, fishing for information.

"If you wanted to see a picture of him, why didn't you just ask?" I reply. Apparently, the wine and adrenaline combination makes me sarcastic, as well as flirty.

Flicking through my phone, I pull up his socials.

Most of his photos are atmospheric, moody landscapes, or ab shots, very little that shows his actual face, but eventually, I find a photo of him and Jacob, arms slung over each other's shoulders in front of their car. The background is some huge house that seems vaguely familiar, but I'm not sure why, and I guess it must have been as they set off for Pendleton Prep.

"Here," I say, wandering over and showing them both. Ruby nods and Eileen fans herself, whistling excessively.

"Oomph," she says. "Look at those forearms and that

jawline. That man knows how to show you a good time. It doesn't even matter which one he is, have them both and live your best fucking life."

"Jacob is gay." I chuckle.

"That one is going to make some guy really happy," she says. "I'll watch."

The three of us burst out laughing, and it feels like the first time Ruby really lets her guard down around me enough to enjoy the moment. *Thank God for Eileen, and Nick, I guess.*

"Shit. Right. Let's get these nails done and get you girls out in that steam room. I've got massage tables to coordinate once you're out of my hair," she says, placing Ruby's hand back under the nail lamp.

"Ooh, yay," Ruby replies sarcastically with a roll of her eyes, all sense of that laughter tucked far away.

"Some people have never been pampered, and it shows," Eileen says as I step back, taking one last look at the photo before dropping my phone to the bed beside me.

I don't understand the seed of disappointment that settles in my stomach. Where is Nick, and why didn't he join Wyatt for the half-naked butler routine? This whole thing was his idea after all.

Grabbing a bikini from the drawer, I excuse myself and disappear into the bathroom, getting changed whilst they finish up. It didn't make much sense when he suggested it, but there might be something to letting her in after all. I've seen more interest and happiness in Ruby in just the small hours she's been here than I have in all our other interactions.

Eileen is packed up and gone when I come out, Ruby

sitting awkwardly with her backpack in her lap.

Leaving my clothes on the vanity chair, I dig out a blue cover-up, sliding it over my side-tie bikini, the royal blue cover a gorgeous combination with the turquoise.

"Ivy, we're heading down," Tamsin says from the doorway. "I think Wyatt's going to walk you down, is that okay?"

"Yeah, that's great. Thanks, chick," I reply. "I'm sure we won't be long, Ruby just needs to get changed."

"Don't forget to bring towels," she adds over her shoulder as she leaves, the rest of the girls already on their way.

I guess forgetting to turn the sauna and steam room on in the first place put Ruby and me behind. Oops.

"It's all yours," I offer, gesturing to the bathroom and stepping out of her way.

Clearing away our glasses, I carefully place them in the kitchen, Liselle and Amy mid-conversation in the living room as I make my way through. Wyatt appears from upstairs, clearly having the same thought as he places an empty bottle in the recycling.

"Thank you for this, you didn't have to," I say quietly, hoping to keep this conversation between us, despite the others in the room.

"What else would I be doing?" he replies. "Nothing as fun as this."

Before I have a chance to reply, Ruby pokes her head out of my bedroom door, bag clasped to her chest.

"Two minutes," I whisper, waving to get her attention. "You can leave that here, it'll be safe in my room."

Nervously, she looks towards Amy then back to me, and one of Eileen's colleagues appears from the entranceway, massage table in hand. *Good job those things fold down, they look heavy.*

Ruby nods, disappearing back into my room as I pull a couple of towels from the stack Aimee left out in preparation and head towards the glass doors and our supposed relaxing afternoon. Ruby reappears, the black chiffon cover-up almost floor length and coming to her elbows. She's got it tied as tightly as she can manage, but the see-through fabric doesn't help her in that respect.

Her black high-waisted bikini bottoms almost meet the matching tankini, seemingly attempting to cover as much skin as physically possible. I get it, not everyone is comfortable in their own skin, it's a work in progress.

"Let me just get some scissors," I say, stopping us all in the doorway as something catches my eye.

"Here," Wyatt says, pulling a pocket knife from his trouser pocket and opening it up.

I gesture to the tag, a blush creeping over Ruby's cheeks. Whether that's embarrassment at her brand new attire or the proximity of Wyatt and his exposed muscles, I'm not sure, but her voice is breathy when she asks, "So, which Devil are you?"

# SEVEN

## Nick

"**L**eo says she's fine, just looks a little shaken up," Jacob says, placing his phone on the table as he grabs a drink. "But she's otherwise totally fine."

"He better keep his hands to himself," I grumble, attempting to cover the relief that pours through my veins.

"I'm just surprised you let him go at all," Taylor comments.

"Or Wyatt for that matter," Oliver adds, fucking around between matches. "There's no way I'd be letting them anywhere near my girl, especially not missing half their clothes."

"Don't trust her?" I ask with the cock of an eyebrow, turning back to the screen to adjust my loadout.

Of course I wanted to fuck up Wyatt's face for scaring the shit out of her in the first place.

And we'll certainly not talk about the desire to rush over there like some insane stalker and demand she confirms everything's okay, and maybe get a sneaky peek at how the whole thing is going for myself. But I can't control *everything,* no matter how badly I want to.

Or at least that's what Jacob says.

The guys bluster various words of disagreement, but who cares? Leo and Wyatt are over there and I'm not.

The decision was made to let the single guys go, they need all the help they can get to secure an Angel. Not that Leo is exactly single, as such, but my spineless *little brother* did nothing more than shrug his shoulders when it was suggested, so fuck knows what's going on with them right now.

"I'm not worried," Taylor gloats. "Tamsin finds any excuse to get me alone, she's insatiable. Remember the mixer? Well, she called me up later for me to *stop by,* if you catch my drift, and that was only the first night."

"What, with Ivy right there?" I ask.

"We were quiet and quick," he explains, finally picking a match. "I had to get back to the clean-up mission."

I pause, my character stopping on the screen before getting shot dead.

"Wait, you're the reason that building was missed, why it was such a complete shitshow," I say, turning to glare at the side of his head.

"Sorry, man." He shrugs.

"You're the reason George lost it, got his leg broken, and then just fucking disappeared. That's all down to you…" Jacob attempts to confirm.

"George lost it because he shoved too much white powder up his nose and then didn't sleep it off," Taylor argues.

"And it was his mouth running that got his leg broken,

and his shitty treatment of Charlotte that got him kicked out," Oliver counters. "None of that is down to Taylor. That's on George."

"No, but me having to haul ass across campus with ten minutes to go and Leo fucking Windsor helping me out is."

"Bitter?" Oliver asks with a smirk.

"Fuck you."

The game goes from bad to worse as I mentally categorise every move he's made from then to date. Was he late? Away when he wasn't supposed to be? What other things that have gone wrong can be put down to his damn dick?

And, oh fuck, I told Ivy he was in it with Tamsin. I guess he is… but if he's thinking with his cock and not his head, how long is he going to last in this game we're playing, and what will happen to her friend should he not end up in the final three?

Shit.

There's no way in hell we're all going to get through this in one piece.

"I'm out," I say, shutting my console down.

I'm done with their shit for the day.

"Take your book with you," Jacob says, grabbing something out from under his phone and thrusting it in my direction. "Leaving your shit in Leo's room is fucking weird, bro."

"Yeah, that's not mine," I reply, slapping him around the head with it.

"I thought brain teasers were your jam," he continues as I look over the book, flicking through the pages.

"Some idiot wrote the answers in here."

"Leo thought—"

"Don't even fucking finish that sentence," I clip out, cutting him off.

He mimes zipping his lips together and throwing the key away before getting hold of the pad and concentrating on the game at hand.

"I don't give a shit what he thinks, and I certainly don't want to know what you were doing there to end up looking after this piece of crap for him." Oliver whistles. "But I'm sure this red edition of Code Breaking for Dummies that someone's already completed—badly, might I add—is not mine."

"Ah, keep hold of it," Oliver says. "You can go through and edit the answers."

"Hard pass," I reply, dropping it onto the table with a slap. "Maybe one of you fucking comedians needs the help."

Their laughter follows me as I head out, my phone burning a hole in my pocket. I could just text her and hear directly how it's going. No need for Jacob and his… whatever, to get involved.

Pulling it from my pocket, my fingers hover over the buttons, ready to unlock and send her something… anything, before throwing it across the room, the damn thing bouncing against the pillow. *Fucking pathetic.*

That's exactly how I'm acting.

Like some pussy whipped little bitch

And that's never been me. Never will be.

Except my gaze lingers on the phone…

Not only the thought of her in some tiny bikini, hot and sweaty, playing behind my eyes, but also of Wyatt, and Leo, their perfect bodies on display…

I'm not blind or stupid, I see how she looks at them when they're around, and the attraction is reciprocated. It only infuriates me further.

Why the hell did I agree to stay here? What an idiot.

My fists clench and unclench at my sides as I stare down the inanimate object like it's personally done something to piss me off. Jacob was right when he said the need to fuck or fight is real, and neither one is an option right now.

If I go for a run, I'm going to end up at her house. I need to stay here and work this out, don't I?

Grabbing the phone, I load it up, bringing up the app and the tiny camera that we stashed somewhere we shouldn't have. Two women are laid out on tables, massages being had, and that's all it takes for me to snap. Turning it off, I shove it in my back pocket and stalk my way downstairs.

They've had enough time.

I'm done.

Taking the stairs two at a time, I thunder down them, bursting into the den.

"Boys, you ready?" I ask.

"For what?" Taylor asks, not breaking his concentration from the screen in front of him.

"To go get our Angels."

"Hell yeah," he replies, throwing the controller down. "I've put my request in. I'm going to claim Tamsin."

"It's serious then, huh?" Oliver asks. "I'm not there yet."

"No?" Jacob asks. "You're happy to go to war for the girl, but not wife her up? Harsh, man."

"Maybe later, once I know her a little better. Once I'm sure she's not going to fuck me over."

"Deep." Taylor nods as he winds their game down. "Let's do this."

I offer Jake an out, not that he takes it, and then the four of us lock up and head around the building, down the path through the woods and to the pool house front door.

It's unlocked when Oliver tries it, pressing his finger to his lips, signalling us to be quiet as we slide into the house and stalk our way down the corridor. The house is surprisingly quiet as we enter, but rounding the corner and peeking into the living room explains it pretty well.

Half a dozen massage tables are set up around the small space, two women loitering outside the glass doors and chatting, drinks in hand.

There's incense in the air and some kind of wave sound playing on speakers spread throughout the room, but as I move from one prone, covered in nothing but a towel body to another, I quickly realise that Ivy isn't in here, and neither is Wyatt.

My confusion must be clear as I continue to look around, until Leo looks up from the body he plies with some kind of oil, gesturing to Ivy's bedroom door. *I swear to God, if Wyatt's hands are on her skin, I'll break every fucking finger and enjoy every single second of it.*

Tentatively, I make my way to her room, more concerned about what I'm going to find once I'm there as I peek around the doorway, the lights dim, and the room feeling far too intimate. My heart rate picks up as I find Wyatt, hands oiled up and rubbing up and down on the back of a brunette… but as I look closer, it's not my brunette—or ours, I suppose.

No, her hair is too light, her body too petite, but the woman beside her isn't. Luckily for everyone involved, she has an actual masseuse, one who manages to smirk in my direction, her gaze sliding up and down me without so much as missing a wave across Ivy's skin.

I gesture to Ivy, silently asking if I could take over. If Wyatt and everyone else are at it, why not? But I wait until she adjusts her wrists and cracks her neck before agreeing. Rubbing my hands together, I pour some of the oil on my palm, working it into my skin and warming them up before waiting for her to say so and taking over.

Ivy's skin is soft and supple beneath me, my skin sliding against hers in a way I never imagined. Rubbing the tension from her back and shoulders is more sensual than I ever imagined it would be, and when the music changes, the masseuse taps on my shoulder, showing us how and where to adjust the towels, pulling the warm fabric over her exposed back whilst drawing it back to give access to her leg.

Talk about timing.

She guides us from the middle of the room on how to work the muscles down the back of her thigh, and all my brain can fixate on is the fact there's nothing but a barely-there blue bikini between my hands and her pussy. The ties could be undone and the fabric gone in seconds, and she wouldn't say no, I don't think.

And isn't that half of my problem?

I can't be sure.

I want her. She wants me. But she's also interested in Wyatt, and Leo, and then God knows how Jacob fits into this tangled mess.

We've shared partners before. A bi couple looking to expand their horizons or whatever. I'm not interested in anything with my brother, not my kink, but I have no issue with watching him get his, and vice versa.

Maybe it's exhibitionist of me, maybe it's my calmer nature when I've got him to temper me, maybe it's none of those and we're just connected differently. I don't know, and I don't care to dive into it too deeply.

But as I run my fingers up the inside of her thigh, my thumb pressing against the muscle, I'm reminded that I'm nothing more than a breath away from the sweetest place on earth, and it's almost enough to make me forget about everything and everyone else that wants to get involved.

To forget about the legacy that Jacob and I have unknowingly walked right into. The expectation that a Barrett man will walk out of this victorious. And we will, together. One way or another, I'll get ahead of this and make sure of it. After all, it's the reason Wyatt suggested mirroring Ivy with me in the first place, isn't it?

I questioned him on it, of course.

Why would he suggest it to me rather than taking the opportunity himself? They have a connection, as much as it kills me to admit it, but it pales in comparison, and I think he knows it. Knows that I'd go to war for her.

The massage takes a much less professional turn as I brush my pinkie finger against her core, not just once, but again and again, sweeping up the back of her leg one last time before covering it up and swapping over to the other one.

She tenses as I uncover her left leg, the air slightly cooler than the warmed towels she's been cosied in, but as I move her leg to the side, drawing it slightly wider than really needed, she leans into it, adjusting her hips to get comfortable.

I swear to God she better realise this is me, because if she's interested in accepting this from the dazzling woman who's been guiding both Wyatt and me through this then we might need to talk.

She releases a heavy breath as I work along the back of her calf, flexing her toes.

I've never had the opportunity to watch her get turned on, our tryst in the woods like paper on fire, burning hot and fast, gone almost as quickly as it began, but I imagine it would start like this.

I take note as we start again, the oils in the air a heady combination with the way she moves. Her breathing has changed, her toes curling, and then there's the way her body moves on the upstroke and sags as I trace back down.

I wish I could see into her mind, understand the thoughts and feelings she has right now, make sure it's me she's thinking of, but I have no desire to burst this bubble. So, instead, I cover her legs, giving her perfect ass one last squeeze before moving on to her feet.

If I remember rightly, there's something to do with pressure points in your feet being connected somewhere else... to other things, or places. I'm sure my sister tried to explain it, one time… either way, the tiny moan that slips free from her would have been swallowed up by the music, had it not been for a perfectly timed pause in the beat.

I pause, my panicked gaze flying to the massage woman and Wyatt, but they're too busy to care, clearly not noticing or giving a shit about what's going on over here, so long as it looks like I'm doing what I'm supposed to be doing.

Wyatt is way more focused than he ought to be, concentrating on his technique and not in the slightest about Ivy. I guess he's got to spend the entire day being the saviour, why would he care about this?

The music draws to an end, and the masseuse comes back to show me how to wrap Ivy's feet in a warmed towel, explaining how they should take a few moments to relax before gently starting to move and making sure to stay hydrated.

"I'll go grab some bottles of water," Wyatt says quickly, always the overachiever.

I take a seat on the edge of her bed, watching Ivy stretch her arms out before reaching around to fasten the tie on her bikini top and sitting up. She blinks a few times as her eyes adjust to the dimmed lighting in the room.

"Good massage, sugar?" I ask, stopping her in her tracks as she turns my way.

"Eileen is super good with her hands," she replies with a wicked smirk.

"Yeah? Get right in there on the balls of your feet, does she?" I ask, knowing that's the point that finally tipped her over the edge. "Good on those inner thighs too, I imagine."

"It was you," she says, her smile faltering. "Of course it

was. She wouldn't be so damn unprofessional."

"No, she wouldn't," I agree. "It's interesting how much you seemed to enjoy it nonetheless."

She straight-up growls.

And just like that, one comment is all it takes to have her hackles up again. I might not be a pussy sitting and waiting for her call, but I'm a damn idiot when my mouth gets within a foot of her.

"I'm going to take a wild stab in the dark here and go for third time lucky," her companion starts. My gaze flicks to her, the fact that I'd completely forgotten she was even here is not a good sign. "You must be Nick, the not-a-boyfriend?"

"The one and only," I agree. She secures the side of her black cover-all as her eyes narrow, seeming to analyse and categorise my every breath as the seconds stretch out. "And you are?"

"Ruby," she replies, getting up and heading to an old backpack stuffed under a chair in the corner. "I'm Ivy's official Little Sister."

# EIGHT

"Oh God," Tamsin moans as she flops face-first down onto her bed. "That massage was heaven."

"Did yours come with a tattooed assistant?" I ask, closing up my book.

"Unfortunately not. It would seem he's not up for massages that don't finish with a happy ending, and in a room full of other people doing the same thing, that wasn't going to happen, so no such luck. You?"

I'd intentionally asked Wyatt to go with Ruby, hoping that her obvious interest in him might mean she left with a smile on her face and a good memory, ready for more positive interactions in the coming weeks, not counting on the lack of patience the rest of the guys have.

I should have known better, because I was aware the second he entered the room. The hairs on the back of my neck raised at nothing more than the sound of his boots landing heavily on the soft carpet, never mind the cologne that swirled around me. That's a warmth that doesn't come with incense and essential oils.

But similarly, his hands are twice the size of Eileen's,

and even with her clear guidance, the movements weren't the same.

She wouldn't have rubbed her fingers against my swimwear for a start.

The first time, I thought it was a mistake, a little unintentional straying. By the time he swapped to my other leg, my nipples were rock hard, and I'm surprised he couldn't tell how wet I was through my bikini bottoms. Who knew something so fleeting could cause so much chaos?

I mean seriously, girl. Get a grip on yourself.

Of course, he was only taking the opportunity to wind me up, just to open his mouth and piss me off again. I think a mute version of him might almost be perfect, except for the manhandling…

Yeah, maybe that wouldn't work either.

"And Ruby?" Tamsin asks, drawing my thoughts back to the conversation at hand. "Did she have a good time? It looked to be going well when I saw you guys in the steam room."

"Well, I'm not sure if she was just glad that it was too hot for me to force conversation on her too much, or whether she was actually enjoying the quiet. But she was certainly enjoying her massage."

"Yeah?"

"Wyatt was doing such a fabulous job with her. You should have seen the way she looked at him, it was almost as if he hung the stars in the sky. But then, Leo had popped in earlier, and then when Nick turned up, it was back to twenty questions about The Devils. It's like they're so super exciting and that's all she's interested in."

"I'm not sure you're going to like this, but it makes sense…" she offers, turning onto her side and propping her head on her hand. "They are kind of stupidly hot and she's a teenage girl… I mean, these are some of the finest pieces of masculine energy *we've* ever come across, and that's saying something, considering the circles our families run in."

"I'm not sure those circles are full of *masculine* energy," I argue with a chuckle, thinking specifically of Spencer's hideous golf outfits. "But I know what you mean."

"Sure, they're clean-cut guys, but you can't tell me that fine as hell diplomat that came the other year didn't have big dick energy. I swear they sent a young one instead of that doddering old fool intentionally, and then for my parents to host him *in our home*. Seriously? They were just testing my ability to keep my underwear on. And it was hard, my friend. So fucking hard."

"And yet, you managed it." We high-five across the beds, neither of us willing to move.

"Either way," Tamsin continues with a wave of her hand. "Our Devils are probably the closest these girls have ever come to hot, rich, tattooed, sexy beasts. So, maybe just cut her a little slack? To be fair, Mercedes had a lot to say about Taylor, but I draw the line at touching."

"Fine," I agree with a sigh. "Anyway, it seemed to go well with her. I'm just hoping I don't have to get the boys in to help every time we meet with the Little Sisters. Eventually, I'm going to run out of reasons, or excuses."

"I'm sure it'll settle out just fine. Try not to worry about it. I know you've been stressing these last couple of weeks, but you've totally got this in the bag. You're ahead on the reading, your assignments are up to date, the girls in our house are nice, the hottest guys on the planet are arguing over you, and the best thing yet… you've got your amazing, funny, sexy best friend here to enjoy it all with. There'll be plenty of time to stress out about stuff, but now isn't that moment."

I eye her warily.

If only she knew what I know.

"I guess you're right," I reply on an exhale of breath.

I can't tell her, it's not my place.

Now that I'm claimed, mirrored, or whatever it's supposed to be called, I get access to more information, or at least that's how Wyatt explained it. Being linked with them gets you closer to the inner sanctum.

I guess she'll find out the truth soon enough.

"Always." She nods seriously. "Now, do you have time to help me plan this ceremony? I want it to be perfect."

"You've requested one of these for Taylor?" I ask, shaking my wrist and attempting to tamp down the panic.

"Of course," she replies, dragging a sketchbook from her bedside drawer. "I said I would."

"Yeah, I just thought you'd wait a little longer. You know, be sure?"

"He's the one for me, Ivy," she says, excitement twinkling in her eyes. There's no hesitation, no fear. The only thing she sees right now is love and opportunity—hope.

How quickly is that going to be dashed once reality sets in? Too quickly.

"Okay," I agree.

It's not what I want for her, this *opportunity,* and I can't think too hard about who might make it though and who won't, and what that may or may not hold for them, but she's here, we're here, and we've got to forge a path forward. Holding on and waiting isn't going to get her into the final run, and if she's happy with him, who's to say there's a better option for her?

"Good, because, girl, I have plans."

I shuffle over on the bed as the book lands just inches away from where my feet just were, Tamsin joining as she flips open the book.

"When did you have time for this?" I ask, flicking from one page to the next, a plethora of mood boards enclosed within. "This isn't a wedding, you know? You get to do that separately, later." I hope.

"Oh, I know. I just wanted to be prepared." She smiles, fondly running her fingers over some of the pictures. "I'm just trying to work out which Devils we should invite to be the ones to officially witness, or whatever. Does something official need signing?"

"Well, I was completely unconscious after he declared me his in the pitch black, in the middle of the night, so I'm going to say no."

It's a detail I'm not sure she was aware of as her critical gaze narrows in on the soft leather around my wrist.

"I'm sorry you didn't get the magical moment, chick," she admits quietly. "It could have been so much better."

"I know," I agree. "But I guess it's kind of fitting, really. He took, I gave. Fear, lust, and an audience. That about sums up my relationship with Nick Barrett."

"So, you do like him after all." She smirks.

"Of course that's what you took from that," I reply with a roll of my eyes, adjusting the pillow behind me, an unwanted waft of cologne from the man in question puffing up from the fabric where he made himself comfortable earlier on. *Jackass.*

"Obviously, I want you there." She continues her train of thought like our sideline conversation didn't even happen. "And Taylor will want Jasper…"

Her sentence runs off as she smiles, a blush creeping over her cheeks.

"Taylor isn't the only one who wants Jasper there though, is he? Don't tell me you did what I think you did… with both of them?"

"Well… that night, at the party, drinks were had, things were said, it may have gotten a little… complicated," she hedges.

"Complicated?" I ask. "How on earth did that even happen? Considering you supposedly borrowed Leo's room for privacy," I ask, not in the least bit surprised now I think about it.

Tamsin has always been free with her affections, it's how we became friends after all, and she's definitely been sending interested vibes his way. Well, since the masquerade party at the house, anyway. I guess I'm more surprised that she went through with it than the idea of it happening in the first place.

"Well, I just said that so you didn't freak out. It kind of seemed like you were in the middle of something with all the guys and whatever… Anyway, everyone was out when we got back, so we just got a drink and went to bed, only, a little bit later, Jasper came in. Roommates and all that. I guss they don't have the sock on the door routine down or whatever…"

"So he came in while you were…"

"Yeah…"

"That must have been awkward."

"You'd think… but not really," she replies, flicking the page over. "Okay, it was, for like two seconds, and then he just sort of started talking, and Taylor started doing, and then it was actually kind of amazing."

"So, the three of you are a thing now, or not? Did you request a band for him too?"

"Oh no. It was just a one-off—well, a two-off, if you count the time we did it before… but it won't happen again." She says the words way too fast for me to believe her. "If I hadn't been so warmed up from all the booze and the sexy way he managed to drop those thoughts into my head all night long, I'd have never even considered it, but man was it hot."

"You totally considered it that night at their house, just for a second," I argue light-heartedly.

"Maybe," she admits. "But I wouldn't have gone through with it."

"Oh, of course not. Now spill…"

"Well, you've seen him, you know exactly how hot he is, and he was the first to volunteer upstairs with Aimee, so I'm sure he's not hanging on for us either, but that man sure as hell knows how to work his way around a woman's body, and her mind."

"I feel like you're intentionally being vague here."

"No." She chuckles. "But you're not getting any more out of me than that. It was amazing, I'd probably do it again if he was interested, but Taylor's the one for me."

"Even after he lured me out into the dark for his friends?"

"Not his finest moment, I'll give you that, but he was asked by Wyatt… and we all know he's a good guy. I guess he was just doing what he thought was right, and he didn't know it would go down like that. You can understand that, right?"

"Yeah, I'm just winding you up." Sort of. "But an apology wouldn't go amiss."

"Did you get one of those from anyone else?" she asks, eyebrows raised.

"Oh, yeah, tons," I reply sarcastically.

She's more than aware I haven't.

"Thought so." She flips the page, back to the task at hand. "Anyway, witnesses… any suggestions?"

"You could leave it with Taylor and see who else he wants?" I offer. "Does it really matter *who* it is, as long as someone is there?"

"No, I guess not." She sighs, defeat permeating the sound as she drops her head back.

"Do you have a timeline for this?" I ask, looking at the lace she runs her fingers over absentmindedly. "If we're going to go shopping at some point, we're going to need to book that in, and the diaries are getting busy quickly."

"The guys were talking about another party at the house, to get everything back on track after their late-night adventures, you know?" I nod. "So, if the bands are here by then, we could do it at the same time…"

"What, just have half of us sneak off somewhere quiet? Or do you mean to have it as part of the *event*?"

"Yes, one of those."

"You have no idea yet, do you?"

She shakes her head, flicking the page again. "I know it's a little bit silly, it's a bracelet tying us together… nothing more than a promise ring made of leather."

"And yet…"

"And yet I can't help but feel like this is more significant. I know it's not a wedding, it's not even an engagement, but it's something… something I want to be celebrated."

"So, let's celebrate it then," I say. "If you want an intimate ceremony, then let's do that. We could just have six or seven of us, if that's what you want, and then announce it back at the party and make that your very own celebration. Have both…"

"That would work," she agrees, perking up with a smile. "I knew you'd get it. You're the best friend a girl could ask for."

"Back at you, chick."

If only she knew what she was really letting herself in for.

# NINE

## Nick

"You have got to be kidding me!" I laugh, the sound so unusual. It's like I've actually forgotten how to laugh in the short time I've been here and I didn't even realise it until the noise echoes around the cabin as we wait for the garage door to silently slide open. "There's no way in hell he said that."

"To my fucking face, man. He said it to my face. Honestly, the balls on the guy must be stupendous," Oliver says, his fingers tapping one after the other against the window sill.

It's been a few weeks since we all went on our revenge mission, but nobody's really broached the subject since. Well, Jacob had some sort of conversation with Leo about him pushing him out of the way. *"I'm not some damsel in distress."* Or some other such shit. He wouldn't have thought that if it had been me watching his back but whatever.

Wyatt and I have been busy dealing with what came after that, and the fallout with Ivy, so it's almost been forgotten, until Oliver brought it up on the way back to the house.

"I'd have smashed the shit out of him too," I agree, rolling the car in and turning her off. "He clearly knew who or what you were there for in the first place, so why poke the bear?"

"No idea," he replies, climbing out and closing the door.

"It didn't do him any favours either though, did it?" I ask, holding the door to the boot room for him as he slings his backpack over his shoulder.

"Nope," he replies, popping the 'P'.

We manage a few steps before the silence registers, Jasper's usual music not currently pumping out of the den.

"That's weird. Is Jasper at a class this afternoon?" I ask, Oliver picking up on the tension too.

He shrugs as the two of us stop just short of the entranceway door, eying it warily. There have been a lot of unusual things going on around here, and none of them have been good. There's no way  something as innocuous as no music being playing is  a coincidence. There's no such thing when it comes to The Sect.

No, everything is perfectly planned out to the minute—to the second.

We both drop our bags to the floor, shoving phones, keys and money in our pants ready to fight or run before moving them to the side and gingerly opening the door to step through. But there's no one there. Which isn't unusual in and of itself, but there's a stillness in the air that is.

There's no TV playing somewhere, no conversations carrying from the back or upstairs, there's no banging and clattering from the kitchen.

"It's nice of you to join us, boys," the Chief of Police

says, stepping out of the dining room and making his way to us. "Go get your masks, you're the last two to go."

Oliver looks at me, and I look at him for the longest half-second ever. We could ask… *To go where? Why? What does it mean that we're the last two? Is that good or bad?*

But there's no point asking any of those questions, not only because this is the man that broke George's leg clean in half with nothing more than a single swing, he didn't even break a sweat or give it a second thought but because we never get answers anyway.

Instead, the two of us lope up the stairs in double-quick time, grabbing our masks before meeting back downstairs as requested.

"School trip time, boys." He grins, gesturing to the front door. "After you."

We walk out, a black SUV parked out front that definitely wasn't there a few minutes ago. We get in the back, he climbs in the front, the locking mechanism engaging as soon as the car pulls away.

"I'll need those phones too," he says, turning around and holding his palm out. "We wouldn't want anyone to cheat now, would we?"

Once again, I have more questions on the tip of my tongue. *Cheat at what? How? Why?* But none of them are helpful when he won't answer. So, with a resigned sigh, I fish it from my pocket and hand it over.

What's the worst that can happen? He sends nudes to my family after using my dead fingerprint to open the thing… I'm not going to be taking the rap for that, so who cares?

Okay, so that's probably a little morbid, or dark, who

knows? But with our phones secured, he turns around, leaving the two of us to stew in our thoughts until we arrive wherever the hell it is we're going.

A long way away, that's for sure. Too far for either of us to remember the route, and I guess that's half of the point as, finally, we drive under a set of roller shutter doors, the rest of the guys from home standing from their chairs as the engine idles before finally shutting off, the four of us climbing out.

Oliver and I join everyone else, two guys in plain black masks moving to stand in front of the doorway as the rollers slowly but surely make their way down, slamming against the concrete with finality.

"Good afternoon, gentlemen, and thank you for joining us." *Like we had any choice.* "Today, we have a fresh challenge for you. It's going to need teamwork and determination, and unsurprisingly, you're against the clock," our masked leader states, moving to stand in front of two doors.

He nods as we're separated into two teams, more of their faceless masked security doing their bidding. Jacob ends up on the other team from me, but at least Wyatt is with him—that's a good sign. Unfortunately, that lands me with Leo, but also Taylor and Oliver. A decent group, I suppose… depending on what we've got to do.

"Today, you're going to be undertaking a series of escape rooms, and we're going to begin with two teams of four. They're reasonably straightforward, providing you can work together well, but there will be sanctions for those that can't. The first team to leave their room goes free, the second one moves on to a second, and then third room. Good luck, boys."

The doors open and silently, we step up, each one of us receiving a laminated card as we do so. The door lock thuds behind us as a countdown timer bursts into life above what I assume to be the exit door.

Oliver tries the door behind us, and then the one opposite with a shrug. "Just checking."

It's almost as if we've stepped back in time as I look around, the hideously pattered burgundy carpet old underfoot, the musty smell of aged wood permeating the air, and the click-clacking that echoes around the room.

"What the hell is this?" Oliver grumbles, turning the card over before reading it. "Welcome To Timeless Trains nmbr 4702."

The floor begins to move underfoot, and instinctively I reach out for one of the tables, hoping for something solid to ground me. There are two tables, and benches on either side of them lining the right-hand side of the room, with windows above them and scenery flying past at speed. It's almost as if we are hurtling down the rails ourselves.

"There has been an escap at a Local penitentiary, a murderer is on the loose," Leo reads. "Fucking great."

"He's coming your way wth only An hour to spare," Taylor says with a roll of his eyes.

"The clues are Hidden in plain sight," I continue. "So there's no need two gt a fright. Seriously, it's as if they couldn't even be assed to spell-check it properly."

"This is an urgent announcement, courtesy of Timeless Trains," a voice begins, crackling over an ancient sound system. "A madman has escaped from a local penitentiary and was last seen crossing onto one of our trains. We have been unable to contact the staff on board, but this is no time to panic. As a precaution, each of the carriages has been locked for one hour, at which point, we hope to have more information."

"Great," Oliver grumbles, moving towards the bar that lines the left side of the room, leaning up against it. "Glad they could confirm the shit they already told us."

"Once the timer runs out, he could be coming your way," the voice continues. "Solve the clues to exit the carriage, and do it before time runs out on more than just the clock."

An ominous sound crackles over the system before it goes silent, with nothing but the click-clack and the rocking of the room to console us.

"I fucking hate puzzles," Leo gripes, looking around the room, but his casual indifference doesn't last. "Okay, there's a lock over here," he says, crossing the room to pick up a padlocked box resting on a shelf beside the bar optics. "I guess that means we're looking for four numbers."

The other three of us look less than convinced, but after he waves his hand around the room, irritatedly gesturing for us to look around, he puts the box on one of the tables and makes a start looking around too.

"Those cards have probably got some kind of clues in them," Leo continues, gesturing to where we abandoned them. "But I guess we can't decipher them until we have more to go on. If we put everything we find together on that table, we can work it out between us. Just remember to keep it simple, yeah?"

"Who made you God's gift to escape rooms?" I ask, attempting to get my bearings.

"Yeah, why should we be paying any attention to you?" Oliver asks, crossing his arms over his chest.

"Are we looking for something like this?" Taylor asks, ignoring our bickering and picking up a teacup, upending it, a letter written underneath.

"Yes, exactly like that," Leo agrees, completely ignoring the pair of us. "But this lock wants numbers, not letters. So, I guess we've got to find the lock that goes with those too."

"Yes, sir," I say, turning and looking around, not a clue where to start until the lights flicker. "Check the artwork," I suggest, looking at an ancient depiction of some sweet chocolate box landscape pinned up between the fake windows. "There's a number two hidden in the chimney of this one."

It's not obvious, and I'd have missed it if it weren't for the flicker of the lights and the jolt of the train we aren't really on, but now I've seen it, I can't unsee it. Leo nods, gesturing for me to hand it over as I unhook it from the wall, checking there's nothing else on the back before giving it to him.

Who died and made him in charge, I have no idea, but he's gathering stuff together in some kind of planned and organised manner, and whilst I have absolutely no desire to find out what happens if we don't make it out of here in an hour, I'll be damned if I'm going to get in his way.

Before long, we have a reasonable collection of items, but no idea how it all goes together as Leo takes the letters we found, putting them into a wall lock before the door clicks open, a red piece of paper inside. "This Lock is Complete. Only Two More To Find," he reads.

"Well, that's helpful," Oliver grumbles, turning over the cup he's already checked twice. "Where the fuck is this other number?"

"I don't think we need it," Taylor says, picking up the key lock. "Sometimes they don't have to be in order."

"Please discard all used items in the bowl beside the exit door," booms from the overhead speakers, making us all jump. It shouldn't come as a surprise that we're being watched, but with no obvious cameras hanging around, it kind of does.

"If we put in the ones we already have, there are only ten other options it could be," Taylor continues.

"Good thinking," Leo agrees, discarding the pictures and notes. "Give it here and I'll try."

"Nah, I'm good. I'll do it," Taylor says, leaning back.

With a shrug, Leo drops down to take another look at the ancient safe beneath the wooden bar top. The lights flicker, the sconces on the wall very good replicas of what may have existed on one of these ancient trains, if any of it were real.

"Additional clues can be provided," the speaker interrupts again. "For a cost of five minutes."

"Yeah, we're good, thanks," I reply glumly, looking around the room again. *Presumptuous bastards.*

"To be fair, that clock's ticking, and we've still got two to go," Oliver offers as Taylor clicks away at the keypad, to seemingly no avail. That is until, finally, the keys slot into place, and with a huge grin, he opens it to pull out a brass key.

Leo takes a quick peek at the flaring red count-down clock as the lights flicker once again, before grabbing the key and sliding it into the lock, turning the wheel as the cogs turn and turn, it feels to go on forever before it eventually snaps into place, the door opening with a loud creak.

But instead of the key to freedom we expect, it's another fucking box, another challenge.

"Fuck." I sigh, dropping onto the seat bench as Taylor puts the lock box, key, and cups in the bowl by the door that we're so close and yet so far from opening. "We don't have any more clues left."

"This one is letters again," Leo declares, placing it on the table beside me, the note I originally found sitting proudly beside it.

The three of them begin to look around, an almost frantic manic edge to the way Oliver pulls cushions and rips the bottles off the optics.

"We're missing something," I say, picking up the note and looking over the words for patterns or something. God knows.

"We could just buy a clue," Taylor says. "We've got time…"

"Such a cheat," Oliver says, rolling his eyes.

"I'm going to see if I can work on anything from here," I say, turning the keypad towards me alongside the note. "You guys see if there's anything out there that makes sense."

I start with the first letter of each line, unsurprised when that doesn't work. I get the same result when I try the first letters from each sentence and all of the random words that start with capital letters. *There's a clue in here somewhere, I just can't work out what it is.*

"Fuck it, let's do it," I say, throwing the note down in frustration. "We're running out of time to buy the damn clue. If we're going to do it, we need to do it sooner rather than later."

"No," Leo argues. "We can do this."

"Sure we can," Oliver agrees. "But do we have the time?"

Leo turns, glaring at the clock as it ticks down the seconds, one after another. Annoying as it is, I know he's right. We can totally get this, if we didn't have that damn clock literally hanging over our heads.

"Well, I'm in." Taylor nods, taking a swig from a bottle of tequila he pulled off a shelf.

"Fine, let's do it," Leo agrees.

Five minutes disappear from the countdown clock as a voice comes over the speaker to say, "The clue is in the lights."

Oliver goes straight to one, fumbling his fingers inside the shade and trying to find something, anything, burning his fingers as he attempts it.

"I could totally pull that off the wall," Taylor says, rolling his sleeves up in preparation.

I don't know why those five minutes disappearing in an instant has my hackles up, the concern that's been building twisting into something closer to worry as each second ticks away.

"It's not literal," I say, reaching out a hand to his chest

before he does something stupid. "The clue is in the lights, they're flashing. Does anyone know Morse code?" I ask, my gaze connecting with Leo's.

How and why I instinctively know this is a skillset he has, I'm not sure. But he does, I can feel it.

He nods, confirming my suspicion before he sits down at the table opposite me.

"Boy scouts?" I ask with a raised eyebrow, but he shakes his head.

Not surprising really.

I have no idea what Taylor and Oliver are doing, whether they're still looking for something physical to help with this, to hopefully find a final clue, or if they're just standing and watching the two of us stare at each other.

"Find me a pen," he finally says, the click-clacking of the train registering as the carriage rushes back into my field of vision.

A cupboard door slams and a drawer is left hanging open, but nobody can find anything. There's not so much as a rogue pencil left behind when the lights begin to flash again, but we're not quite quick enough to catch it, too busy scrabbling for something we can't find.

"Four," Taylor declares, a bottle of vodka in hand. "There were four sequences then and there are four of us. So, if we each remember one sequence, then you can work it out, right?" he asks, looking hopefully at Leo.

Nobody dares to look at the clock as it nears the end of its timer. We're down to our last fifteen minutes and the pressure is really fucking on, heat seeming to blossom out of nowhere.

"Yes," Leo agrees. "Or I could use that," he says, pointing to the bottle.

Taylor takes one final pull before handing it over, Leo holding it as we wait, each of us watching the wall lights in anticipation of the moment they finally blink again. Hope swells in the pit of my stomach, and I'm not sure how well placed it is, but together, we've worked this out, as a team. As odd as that may seem.

"Are you sure we shouldn't try something else?" Taylor asks.

"Give me those notes and I'll see if I can find something," Oliver suggests, holding his hand out.

"Sure," I say, handing them over.

But he's not going to find it, not if I didn't.

No, we have to wait for Leo, he's got this.

The seconds tick on, as do the minutes, and the hope sours and sinks like a stone, a lump forming in the back of my throat, but still, we wait, silent and patient, until the lights go again.

Then Leo pours a series of puddles on the bar top, nothing that makes any sense to me as he mumbles away to himself, heading straight to the lock box and punching the letters into the keypad. His concerned gaze turns triumphant as he pulls out a key, a raucous sound of elation tumbling from the rest of us as he goes straight to the exit and slides it into the lock.

Oliver jumps on his back as he swings the door open, and Taylor loops his arm over my shoulders. Eight minutes and thirty-seven seconds to go on the now stopped clock as we walk out, following the arrows to the left and the lit-up

'EXIT' sign.

"Thank fuck for that," Taylor says on an exhale of breath. "Can you imagine the shit they'd have given us if they came out first?"

"About as much as we'll give them?" Oliver asks, pushing open the door and stepping out into the warehouse.

There are seats and bottles of beer waiting for the victors, and as I look around at the deathly silent room, I realise that must be us. Leo grabs a couple from an ice cooler, handing one to me with a nod before grabbing a chair and sitting down.

It looks like friendships can be forged under pressure, but as I take in his posture, it's clear to me, he's as nervous as I am about the fact that we're the first ones out.

Where's Jacob?

# TEN

## *Jacob*

"I don't know why you're even bothering with that stupid note," Jasper says, exasperatedly tugging his hands through his hair. "There's nothing else there."

"It had the info for that one, and this one," Wyatt replies, gesturing to the two locks we've managed to complete so far. There's a calmness to his voice that's soothing, and completely at odds with the insane way my heart pounds in my chest, the final minutes ticking down on the clock. "There's nothing to say that it won't have more in it if we can just work it out."

The lights dim as we go over a bumpy section of the track, figuratively speaking, as I cling to the hope that Wyatt's going to find something, anything, before the time runs out.

Sliding out of the booth, I run my fingers under the edge of the table, again finding nothing. Only, as I turn my head, something catches my eye on the bottom of a saucer.

"Did you say there wasn't anything over here?" I ask, heading to the pile of discarded crap, a bottle of scotch upended and leaking all over everything.

"Nah, just junk," Emmerson replies.

Pulling the saucer out, I tip the alcohol off the surface before turning it over. *Useless crap my fucking ass.* Excitement courses through my veins as I rush to the table, placing it face down.

"Fucking idiot," Jasper growls, finally seeing the same letter I am. The two of us head straight back over and rummage through the mess, searching out the rest of the cups and saucers, hoping to God the letters haven't been washed off with all the booze.

Finally, we manage to get them all together and attempt various combinations, but to no avail.

"Try N.E.W.G," Wyatt offers, his fingers pressed against some letters on the note.

Unsurprisingly, the code accepts, and we pull the key from the box, rushing to the door with only four minutes to go. It's closer than I'd have liked, but at least we're out. But all the anxious anticipation fizzing around my body solidifies when the key won't turn.

Fuck.

It doesn't fit.

With a groan, Emmerson says, "Boys, what about this?"

He stands in front of an ancient cast-iron safe, the kind you'd expect in an old Western movie. As everyone stands there, stock still, disappointment pouring from them in waves, I grab the key and stuff it in the lock, spinning the wheel as fast as I can, praying, once again, that this doesn't have yet another riddle in it. *I should have paid more attention to that book the other day.*

It feels like a lifetime, but it's not even a minute before

I'm pulling the door open to find another lock box and no clue where to start.

"Fuck," I yell, slamming the damn thing loudly on the table before gathering everything else up and placing it in the rejects pile. *That's the very place we're fucking going if we're not careful.*

"We don't even have enough time left to *buy* a fucking clue," Jasper says, as if we aren't all astutely aware of this fact, sweat slicking down my back.

Exasperatedly, I look around the trashed room, more and more aware as each second ticks away that the air must be getting hotter, and thicker. Four men trapped in a small room for an hour will do that to you.

But there's nothing left here that could even hold a clue. Emmerson zeros in on the seat bench, attempting to pry the cushion top off like there might be something hidden beneath, but there won't be. Even so, there's no point in telling him that.

"Two minutes," Jasper says.

I throw him a glare, but all he manages is a shrug in reply. He's given up, and to be fair, I kind of have too. I'm hanging all my hopes on Wyatt finding something inside this note. He's been bang on the money for the last three, so why not for one last time?

"I can't just sit here," I grumble, looking around the room yet again. Getting up, I open the cupboard doors, checking through the discarded pile again. It worked last time...

"One minute," Jasper counts down.

What happens when that timer runs out?

This is just a game, right?

There isn't really going to be some kind of gun-toting axe-murderer coming through that door, is there?

I guess Emmerson thinks there is as he grabs one of the discarded metal optics brackets and gives it a few testing swings, but all eyes fly to Wyatt as he grabs the box, punching in a code.

I'm sure the entire room holds its collective breath as we wait to see if it opens, but it doesn't.

"Shit," Jasper hisses, edging closer to the exit and eyeing the door we came in warily. "If anyone has any last-minute ideas, now would be a good time to share them."

"Hold up," Wyatt says, punching in another set of letters. "I think… I've got it."

The lock box disengages as he yanks it open and pulls out a key. We're all huddling by the door, the seconds counting down in single digits. *Talk about cutting it fine.*

Wyatt turns the key just as the numbers stop and the entrance lock disengages. My gaze flicks to the mild panic hidden in his as he pulls the door back, the opposite one mirroring the motion as he takes the key and the four of us file out.

But before we're in the all-clear, a dagger flies past my shoulder, embedding itself in the wall ahead of me.

Stalking through the entrance door is someone else in a black mask. Red crosses the face in a wicked slash, and the eyes behind it are cold and dead. He's here to kill, and that was a warning shot.

Wyatt is barely through the door as Emmerson starts pushing it closed, almost trapping him in it, or worse, on the other side, as I grab him by the shirt and yank him through. After all, it's Wyatt that literally just saved our asses.

"Are you fucking kidding me?" Wyatt yells, shoving him in the chest.

Electricity crackles between them, blood in the air, until the door handle moves and all attention flies to the key in Wyatt's hand. Bracing my body against the door, I push it, Emmerson joining me as Wyatt attempts to get the key in and turn it. But every time I think we're almost there, the door jiggles and the lock won't engage. Infuriating.

It feels like a million years before we get the door secured, and my body sags against it, resting my head against the wood until whoever is on the other side bangs it harder than my heart is hammering in my chest.

We all take a beat, nothing but the sound of our panted breaths echoing in the enclosed space, but we eventually get our senses together and look around. I realise we're in nothing more than a corridor, two doors beside us with writing on.

"Only two may enter," Wyatt reads. "Well, that's easy, Jacob you're with me. Like fuck I'm going with the guy who just tried to push me into a room with a killer to save his own ass."

"Hey, what about me?" Jasper asks, his offence clear.

"Wyatt is my brother's roommate, I'm kind of obligated to keep an eye on him," I intervene. "Can you imagine the shit Nick would give me if I left this fool to figure it out without me?" I scoff.

But it falls flat.

I'm not even buying this fake bravado shit myself,

never mind anyone else.

"Look, I'm sorry. It was instinctive," Emmerson says, his very own attempt at an apology. "I didn't realise you were still in the doorway."

"Sorry, bro, the damage is done," Wyatt clips. "Good luck, Jasper." He shrugs, grabbing my arm and shoving me through the closest door before slamming it shut behind us.

The second we enter, a new timer glows, forty-five minutes counting down above an old wooden door. The soft carpet has been swapped for concrete, the stained oak panels are now nothing more than planed wood, and with a stack of hay bales piled in the corner, it's a long way away from the train carriage we left.

Double-checking the door behind us and the one opposite, I shrug my shoulders. "Emmerson was right, it's worth a check."

I follow as Wyatt strides towards the bales, picking up the bright yellow note I missed and reading aloud.

"Congratulations on making your escape from Timeless Trains," he begins. "Unfortunately, in your last-minute escape, You were spotted, and the escapee is hot on your trail. Take solace in this abandoned Barn, but not foR too long…"

"Ominous," I reply with a sigh. "But at least the floor isn't rocking here. I swear I was starting with some kind of motion sickness by the end."

I huff out a laugh, but I guess neither of us really find it funny, instead looking around and considering where we should start. There's not much to go on, some old tools piled up in a corner, this bunch of hay, and some sacks of grain, or feed, or something.

"I'll go see if there's anything in those tools," Wyatt says. "Can you have a look in and around these bales and see if there's anything here? It's just a side door, so a normal-looking key is what we're after."

"If we have to search through all those bags, I might go insane," I comment, watching him move away as I stuff the note in my back pocket, running my hands over the top and ends of the bale.

"Looking for a key in a grain sack is not my idea of a good time." He winks.

"Agreed."

The two of us work quickly but efficiently, piling anything that looks like it might be of use in the middle. It might be counter-intuitive to follow someone else's lead, but he was right with everything last time, so why not?

I find three coloured squares in the hay bales, and a number sentence underneath, and Wyatt finds a lockbox stuffed right at the back of the tools and a couple of numbers on the tools themselves.

It's an odd selection, that's for sure.

"So, if we put the numbers in the equation, that should give us the combination for the lock box, right?"

He nods, clattering the tools together as he drags them across the room and puts them in the simple number sentence.

"Assuming there's a key in there, what's it for?" I ask.

"It would be way too simple for that to be the exit key, and it wouldn't make use of the coloured squares. As much as I'd like to think they're a dead-end like that wall lock was, I'd be surprised if they were," Wyatt says as he moves the tools into place.

Grabbing the lockbox, I put the numbers in order, but it doesn't work. Putting them backward yields no results either. I try it again, just in case, but get absolutely nowhere.

"Here, you try," I say, handing him the stupid fucking thing. I'm already getting crotchety and it's only been just over ten minutes. *We're almost a third of the way through the time with nothing to show for it.*

There are half a dozen bags of grain seen piled up at the side, and whilst there isn't anything obvious on or around them, it doesn't mean there's nothing inside them…

"I'm going to tip those bags out," I decide out loud. "This isn't getting us anywhere, so it's got to be worth a shot." I can't just sit here and do nothing, I've spent way more time doing that than I should have done already.

Wyatt shrugs, getting no further with the box than I was as he abandons it and follows me over. "Two sets of eyes are better than one."

They are, but time is running out…

Either way, I grab the first bag and tip it up, the grain whooshing out like sand.

"Slowly," he says. "It'll be easier to see something that's not supposed to be there as it falls than scrabbling around in it once it's on the ground."

Slowing it down is easier said than done whilst it's this heavy, but it gets easier as time goes on. Disappointingly, he's not found anything, and neither have I as I turn the empty bag in my hands before throwing it to one side.

Wyatt picks up the next one, doing a much better job

than me of slowly pouring it out and spreading it thinly over the ground rather than in one big pile. *Good thinking.* Except, as he gets to the end of that one, it's got nothing in either.

The wind whistles 'outside' as we repeat the process, alternating pouring until we're on the last one. The amount of time this has taken is ridiculous and neither of us can help the panicked looks we keep sending to the countdown clock; there's got to be something in here somewhere. There has to be.

The box lands with a thud, and the relief I feel is unbelievable.

Not that I had any concerns.

Not really.

He finishes tipping the bag, double-checking it and the contents meticulously as I sit back, clearing space in the dirt as I look over the coloured combination lock on the otherwise innocuous-looking wooden box.

"Three numbers and three colours," I say, showing him.

"Well, you've got the three colours already, so that's straightforward, but this equation is four numbers…"

"Yep," I reply, popping the 'P' as he reads the exact thought running through my mind.

With barely ten minutes left to figure this out and get out of this hell, we could have hit a brick wall.

"Fuck."

He drops to the ground with me, not even bothering to move the corn before his knees hit the floor. Looking around holds no more clues, there's nothing else here. Nothing on the walls. Nothing on the floor. Nothing except the items themselves.

"The items themselves," I ponder aloud. "Three hay bales, six grain sacks, and how many tools were there?" I ask, hoping I'm finally grasping the right straws.

"Five," he replies, watching with interest.

"Any thoughts on the combination?" I ask, trying three reds, six yellows, and five blues. *No luck.*

"Give me that note," he says, gesturing to my pocket. "There might be something in there."

Carefully placing the box on the ground, I shuffle, pulling it out and handing it over before trying another combination to no avail. Sparing a glance at the ticking time bomb on the wall has my heart racing to a different tune.

The heat is on, and not just figuratively, and this time, we know the threat is real.

"Do you think they made it through the first one okay?" I ask, finally voicing the one thing I've tried my best not to think about.

"Huh, who?" Wyatt asks.

"Leo, and Nick…" I offer, realising only belatedly that the question slipped from my lips. "I mean, they're not likely to tackle a two-person challenge together, but do you think they made it through the first one all right?"

"Determined, Charming, Ruthless, and Reckless?" he asks with the quirk of an eyebrow. "Of course they did."

"Is that really what you call them?" I ask, the tension in the room reaching boiling point.

He shrugs. "Sometimes."

I dare not ask which one is which, I'm not sure I want to know as I go back to attempting various combinations of numbers and colours, Wyatt re-reading the note. Finally, he reads the correct set out just as I punch them in and the lock clicks. Excitedly, I pull off the lock, opening the wooden box to find another lockbox. *This must hold the key.*

"Okay, let's try this again," I say, exhaling a breath as I click in 5, 7 and 12.

The lock disengages with a click, and I slide it open to find a key.

"Do you really think that could be it?" Wyatt asks, looking around like we've missed something.

It can't be that simple, can it?

Just one misdirection.

A single box with nothing useful inside.

A number sentence, some badly hidden colours, and a bit of common sense and we're out?

"There's only one way to find out," I reply, jumping up and heading straight for the exit door and sliding it in. When it unlocks and pushes open, my released relief is audible.

"What on earth was that stupid box with the tools for?" I ask as we step out, locking it behind us.

"No idea." He shrugs as we turn around in the darkened space.

The only thing lit up in here are the arrows in front of us, pointing to the left and an 'EXIT' sign. *It can't be that simple, can it?* There's something on the wood in front of us, and as I glide my fingers along the edge of the rectangle, I squint my eyes to see the wording; only one may enter."

I guess that means Jasper and Emmerson aren't done yet.

The two of us look at each other before looking again

at the door. Clearly, we've dodged a bullet here as we head straight for the exit, pushing open the door into the harsh fluorescent lighting of the warehouse.

Whoops and cheers ring out, and as my eyes begin to adjust, I see the guys heading our way.

"I knew you could do it, little bro," Nick calls out, and I think it's him pulling me in to slap his fist against my back until Leo's cologne hits my nostrils and his lips crash against mine with urgency.

Any thought of the panic that gripped us all at the end of that first room, or the near constant state of panic the last half an hour or more has held disappears as his tongue tangles with mine. My fingers thread through the loops of his belt, dragging his hard body against me as he deepens the kiss.

If anyone is surprised by our open and obvious display, they don't say it, leaving us to our moment, and even though I'm ready to let him go and check on everyone else, he isn't quite there yet, instead resting his forehead against mine, our intermingled breaths coming out panted, lust filled, and wanting.

"I guess your brother knows," Leo comments, eyes closed.

"I guess he doesn't care," I reply, peeking over his shoulder to where Nick, Wyatt, Taylor and Oliver laugh together over a drink.

"I'm glad you're okay," he says, opening his eyes, darkness swirling like the midnight sky.

"Me too, that dagger was really close." I huff out a laugh, watching the darkness in his eyes solidify, along with every muscle in his body as he tenses.

"I'm sorry, say that again…"

I pull back, looking over the unscathed exterior of both my friends and my… Leo. His hands drop from my face, not that I'd even registered the reverent way he held me just seconds ago until the contact was broken. Grabbing him through one belt loop, I drag him back to where everyone else waits, ready to remember we're out and safe, for now.

Reluctantly, he comes with me, no less rigid, no less taut as he waits for an explanation with more patience than I expect.

"It sounds like these fuckers made it out with ten minutes to spare," Wyatt says, filling me in as I grab a beer from the closest cooler.

Leo takes it from me, opening it before handing it back, dragging a chair along and placing it beside where he's been so obviously sat stewing away. I sit with him, revelling in the simplicity of sitting with friends with a beer, as Wyatt begins to regale the tale of our last few hours.

But I can't help how my gaze keeps flicking back to the escape rooms.

Did Emmerson and Jasper make it out in time? Are they on to the final, individual challenges? Who's going to make it out and to the end? And who won't?

# ELEVEN

## Ivy

"**S**o, is this all you do? Have pamper parties and drink coffee?" Ruby asks over the rim of her mug.

I think I prefer her casual indifference.

"Oh no, we're having an actual party with the Devils at the weekend," I reply, the words dripping with sarcasm.

Well, we are, but if she thinks that's the sum of what's going on here, she's got a lot to learn.

"Fun."

"It's about time we had a break from the rigorous lecture schedule and all this mentoring stuff." As much as this feels like hard work right now, it's not a chore.

The Big Sister training is only a couple of hours each week, and we've just started doing it by Zoom, which is much easier. No getting through the door, turning around and heading back out. Now we actually have time to turn around, it's nice.

Or as nice as peer training can be, I suppose.

I was hoping the pamper session would have thawed her out a little, making it easier to talk, or at least be something more than trying to get blood from a stone, but it's not quite worked that way.

There was definitely an interest in the Devils, Wyatt particularly, but her shyness around Leo is what caught my eye. She was bold around Nick and Jacob, and didn't really pay any attention to the rest of the guys, but whenever Leo was in the vicinity she almost shrunk into herself.

He didn't notice, but when do they ever? And I missed a lot of their interactions, too distracted by his dark eyes and the ripple of attraction that rolls between us. Perhaps that's what she's picking up on? Although, there's a similar feeling around Wyatt and she's definitely not noticing that.

God knows.

All I need at this point is for her to start getting to know *me* a little better, and vice versa. I'm sure we're not going to be tested on it, but this feels like something we're being observed and marked on. Maybe not with an in or out decision like the Devils, but this isn't without cause, I can feel it.

"Sounds taxing."

"Hmm," I reply. "And what do you do outside of attending college and meeting us?"

There's got to be something exciting happening in her life, somewhere.

"Oh, you know, sex, drugs, and rock-and-roll."

"Obviously," I reply with a nonchalant shrug of my shoulders.

The conversation dries up, not that there's been much of that as she snipes at every word from my mouth. My attention is grabbed by Stephanie gesturing her arms around wildly as she animatedly explains something at the other end of the coffee shop.

*Why can't our friendship come so easily? Why is this such a task?*

"Do you know, Nick brought me here once," I muse aloud. "When I first met him and Jacob, I didn't realise they were twins. I'd only noticed one of them, so don't hold it against me, but it took us all a minute to figure it out." A smile creeps over my face as I remember the amused confusion on Jacob's face as he joined Nick and me in that corridor.

The three of us were a boulder in the steady stream of people coming from their classes, and it feels like a lifetime ago. A group of barely adults dropped off, pushed out, or running from their families, seeking out a year or two for themselves. It's hard to imagine that for some, this is all the freedom they'll get.

Some of the students at Pendleton Prep will be heading to corporate jobs in firms created by their parents, or further back in their family history, going to roles that were selected for them a long time ago. *At least I don't have that to contend with.*

No, in that respect I'm luckier than some.

"Anyway, he brought me for coffee, to get to know each other better after the mix-up," I continue, attempting to shake off the memory.

*"I think you like it." He smirks, something more than just mischief twinkling in the depths of his hazel eyes. "You like it when I'm a bit of a dick, when I don't give you what you want."*

*My breath hitches, a blush creeping across my cheeks, and I can do absolutely nothing to stop it. The goddamn audacity of the man.*

*I'm not annoyed at him, or I wasn't, not until he started rattling on about me flirting with everyone but him. There's something about this fraternity that's so close to the answers I'm looking for. They know why I've been sent here, but nobody is willing or able to give me the details I need, and it's infuriating.*

*Almost as infuriating as the heat that rushes through me from merely being in the presence of Nick fucking Barrett, never mind being in an enclosed space. His heady cologne hits the back of my throat, his intense gaze laser focused and directed solely at me as he stalks my way.*

*My hand goes to his chest, and I'm not sure whether it's to stop his advance, as if I really could, or to draw him closer, but my back hits the counter with a finality I'm more than ready to explore. There's nowhere left to run.*

*"You're so used to men dropping to the ground you walk on to worship at your feet that you have no idea what it's like when someone wants you and isn't willing to bend."*

Arrogant fucker.

*"You don't know anything about it," I whisper.*

*The words were supposed to come out strong and determined, and yet, all I hear is the lust thrumming in my ears, the two of us walking along a rope pulled so tightly it's going to snap at any given moment.*

*I don't know which one of us moves first, my hand twists in his shirt as he surges forward, our lips coming together as inevitably as two magnets.*

"That must have been some good coffee," Ruby comments, dragging me back into the here and now with a crash.

"It wasn't actually."

I honestly couldn't tell you, I have zero recollection of the coffee itself, but, much like with Nick, I can't help but verbally spar with her. For some reason, being nice gets me nothing but the cold shoulder, but this back-and-forth is exactly what she needs to pull words from her, no matter how exhausting it is.

"Great story," she says, turning the phone over in her hand and effectively drawing the conversation to a close.

The silence stretches out between us again, but I refuse to let this become awkward.

"So, who's the guy?" I ask.

"What guy?" Her astute gaze flicks around the coffee shop, perhaps thinking I'm talking about someone here.

"You said there was someone special in your life, a friend, but that I'd never get it. That's got to be a guy, right? Because I'd never have a clue how to be friends with a guy," I say calmly.

"You're friends with Wyatt." She says it like an accusation, like I'm reaching for a connection, for something to tie us together, but I've seen the crack in her facade as she checks her phone once again.

"I am," I agree, although, it's more complicated than that. There was that kiss, and the way he held me when I scared the shit out of myself by the sauna, the heat of his hands on my skin, the salty freshness of whatever shower gel or aftershave he uses, the sizzle of attraction that's never far away when we're together.

"And… other people," she adds.

She means Leo.

I can almost see his name on the tip of her tongue, except she doesn't let it loose, playing it safe.

"*Other people* are complicated," I reply, taking a sip of my latte.

And it's not like things between Wyatt and I are simple, or straightforward. How could anything be simple in this melting pot we've found ourselves in? But if she wants to give me cagey answers to keep me interested, I can play that game too.

"So, you're stringing them all along, huh?" She smiles a knowing grin, thinking she's figured it all out and holds all the answers. *Oh, if only she knew.*

"It's that black and white in your world, is it?" I ask. "I'm either with them or stringing them along." The words were supposed to come out cool and calm, collected, but there's an edge to the statement I wasn't expecting. Something sharp and prickly I'm not ready to address.

"I'm just calling it as I see it." She shrugs.

Sure. Whatever.

I nod, thinking quickly.

"Why don't you join us on Saturday night? See how it really is. You could bring your friend with you too," I say.

"He's not the house party kind of guy," she replies. "And he wouldn't be caught dead somewhere like Pendleton Prep."

"Fair enough. But you'll come?" I do my best to keep the triumph off my face and out of my voice as she reluctantly nods.

There is a guy. Someone special. The same person she's no doubt checking her phone for again. It's not a lot, but it's a start, and it makes her reaction to Wyatt all the more interesting.

"Ladies," Amy says, clapping twice like a cheerleader. "It's time for us to head home. Finish up, please."

We both stand, more than ready to get this sparring session over and done with.

"I'll send you the time and place," I say.

Tamsin hugs Mercedes, but I get nothing more than a chin lift as Ruby heads towards the front doors and back to her life.

"We should totally double sister and go to a movie or something," Tamsin says, wrapping her arm in mine as we head to the waiting SUV. "Mercedes is so sweet, she'll totally get Rubes to open up and you guys will be the best of friends in no time."

"I'm good," I reply. I might be tired of fighting with her, but I'm making progress. "I've invited her to the party though, is that okay?"

"I'm sure it'll be fine. I would check with Taylor, but he's not been replying all afternoon. Have you heard from Nick?"

"Uh, no, but that's not unusual." Grabbing my phone from my bag and checking shows that I have no new messages, and whilst that's not unsurprising, it's still a little disappointing.

"He usually replies straight away but it's been hours," she continues.

"Is he in a class?" I offer.

"Shouldn't be…"

"How odd. Maybe he's at the gym? Gone for a run? Dropped his phone in the sink… There are a million reasons he might not be answering," I say, refusing to even consider the alternative.

The car bumps along the road, just seconds from turning onto the campus grounds as she holds her phone up, moving it from one side to the other, as if there was anything wrong with her signal. There isn't.

"Why don't we stop by the house?" I offer. "One of the guys will know where he is."

It takes the guy in the front of the car nothing more than a few messages to get the approval required, and then we're deposited outside the doors of the main house. Why he needed approval when we could have just walked back up, I don't know, but here we are.

Rain threatens, the stillness in the air that comes before the heavens open and the rain pours washing around us as we stand, watching the cars disappear down the driveway as an awful thought flits through my mind. What if he's not here?

She bangs on the door and we wait. *Nothing*

I ring the doorbell and we wait. *Nothing.*

She curses, I bang on the door and she rings the doorbell again, and still, we wait. *Nothing.*

Nobody comes.

"Well, they're either all gone and we're free to get on and live our lives… or they're busy," I say, trying to inject humour rather than blind panic into my tone.

They're not *all* gone, are they? They can't be.

The signal is fine as I check my phone, sending a quick message to Wyatt, knowing that he's the easiest of the Devils to talk to, and the one least likely to give me shit about the panic attack I'm currently staving off, but the message remains unread.

Shit.

Maybe Tamsin really does have a reason to be concerned.

"It looks like nobody is home," I comment, trying the doorbell one last time. "They must be busy or something."

"Yeah, I guess so," she replies unconvincingly.

The house looms over us as I search out a reason, something, anything.

"We've been out together all afternoon, so maybe they're doing something similar, a team-building exercise or whatever," I offer, linking our arms together and heading down the stone steps.

I need to get out from under the oppressive feel of the building, the prickle of someone watching us as we stand alone in the cold creeping along my neck unnerving.

"Yeah, maybe," she replies as I do my best to push the panic down.

"Why don't we head back and get everything finalised for Saturday night? Maybe those beads you were waiting for have arrived?" I offer.

At this point, I'd do or say anything to get us away from the foreboding silence and the concern that swirls in my gut. Sure, they could all be at a team-building exercise, maybe they went paintballing or axe throwing or something, but what if they didn't?

"Yeah, the beads were due today." She repeats the words almost on autopilot as we head around the building and back towards our house, our now empty SUVs coming back in the opposite direction.

It's lucky really that it's not throwing it down, considering that not a single one of them slowed down, never mind stopping to offer us any help, we'd be out here getting soaked if it was. A cold wind whips around us as we turn the corner, the tumultuous breeze not far off the spin that's going on in my stomach.

Tamsin is doing a better job of tamping down that panic that was so close to tumbling out as we arrive at the pool house, sliding her shoes, and the concern, off at the door as she picks up the parcel.

"This must be them," she says as she worries her bottom lip

Together, we head straight for the kitchen, grabbing the scissors as she peels the paper back. The delicate beads glisten, even in the rubbish lighting in here, and she smiles, opening the boxes to check them out individually before we head back to our bedroom.

Silently, I sit on the edge of my bed and watch as she sets about her preparations, pulling out the design books and draping them over the bed. The fabric comes next, already cut, sewn and sized to absolute perfection, and then, the sewing kit.

This isn't going to be something you can do on a machine. No, this is going to be hours of tireless labour, the perfect way to ignore what is potentially happening in or around the huge building that looms over ours, its presence as forboding as the men who live within its walls.

"Do you need some help?" I ask, knowing this is a very personal project and perhaps this is something she'd prefer to tackle alone.

"There's no way I can get this done without a little help from a friend," she replies, an anxious smile on her face. "Get your ass over here."

We place our phones on the desk, close enough to hear but far enough away to avoid checking on them twenty times a minute. A thought flickers through my mind—maybe there's something worrying going on with Ruby's man, friend, whatever…

I have my own men, friends, whatever to worry about right now, and a friend who needs my help. Anything else can wait.

# TWELVE

## Nick

A door slams somewhere, and all the laughter dies, ears pricking up as our gazes search down the side of the warehouse. The last time that happened, Wyatt and Jacob came tumbling out like little lost lambs, and yet, there's no one to be seen.

"Hello?" Jasper calls, the sound echoing around the building but giving no indication as to where it's coming from.

"Yo, Jasper. We're round here, man," Taylor calls out excitedly as we all jump up from our seats. "I knew he had this in the bag," he whispers before heading off at a jog.

"Sure he did," Wyatt says quietly, clearly much less convinced than his roommate.

"Yeah, baby," Taylor whoops and cheers, coming back with Jasper tucked under his arm, the same bewildered look on his face that Wyatt and Jacob had. I guess going from one to another, and then another does a bit of a number on your brain.

Oliver hands the guy a beer, Leo still hovering protectively near Jacob, when another door bangs closed.

The security, who's been silent and stoic the entire time stands to attention, standing straighter, quieter, almost sinking into the background completely as two masked men appear.

"Thank you for your time, gentlemen. Please leave your masks on until you arrive back at the house," one of them says, loitering by the entrances to the escape rooms.

"Wait, that's it?" Oliver asks in disbelief.

That was way too easy for it to be over. Well, for us, at least. Jasper looks like he's been through hell and back.

He nods, the SUVs starting up beside him as one of the garage doors begins to peel upwards.

"What about Emmerson?" Jasper asks, looking around and not finding his finale counterpart.

A stone sinks in the bottom of my stomach. How could we have been so blind to notice that we're being dismissed but one person hasn't come back yet?

"His time in this competition has come to an end. You're free to return to the house."

A heavy silence drops over the group. The elation that surrounded us after we came out of the room, then as Jacob and Wyatt arrived, and now Jasper, turns bitter at the back of my throat. We were out here drinking and celebrating whilst they went through the wringer, and now Emmerson isn't even coming out—coming back.

Silently, and as if on auto-pilot, we head to the cars. Grabbing Jacob, I shove him in the closest one, Leo following with nothing more than a scowl before Wyatt climbs in too. Pulling the seat forward takes twenty million years with us all smashed in the small space, but I clamber in the back row regardless. I'd rather be squashed in the back knowing he's safe than in a car with the others, or on my own.

A shiver ripples over my skin. Being alone in this game isn't an option.

"When will we get our phones back?" Leo asks, his arm casually thrown over the back of the seat.

"They're back at the house," the driver replies.

"Are you waiting for something?" I ask.

"I just want to know where it is," he clips out without turning his head. "A clue on what time it is wouldn't go amiss either."

"It's a little after seven," the driver replies.

Well, I guess it's good news that they do speak, that they are humans. Seeing them loitering around the pool house and Ivy and the rest of the girls had definitely caused concern.

Not that any of these blank-masked guys have done anything to cause that, but they answer to someone beyond us and obey without question, and that can't be fully trusted.

"We've missed dinner," Jacob comments idly.

"We're heading back with a lot less than an empty stomach," Wyatt says quietly. "Even if he did try to push me back through that doorway."

The car falls quiet, with each of us lost in our thoughts. We all made it out in the first two rounds, so how much worse does Jasper feel right now knowing that it could have been him?

Jacob tips his head back between the headrests and I shuffle forward, pressing mine against his, eyes closed as I rest my arms over his shoulders. *No matter how close or far it felt today, we've got this.*

After a few minutes, he taps my arm, sitting back up properly as I move back in the seat. We might be amongst friends, but we still can't show weakness, plus it's a long way back, and that shit was uncomfortable.

Eventually, the Pendleton Prep campus comes into view, our familiar driveway dark and empty as we thread under the trees. Somehow we're the first ones back, and I idly note how lucky it is that both Oliver and I shoved our keys in our pockets before leaving, although I have a feeling the man in the front would have had a solution for that.

The house is silent as we enter, peeling our masks off, but nothing is seemingly out of place as we turn on every light and head to the kitchen, secretly praying for food, or at the very least a take-out menu. Neither of which we find.

Luckily for us, Jacob still has the list Ian gave us before we moved in here, thank god for friends outside of The Sect, and runs upstairs to grab it. The phones are  lined up on the kitchen counter as we get there, and the temptation to take them all and flick through them is a lot… even without their passcodes

"Nick, did you hear from Ivy?" Wyatt asks, looking at his.

Flicking out of my notifications, I check my messages again. "No, why?"

"She text me a couple of hours ago to check that everything is all right."

"Fuck, okay. Well, reply to her then," I say, my heart pumping.

"I already did," he says. "I just let her know I'm home safe and sound."

"And…"

"And she asked after you."

*Yes!*

"And Leo, Jacob and Taylor."

*Not so yes.*

"Apparently Tamsin had a minor freak out, and now they're sewing," he continues, typing away.

"And she texts you rather than me because…"

"Because you're a dick," Jacob offers with a grin, Leo barely containing his laughter as he necks half a bottle of water leaning up against the kitchen counter.

"Thanks for that."

"Honey, I'm home," Taylor sings as the rest of them burst through the doorway. Clearly, his funk over this whole thing has been and gone already.

"You might want to ring Tamsin," Jacob says. "She's worried she's not heard from you."

Way to soften the blow.

Opening my message back up, I can't help but send something her way. I know she's got her phone to hand if Wyatt's furious fingers are anything to go by.

**Me: I'm not sure if I'm disappointed that you didn't check in on me, or impressed that you know I can hold my own. Emmerson didn't come back.**

Three dots bounce in the corner, then stop, repeating a few times before one single word arrives.

**Sugar: Wow.**

It irks me that when she needed reassurance, Wyatt is

who she went to. It would have been even more annoying if it had been Leo, or someone else, but still… it's always one step forward and then two steps back with this woman, and it's fucking infuriating. She's infuriating.

**Me: Are you working on Tamsin's outfit for Saturday night?**

I ask her a question, changing the direction of the conversation to try and get us back on an even keel, even if I have to use the details Wyatt gave me to do it.

**Sugar: Yep, busy. I can't talk now.**

Great.

Wyatt still texts away like I didn't just get completely blown off.

We spent an awkward hour or more on the way there, an hour in the escape room, then all the time the other guys were in, plus that hellish journey back, and it's done nothing for my nerves. I need a break, some peace and fresh air.

"Shout me when there's food," I say, leaving the bustling kitchen in search of some quiet.

Heading out the front door feels the easiest, and as I sink onto the cold concrete, I know it's the right decision. There'll be someone on the back patio having a smoke, someone else laughing and joking as they join them, and all I can concentrate on right now is nothing.

There are at least two assignments I should be working on for class, an Angel that I'm supposed to be supporting but who won't speak to me, and then there's Jacob, and The Sect, and whatever expectations they have of me.

You'd think there would be a billion thoughts and ideas running through my head at any given moment. Instead, there's nothing. A numbness that can't be good.

She went to Wyatt over me.

Wyatt.

Like, I get it, they're cool or whatever, but I thought we were getting somewhere, and it grates.

Sure, we had that shit locked down. We were in and done in good time, so maybe she had no real *concern* for me, or perhaps she was really asking for Tamsin and she knows that Wyatt and Taylor are friends. Fuck it, it's not my issue.

The wind curls around the entrance as I turn and lean my back against the concrete balustrade, letting the silence and peace wash over me until tyres crunch over the leaves and the gravel, a door slamming to my side.

"Someone ordered pizza?" a guy asks from beside me.

Opening my eyes, I pin him with a glare.

"If you're turning up here with it, you'd better fucking hope so."

The stack wobbles in his hands as he looks from me to the door and back again, but I make no move to help him.

"Uh, I'll just..." He awkwardly steps around me, balancing the boxes badly before ringing the bell.

He shuffles from one foot to another, peeking over his shoulder to find me still watching him. His gaze flies back to the door so fast I'm surprised he doesn't give himself whiplash, and the way his eyes bulge when Jacob opens the door almost has me chuckling.

It's been a long time since we managed to do that, apart from Ivy, I guess, but that surprise wasn't intentional.

*"I'm not hiding from anyone," I argue, crossing my*

*arms over my chest.*

*She doesn't answer, doesn't push for anything more, instead picking at some dirt on the edge of her dress, unfastening her sandal before adjusting one of the straps and refastening it.*

*"Fine." I sigh. "We're playing hide and seek. I guess you missed the game or something."*

*"Yeah, or something."*

*"Why are you hiding?" I ask, a sadness in her voice that I don't like—it makes my tummy twist.*

*"Uncle Derek said I should be a good girl and go play quietly while the grownups did their thing." She rolls her eyes, flicking her hair over her shoulder and turning to me fully. Her hot hand lands on my thigh and she hisses the words out between clenched teeth. "Like I'm some kind of toddler getting in their way. Do I look like a baby to you?"*

*She doesn't wait for an answer before continuing her tirade. "Honestly, he's such a bore. I don't know why he had to come today. Daddy said this would be fun, and now I'm stuck in the middle of this… this garden, and you won't even show me the way out. Everyone here is so mean."*

*Huh.*

*My leg tingles where her hand meets it, her skin way softer than my busted-up knees.*

*"Come on," I say, standing and holding my hand out to her.*

*If she wants fun, I can show her fun.*

*I might have followed her through the gardens and chuckled a little when she went around this same corner for the second, and third, time, but that doesn't have to be all today is about. Today can be about fun, and avoiding my family with a perfectly good reason, for as long as possible.*

*She hesitates, her fingers twitching like she wants to take my hand and go but isn't sure it's safe to.*

*"What other choice do you have? You're already lost," I say calmly, and yet, she still thinks about it.*

*Just when I'm ready to give up and sit back down, she slides her palm against mine, intertwining our fingers before standing up.*

*"If you abandon me somewhere and run off, I swear I'll find out who you are and make your life hell," she promises with narrowed eyes.*

*"You can try." I grin.*

*Pulling her along is easy, and fun, as I head down the same path she has done so many times, only, instead of taking this turn or that turn and looping back, we keep going. Heading past the decorative gardens and the fishing lake, through the archway of trees and around the corner to the play area. My favourite play area.*

*Excitement ripples in the air as she strips off her sandals, abandoning them where I stand as she hurries her steps, sinking her toes in the sun-warmed sand.*

*"There are buckets and things in the chest," I say, pointing it out. Nothing gets left lying around out here, there's always someone coming along and smashing the sandcastles to nothing before packing everything away. "That's one of Sophie's favourite places to be."*

*"Who's Sophie?" she asks, bending down to grab a handful of sand, squeezing it in her palm.*

*"My sister."*

*I don't know why I don't go over and join her, sit on the edge of the pit and wiggle my toes in the sand. It would be nice, I do it with Soph, but something about her is different, and I can't help but watch in awe, waiting to see what she does next.*

*I stand in silence, watching the grains tumble between her fingers as she opens them, the sand tumbling into a little pile next to where she crouches, repeating the process.*

*"She's got good taste," the girl replies with a smile.*

*I smile too, happy that she's enjoying this. More than anything, I'm just glad to remove the frown from her face.*

*"If you say so." I shrug. "She follows me around with hideous dolls and a bag of stuff almost as big as she is. And she's bossy. So bossy."*

*"I guess that's what sisters are for though, following you around and keeping you safe." She doesn't look up from the sand, watching it cascade like a waterfall. "Where is she now?"*

*"Don't know." I shrug. "She'll be around here somewhere."*

*"You should look after her too, you know? That's what family does."*

*"Sure."*

*I have no idea what that would look like, but I guess I could try. I'm not sure how much she'd like it though.*

*"Let me show you something else, it's my favourite," I say as she looks up from the sand, cocking her head as if she'd already forgotten I was standing there. "We can come back to the sandpit after, it's only over there."*

*She follows the direction of my finger, her eyes lighting*

up when she sees the climbing wall. I head straight there, expecting her to grab her shoes, but she's step by step beside me, clearly as excited as I am for a challenge.

"The pegs are coded," I begin to explain. "Green for easy, orange for medium, and red for hard."

"And the black ones?"

"They're daredevil level," I reply with pride. "Those were done especially for me."

Not straight away, obviously, I had to master the other ones first, but having to get someone back out to make a more challenging course just for me was pretty amazing.

"Cool." She nods and heads straight there.

Impressively, she manoeuvres her tiny body from one peg to another with ease, starting with the orange course and finishing with a flourish. She goes straight back to the start, reaching for the first red one before stopping to ask if I wanted a turn. So polite.

"I'm good, you go for it."

I kind of want to sit and enjoy her working out each move, but I'm rooted to the spot in awe. I'm also sure she's done this before, she knows where each peg should be, moving fluidly from left to right, hand to foot; she's good.

She jumps off again, and I can't help the little clap I do. It's just great. She's just great.

She heads back to the start with a smile, placing a foot and reaching for the top black peg. I'm holding my breath as I watch her lithe movements, smooth and graceful. The fact that she never went and got her shoes isn't even an issue, until she gets to the point I always struggle with, it's too far, reaching is too hard for me, and she's even smaller *than I am. There's no way she'll make it.*

*Even so, I'm practically on tenterhooks as she gets to it, a nervous excitement coursing through me. What if she* can *do it?*

*She reaches, and misses, holding back before trying again, losing her footing and landing on the ground. It's as if whatever tether was holding me in place snaps and I rush over to where she curls up, holding her knee as tears silently track down her cheeks.*

*"You were so close," I say, sitting down beside her.*

*"Not close enough," she grumbles, glaring at the wall whilst swiping angrily at the tears.*

*"Your knee is bleeding," I comment.*

*It's only a graze, nothing in the grand scheme of things, and I'm not sure whether the tears are from the knee, the shock of falling, of landing on the ground, or of failing. I get it, I've been there. We've all failed at something, right?*

*"Let's get you back to the house," I say. "It probably needs cleaning."*

*She grits her teeth, turning her glare on me. "I want another go. I can do this."*

*And it's not that I don't believe her, I do. The determination glowering at me right now is enough to take that wall and mould it into anything she wants it to be, but it's going to be sore if she doesn't get that knee cleaned up and covered.*

*"You can come back another day, this needs taking care of," I explain carefully.*

*This was the girl huddling up in tears because she couldn't find her way back, and now I'm offering her the very thing she was searching for and she doesn't want it.*

*"Come on, I've got you."*

# THIRTEEN

The party is in full swing as the three of us make our way through the gardens, torches in hand.

"I have no idea why you thought a floor-length dress would be a good combination with leaves," Penelope grumbles, side-stepping a large stone with her skirt in hand.

We didn't, she was the one who decided that's what she wanted. It's half the reason both Tamsin and I are in knee-length dresses in the first place.

"We'll only be out here for an hour, tops," Tamsin argues. "And then you can show that dress off to its full potential."

"He'd better appreciate it too," she clips out, her irritation getting the better of her as we dodge wet branches and falling leaves.

Tamsin doesn't bother arguing with her or explaining herself any further. Penelope didn't have to come, she volunteered herself, not that we asked, but here we are. We walk in silence the rest of the way, finding ourselves almost at the clearing soon enough, the sound of male voices carrying over the distant sound of music playing,

"Ooh, I'm nervous," Tamsin admits, shaking her hands out. "No, I'm okay. We're good."

All the work she's done on this outfit is going to be worth it once he sees her.

"We can hear you over there," Taylor calls.

"Fuck," Tamsin hisses, fluffing up her hair. "Do I look all right? No errant twigs sticking from my hair?"

"You're fine, let's get this over with and get back to the house." Penelope sighs.

"You're welcome to leave whenever you'd like to," I say, getting between the two of them before Tamsin loses it, the rope of irritation she's holding onto getting thinner by the second, or maybe that's mine. "We can do this without you."

Penelope rolls her eyes, adjusting her skirts in her hands before shaking her head.

"Are you girls good?" Jasper asks, peeking out from behind a tree. "Your knight in shining armour awaits, and we have carpet… for the skirts."

"Thank God," Penelope says, raising her head to the sky before setting off in the direction he points.

"If you'd like to duck out, I can make up some excuse, you know?" Jasper asks, a mischievous twinkle on his smirking face. "Or you could just swap him out and have me instead. I'm a catch, you know?"

"I'm sure you are." Tamsin laughs, his silliness exactly the thing she needed to calm the nerves and ease the tension rippling in the air between us. "I just need a minute to check my makeup and then we'll be there, promise."

"You know it's dark as hell right now and he can't see for shit, right?" he asks with a chuckle.

"Oh, just go, Jasper. We'll be there in two minutes," I reply, whooshing him away with my hands.

She waits until he's out of sight before asking, "You've got the band, right?"

"Of course," I reply, tapping the bag on my shoulder.

"Good." She nods. "And I really don't have mud up my leg or half a tree sticking out my hair, do I?"

"You look perfect," I reply with a smile.

She nods, excitement replacing the tension that was here just minutes ago, looping her arm through mine as we set off in the direction everyone else went—they can't be far.

"There she is." Taylor smiles as we pass through the copse of trees.

The solar fairy lights we hung a few days ago light up the area beautifully, the butterfly spikes floating around the ground marking a perimeter for the carpeting the guys brought earlier on, something we never even considered.

Excited energy radiates from Tamsin, and I'm transfixed by the serenity of the moment, completely oblivious to the other half of our group, until I hear his deep throaty chuckle. My head snaps their way, my steps faltering for just a second as my gaze zeros in on the red nails pressed against his crisp white shirt sleeve.

Jealously curls its twisted way around my insides, and no matter how many times I tell myself he isn't mine to get jealous over, it still smarts.

"The most beautiful girl I have ever seen," Taylor says,

appreciation laced through the words. "And her best friend."

He places a quick kiss on my cheeks, taking her arm from mine as I step back.

"Yo, boys, you can flirt later," he calls.

"Nick? You chose Nick as your second witness?" I ask, incredulous despite him standing right there.

Nick's sharp gaze finds me instantly, the dimmed light only intensifying the ego on display. If he thinks he can claim me as his with this little bracelet and then stand there flirting with someone else at my best friend's ceremony, he's got another thing coming.

"I've got to show my boy how it's done now, haven't I?" Taylor laughs, aware of nothing but the woman under his arm, my simmering irritation not even on his radar.

Nick, Jasper, and Penelope come over, the distance not nearly far enough as Jasper comes to my side, Nick opposite with Taylor and Tamsin between us. Penelope leans closer to Nick again, whispering something in his ear, even as his gaze stays fixed on mine. Whatever she said must be amusing as the corner of his mouth lifts in the barest of smiles.

She stands too close to him, not like Jasper and I, and as Taylor asks his roommate for the band, all attention is finally on the two people between us, the two we're supposed to be here for. Jasper slides it from his pocket, along with some kind of metal clipper thing, wrapping the black leather around her wrist before pausing.

"Last chance to back out, baby," he offers, looking Tamsin in the eye.

She's been silent this whole time, another tell for the

nerves that I know she's feeling right now, but her voice is as steady and confident as the hand she holds out when she looks Taylor dead in the eyes and says, "I'm yours."

His grin is resplendent as he takes the clipper from Jasper, binding the leather together, the silver stripe glinting in the lights. *It won't be the only thing shining shortly.*

The leather is soft in my hands, cream and delicate. Beautiful. Tamsin offers him the same out before wrapping it around Taylor's wrist and letting Jasper clip it together.

"Cool, well I guess that's it," Jasper declares, pocketing the tool.

"That's it?" Penelope says, accusation dripping from the words. "I expected more."

She picks her skirt up, turns on her heel and stalks off into the darkness of the woods without another word.

"Pen, baby. You'll get lost," Jasper calls as we all watch her disappear through the trees.

"It's Penelope," she calls back.

"Wait up, baby cakes," he says, taking a step her way before pausing and turning to Taylor, something serious settling on his usually carefree face. "You got our girl?"

"I've got her," Taylor replies with a nod before Jasper runs off in search of Penelope—she's probably pissed off and half lost on her way back to the house.

Their light-hearted moment disappears in an instant, and Taylor asks if we'd give them five minutes and meet them by the pool for their grand entrance. Of course the two of us agree with a smile and a nod, and as his hand slides through her perfectly prepared curls, a sexual tension sizzles in the air.

Nick and I take a step out of the circle of light, the darkness wrapping around us like a blanket as I switch on the torch, the air between us charged.

"So, do you wish you'd done it differently?" I ask as we walk side by side, Nick holding a branch out of the way for me to pass.

"Not really," he replies calmly, a waft of Penelope's perfume hitting my nostrils and turning my nose up.

Irritation mingles with the jealousy swarming in my stomach.

Red nails on a white shirt. Her lips too close to his ear. She could have reached up and kissed him, and he might have gone for it. I've no hold over him, no claim. So, why wouldn't he?

"That was cute," he continues, clearly oblivious to the feelings that tumble around me.

I just need to get back to the house. Get a drink. Get some space. Then I'll be fine. Totally fine.

I'm watching the floor, attempting to ignore his proximity and the heat that keeps brushing up against my arm when something suddenly wraps itself around my face and I scream, the sound ripping from me unexpectedly as I claw at whatever the hell it is.

"Help," I yell. "Get it off!"

He's there straight away, his cologne surrounding me, his hands pushing mine out of the way and sweeping gently down over my skin, but there's nothing there, just tatters of something between my fingers as my heart roars in my ears.

"What the fuck was that?" I ask, attempting to focus my gaze on whatever the hell is in my hands, but I can't see anything, the torch lost in my abject terror.

"Spiders web," Nick replies quietly, picking something from my hair.

"Do not tell me there is a spider on my face, or in my hair." A shiver ripples over me as he smooths it back into place, his gentle touch a balm I didn't realise I needed.

His deliberate calmness is such a juxtaposition to the panic that still courses through my veins, my breaths coming out panted as I drop the spider's web from my fingers, attempting to get some semblance of control.

"I guess we wandered from the path," I comment.

"Looks like it," he agrees, his thumbs tracking back and forth against the back of my neck as I finally look up.

His white shirt stands out half a mile in the darkness, but the rest of him not so much. His square jawline, the darkness in his eyes, the way my body is pressed in against his.

"I wouldn't change how I claimed my girl," he says softly, and I still. "My girl was hot, and half-naked, and she wanted me almost as much as she feared me, at that moment. She was absolutely perfect."

All the air is sucked completely from my lungs with his words, seeing the moment through his eyes rather than the fear that coursed through my veins, the same kind I'm tamping down right now.

"Thinking I wanted you is a bit of a stretch, don't you think?" I ask, not nearly as strong as I hoped, the statement coming out breathy.

"If I could go back, push you up on that hood and lick the nectar from your wet pussy the same way I lapped those tears, I would," he admits on a rumble.

The way my body reacts to the words, the voice, the rumble… it's instantaneous. Heat floods my system as the adrenaline morphs into the exact thing his dirty words accuse me of. Lust. Wanting him.

I did want him.

I had him.

In these very woods, somewhere.

And now, I'm supposed to be walking away.

We had a truce, of sorts.

And it slides, that truce.

A pushing back and forth as tempting and delicious as he is.

"I bet, if I push that skirt up and dip my fingers along the seam of the thong I know you're wearing, you'd be fucking soaked," he rasps.

Goosebumps follow the path of his fingers as they trail a blaze down my chest, over my abdomen, and down my thigh. By the time he's hitching my skirt up, I'm widening my legs in anticipation of his touch. My eyes close and my lips part as he holds me firmly in his grasp.

Any softness in the hold at the back of my neck disappears as his tongue lathes a path along my jaw, my already thunderous heartbeat giving me away as need curls low in my belly. His teeth nip gently at my earlobe and down the column of my neck to that sensitive spot where it meets my shoulder, and still, his fingers only dance up the inside of my thigh.

By the time they finally make it to where I need him so desperately, I'm practically ready to beg him for his touch, the need for more so overwhelming that it's all I can think of. His dark chuckle hits me deep as he slides his fingers beneath the wet fabric, slipping up and down.

"Please," I whimper, lost to the feeling, to his touch, to him.

"I don't know how you even dare deny this when you so clearly want it." His spikey words come out smooth and sweet before he pushes two thick fingers in deep.

My exhale is practically a sigh of relief as he fills that aching need, torturous inch by torturous inch, and when his thumb finds my clit, I'm practically grinding myself against him, but he works my body like I'm an instrument he knows all the keys for, a symphony I'm not prepared for at all as my orgasm curls and coils, wrapping tighter and tighter around me.

"That's it, sugar," he rasps. "That's what you need. I've got you."

He sinks his teeth into my shoulder as I grind helplessly against him, the sting hurtling me over the edge as my orgasm crashes into me like a tidal wave. Surge after surge wracks my body as he drags every last sensation he can until opening my eyes has reality creeping in once again.

My forehead is pressed up against his chest, one hand gripping the wrist between my legs, the other twisted in his shirt as he pulls his fingers from me, sliding them into his mouth and sucking my taste from them as he fixes my thong and dress with his other hand.

"Fuck, you're as sweet as I knew you would be," he admits.

I'm struck speechless as his hooded gaze meets mine.

Reaching up, I thread my fingers through his hair, pulling his lips down to meet mine. My taste is sharp on his tongue, and mixed with the coffee he had earlier on, it's different, pleasant, as I tangle and taste. His hand comes back to my nape as he angles the kiss deeper, pressing his thick erection against me.

"I'm not fucking you in the woods again," he says, pulling back. "The next time you come, I want to be front and fucking centre."

"In your dreams," I reply, but there's no strength to it, no conviction. Our panted breaths intermingled as the seconds tick by.

"Or yours." He smirks. "But I expect pictures."

I can't help the laugh that tumbles from me as my knees finally strengthen and there's half a chance I can walk out of here not looking like I've just been fucked in the woods. Again.

"We'd better get back," he says, bending down and picking up the torch. "People are waiting for us."

I nod my agreement, taking the torch and the olive branch it offers and pushing back any and all thoughts of red nails on his white shirt. She might be here for whoever she can get, but he isn't, and with that thought settled in my mind, and a serious post-orgasm haze, I let him guide us back to the pool.

Cheering calls out from the house as we duck out of the cover of the trees. *I guess they got sick of waiting.*

"Shall we?" he asks, holding his arm out for me as I swap out the now muddy ballet flats for the heels we left by the pool. *Planning ahead.* My legs are still wobbly as I accept his arm and the two of us head to the house, sliding discreetly through the French doors.

"I knew there had to be a good reason for missing your girl's big entrance," Jacob comments idly from the kitchen, his assessing gaze astute.

Nick steers us in that direction as Jacob finds us both drinks, but I decline. "Never accept an opened bottle. Girl code," I explain.

"Good thinking," he agrees, throwing his down the sink too and heading to one of the electric coolers laying around, pulling out a bottle of Moet. With a smile and a shake of his head, Nick grabs half a dozen glasses from a cupboard as Jacob opens the bottle. "If you see me open it, that's okay, isn't it?" he checks.

"It is."

Awareness prickles over my skin as Nick's gaze flicks to someone over my shoulder. There are plenty of people here, it's a party, after all, but the hands on my waist give me a moment's hesitation until Leo kisses the side of my neck and steps back.

"You look… gorgeous," he compliments.

"Ravished." Jacob grins, handing me a glass, knowing in his eyes.

"Ravishing," Wyatt corrects, plucking two glasses from the counter and handing one to Ruby, who sneaks in quietly beside him.

"Yeah, whatever. You look fine," Ruby says. "Who has seen Tamsin's dress, though? Now *that* is amazing."

"Oh, she did the thing?" *Already.* "With the thing?" I ask, gesturing to the long train we added.

"Absolute fire." Ruby nods.

"You've all seen it?" I ask, looking at the guys who nod and shrug like it's no big deal. "My fingers are still sore from all the time we've spent on that damn thing."

"Wait, you guys made that?" Ruby asks, edging closer. "Like, the two of you, together, by hand?"

"Yep." I nod. "It's Tamsin's design."

I don't know if it's the drink she's barely touched, her proximity to Wyatt, or being away from Amy's watchful eye, but she's almost another person at this moment. She's interested, excited, and engaged. Running with it, I ask if she'd like to come and take a closer look, and to my astonishment, she says yes, lighting up.

Well fucking hell.

The temptation to reach up and kiss Nick before we leave hits me right in the gut. It would be so easy, so straightforward, but with the feel of Leo's hands still branded on my waist and Wyatt's helpful optimism just a breath away, I don't. Instead, I squeeze his hand before Ruby and I walk away, champagne in hand, weaving our way through the guys and the rest of the partygoers.

"I didn't know you were into design," I comment, attempting to make conversation.

"I'm not really," she admits. "I'm into black, and that dress transformation was spectacular."

Eventually, we find them holding court in the den, chatting with some people I've never seen before. The train glitters and shimmers, even in this rubbish lighting, and as she flicks it out, the pride is indescribable.

She comes over, catching my gaze and welcoming Ruby

but keeping her hugs and air kisses to herself. *The restraint.* Her simple black silk slip matched my red one, and as I disappear, grabbing my own transformational jacket, I know I'll look almost as amazing as she does.

The delicate lace glides over my shoulders, stopping at my elbows, whereas hers is full length and goes to her wrists, a single strap sliding over her thumb. The silver beads and gems we embedded are heavy at the base of her floor-length train, feathering out up to the bodice. With mine being a deep crimson, we went with black beading, and with her being the centre of attention, I stopped mine at knee length.

"May I?" Ruby asks as I join them, gesturing to the train of Tamsin's jacket.

"Of course," she replies, flicking my fingers out of the way to take over my awful attempt at fastening the delicate hook and eye on the front. "Sorry we didn't wait for you," she says quietly. "We assumed you'd given up waiting and come in already."

Penelope sneaks in, passing beside us to join Oliver on a sofa, a smile on her face as that jealous irritation bubbles again. Stephanie isn't going to take her moving in on him well either. After all, he's gone out of his way to make sure everyone knows she's his and kept safe, and that works both ways.

"Sorry," I reply, my gaze flicking to where Ruby studies the hem of her dress, no doubt doing her best to look like she's not eavesdropping whilst absorbing every word. "We got a little… delayed."

"We heard." She grins.

Heat creeps up my neck as I press my lips together,

attempting to hold in the embarrassed smile desperate to break free.

"Are you okay down there?" I ask as Tamsin finishes the last clasp, stepping back to straighten and adjust it over my shoulders.

"I still can't believe you did this by hand," Ruby says, wonder laced through her tone as she turns to look at the detail on mine. "These are totally amazing."

"Thank you." Tamsin smiles, ever grateful for the acknowledgement of her natural talent.

"Why she's wasting her life in philosophy and not design, I will never understand," I say with a roll of my eyes.

"Just because I can, doesn't mean I should," she jabs back with a smile. "This is for fun, enjoyment, and happiness. Something that looks good on your face, for a change."

"Uh-huh. You'd better get back, Taylor's looking for you," I say, tipping my glass in his direction before taking a sip.

She nods, clinking her glass against mine before heading back to Taylor.

"Philosophy?" Ruby asks as I watch my best friend loop onto her man, showing off the leather at her wrist with pride.

I wish I could do the same, but it doesn't feel like a coupling, like a conscious choice. Not yet, anyway.

"Apparently so," I reply distractedly.

"What a waste. That top is amazing, they both are."

"Yep."

It's a conversation we've had more than once.

Her designs are incredible, her creative ability way beyond anything I could dream of, and yet, she holds it back from the world, only allowing them tiny glances; like tonight. If she didn't want to make, why not just design and work with a seamstress? But no, it's not that.

I'm not sure what it is.

Something, for sure.

The fear of failing? Of not being *good* enough? Or maybe she thinks it can never be a reality for her, that she'd never make it anyway, so why bother?

I don't know. She won't talk about it.

And she's happy making designs for herself when the moment takes her; when inspiration hits. So, why push her for more? To *be* more, to take on more. I'd rather she was happy than taking that enjoyment and potentially transforming it into a chore.

"You people are weird," Ruby comments.

"I thought you were one of *our people?*" I reply, moving us through to the dining room and gathering a couple of chairs. It's easier than I expected, the room half empty as I find us a corner to sit in.

She doesn't reply, just follows along with me, silently watching everything and everyone as they move around the house with the practised ease of those with money. There's no keg on the table, no rowdy boys fighting in the backyard, and no humping and grinding on the dance floor. Well, not yet, anyway.

Most of the people here have been groomed for polite company since childhood. Smile, keep quiet, laugh when appropriate, and generally be a good girl. Now, that's not to say they don't know how to enjoy themselves or have a good time. Lord knows Tamsin and I have been to our fair share of raves and good nights out, but they weren't sanctioned by our parents.

"Not quite," she finally admits. "My mother's employer is paying for my tuition. It's complicated."

"Sounds it."

"He's an asshole, and why he's bothering, I'm not sure." She finishes the rest of her champagne in one go, clearly seeming to need it.

"So, you're telling me you didn't grow up with a butler and the talent to design your own stunning clothes?" I ask, attempting to keep the tone light as Wyatt slips in the doorway, winking our way before finding himself in conversation with someone else. "Me neither."

She scoffs out a laugh. "I'm going to need more alcohol if you're going to come out with crap like that. I know exactly who you are, Ivy Rose."

"Yeah?"

I'm not going to stop her, whatever thoughts and ideals she has about me are probably nine miles from the truth, or at least short-sighted enough, based on our limited interactions. And whilst she's talking, opening up, giving me a glimpse into how her mind works, I'm not going to say no.

"You were top of your class, you're a psychologist in the making. Don't think I've missed the way you analyse and strategize me," she says, plucking another glass from the table, her cocktail dress moving fluidly around her.

It's not a designer brand, but still, it fits her beautifully. The black satin crosses over her chest and wraps around her back, the skirt floating from that point in layers to the knee. It's simple and classy, but not showy.

She fits in here better than she realises.

Money is just a number, it doesn't give you elegance. That's learnt, usually.

There's a confidence, an openness that she doesn't usually have as she finishes another glass, refilling it before joining me once again. She'd have stuck out in her jeans and jumpers here, but instead, she blends beautifully, a true chameleon in our midst. Oh, and there's no phone in her hand.

"Why don't you share a few things about yourself then?" I ask. "Even the playing field a little."

She glides to the seat beside me, not noticing Leo come in or the way both he and Wyatt watch her with interest. She's not an Angel, neither of them can pick her in that way, but still, underneath all the irritation and refusal to engage is a brilliant young woman doing her best to survive. I get the interest.

"Or not, that's totally fine," I say, conscious of her lack of reply.

Perhaps getting personal information from her when she's had this much wine is unethical, but this is the most she's opened up in the weeks and months we've been getting to know each other. How can I help her realise her dreams if she won't even let me in enough to tell me what they are?

"Is there a bathroom somewhere?" she asks, ignoring my question. "Too much champagne."

"In the hallway, second left," I reply.

For some reason, she carefully manoeuvres her way around the room, never obviously part of a conversation but close enough to various ones to look like it. Personally, I'd have gotten up and walked through the room, who cares if someone notices and sees you leave?

I guess it's more than just her history that's guarded.

# FOURTEEN

## *Nick*

The beer warms in my hand, not only because I'm aware of our two-drink limit and how spotless this place is supposed to be, even after a party, but because I can still taste her on my tongue, and it's fucking glorious.

Her grip on my arm, her moans, the whimper, fuck, that almost did me in on the spot and had me coming in my pants like a teenager. Not quite, but almost. It's ridiculous how badly I want to fuck this party off and take her upstairs, ignore whatever fancy shit her friend wants for the poncy display of affection, and show her exactly how a man treats his woman.

I'm not here for the show, I'm here for her. I'm here for The Sect. I'm here to become more than my brother, more than my father, and more than anyone expects of the silly little boys who know nothing.

Jacob and I have always been cute and matching, even when we didn't mean to. It's an easy role to play into. Just turn up to the events we need to, smile and be charming, but nobody ever expects anything of us.

Andrew took over Barrett Enterprises like it was

always meant to be. After disappearing for years on end, hiding away and sulking, he strode into the role with his new fiancée on his arm, our sister at his side, and our father behind him. But we were too young, too inexperienced, too… fuck knows what, but whatever it was, we weren't enough to be taken seriously.

And I think, in the end, our mother was just glad to be rid of the burden of us. Not that she's ever been the doting kind, and more recently she's been nothing but a ghost of herself and has spent months wandering around the house in mourning.

But still, we were there, a reminder of a job uncompleted. Two boys that she hasn't managed to get into a good job yet, that she didn't get to marry off to a nice woman from a good family. *Shit, can you imagine?* So, when the opportunity arose to pack us up and send us off to Pendleton Prep, how could she say no?

We'd be out of sight and out of mind, finally making something of ourselves, supposedly. Yes, that's what we're supposed to be doing, not being distracted by pretty girls and tight pussies, but fuck if she isn't worth being distracted for.

As if conjured by nothing more than my thoughts, Ivy appears briefly in the doorway, her simple silk dress transformed with lace and some sparkly shit that shines as she moves. As quickly as she appears, she's gone, lost in the throng of people.

"You'd better wipe that smile off your face," Jacob says light-heartedly. "People will think you're approachable and start talking to you, and we both know you don't want that."

There's no stress ball to throw at him down here, and certainly not in the middle of a celebration, so I just throw a smirk in his direction instead. "They'd soon realise their mistake when they attempt to make conversation."

"Ooh, so hostile," he jokes, moving to stand beside me.

"I have no details I'm willing to share, so don't even bother," I say, cutting him off at the pass. "If you want to gossip, what's going on with you and Leo?"

Don't think I didn't notice him hovering around, always nearby, always watching. I'm not that much of a self-centred prick to think it's because of me and not my twin brother that he has eyes for.

It's that very same attraction that means he has never once got the two of us mixed up. Yeah, sure, people figure it out eventually. We're not the same, despite how our looks might contradict that, but there is not one single occasion he's got us confused, and there's likely a reason for that.

"It's complicated," he admits.

"Because he still wants Ivy."

He's stupid if he thinks I've missed how Leo looks at her, taking almost any opportunity to get up close and personal with her, it's the same thing he does with Jacob, which is probably why it's so irritating. The intent is clear, and annoying as fuck, even more so now she has my band around her wrist.

So what if mine's empty? That doesn't mean anything. She'll come to her senses eventually, I'm sure.

"As I said, it's complicated." He sighs, taking a swig of the beer much colder than mine.

"Well, good catch-up. I'm going to go do a quick sweep

and gather up any empty glasses and bottles. Try to get us ahead of the chaos that comes later," I say.

"Good plan," he replies. "I'll help."

We set off in opposite directions, Jacob heading for the dining room whilst I make moves to the movie room. The lights are half up, the film being played but not watched by the dozen or so people gathered in the centre of the room.

Nobody pays me much attention as I wander around the room, until Leo notices what I'm doing, peeling away from the group to give me a hand before joining them again with nothing but a chin lift. I don't know what his game is, but I'll figure it out.

The bottles land in the nearest bin a little louder than probably needed, but nobody says anything as I gather up the empty glasses and head to the kitchen to drop them off. Jacob winks as we pass each other, him on his way in, and me on my way out.

Grabbing a bag, I head into the entranceway, gathering glasses on a side table and throwing rubbish in the bag when movement upstairs catches my attention.

"For fuck's sake," I grumble. We've been more than clear about it being off-limits, and if I find someone fucking in one of the rooms, I'm going to lose my shit.

Dumping the bag at the bottom of the stairs, I creep up, checking the first room but finding nothing. A bump comes from further down the corridor, the sound of a door closing as I carefully close Taylor and Jasper's door. It wouldn't have surprised me to find them both in there with Tamsin, party or no party, but that noise isn't here.

I check the room next door, not expecting anything, but

there's definitely someone up here, and now, I want to know who, and why. There's nothing out of place in my room, and it's only as I go to close the door, I realise the bathroom light is on.

Closing the door behind me, I cross the room, the sound of running water catching me off guard.

"Hello?" I call, knowing for certain that Wyatt's downstairs and there is no other reason for someone to be in here.

But no one answers, and my hand is almost on the handle, insecurity holding me back when it opens, Ruby turning the light off before she almost walks right into me.

"Woah, shit," she says, pulling up short. "Sorry, Ivy said it would be okay to use your bathroom."

"Uh, yeah. Sure, that's cool," I say, looking quickly around the bathroom before stepping back.

"Someone was in the one downstairs and when you've got to go, you've got to go," she explains, straightening the top of her dress.

"Ah, yes," I agree. "Shall I walk you back down?"

I don't know why, but my gut still tells me something's off. Perhaps she didn't hear me over the water running, and maybe I've just followed her up and there's nothing untoward going on at all, but something inside me says that's not what's happening.

"That would be great." She smiles sweetly, a long way from the snarky girl I met at the house the other week.

Yeah, something is definitely not right.

"Are you enjoying the party?" I ask, guiding her out and heading back towards the stairs.

"It's not quite what I'm used to," she admits, gesturing to the dress. "But it's been different, fun."

"Been?"

"Ah, yeah. I'll have to go in half an hour or so… curfew," she explains with a shrug of her shoulders.

"Right."

"Anyway, thank you for… this. I'll catch you in a bit." She takes the last few stairs quickly, disappearing back into the dining room without looking back.

She never asked why I was there, I ponder, picking up the glasses and heading back into the kitchen, rinsing them in the sink.

"You're welcome, by the way," Taylor says, dropping his empty bottle in the bin beside me.

"Huh?"

"Get her in a good mood with the cutest mirroring moment ever, throw in a little bit of jealousy from a girl she kind of likes, and boom, you're later back than we are." He chuckles, pulling another beer out.

"That simple, huh?"

"Oh, absolutely. Although, it's not just been me and Tamsin these last few weeks. Throwing Jasper in the mix has been a great help too."

"Really?"

I have no idea how adding someone else in is going to make things better, or hotter. Sharing isn't usually my thing, outside of my brother.

"Well, the first time was just accidental, but the second… well, yeah, okay, that wasn't intentional either but fuck man, it's pretty good."

"Wait, that's happened more than once?" I ask, placing another glass on the draining board.

He shuffles closer, dropping his voice so nobody else overhears. "Well, you remember that night we went and did the stupid picture thing? Posting them on all the dormitory doors or whatever?"

"Yeah."

"Well, she messaged me this picture and Jasper saw it. The next thing I knew, the two of us were leaving halfway through and meeting her back at our place."

"What, you never finished it?" I clarify. Not sure why that takes precedence over the threesome he's about to discuss, but for some reason, it does.

"Nah, we figured you boys had it under control."

"And that's why Jasper met us at the side door and you were nowhere to be seen."

"Sorry, bro. I had to make sure she got back to her place safely. She was thoroughly fucked and dishevelled, not fit for public consumption."

"No, just for the two of you," I clip out, attempting to tamp down the irritation.

That's twice now he's skipped out on something for a girl without saying anything, without so much as giving us a heads up.

"Yeah, well, it was supposed to be a one-off, but she kept asking about him whilst we were at that party. You know, keeping everyone distracted so you could claim Ivy."

"I remember." How could I ever forget?

"Well, after Ivy left, for the second time, I brought her back here and gave her it good, but Jasper was back earlier than expected, and you can probably figure out the rest."

"So, you didn't let him know you were home with her?" I clarify, trying to remember what I asked him to do, what's been half-assed for pussy. What's been missed?

"Nah, man. He just turned up."

Thank fuck for that.

# FIFTEEN

## Ruby

"Thank you for coming," Ivy says, holding herself back from the hug I'm sure she wants to give me.

Tamsin, however, does no such thing, wrapping her arms around me, her cloying perfume still a cloud even after all these hours. "We absolutely need to do this again."

"Sure," I agree to both of them, managing to extricate myself and slide into the back of the taxi without any further issues.

"So, next town over?" the driver asks, seeking clarification as we pull away, the gravel crunching beneath the tyres.

"Just outside the main gates here is fine," I correct, waving through the windows.

"But the lady said—"

"I know what she said," I interrupt. "And just outside the gates is fine."

He's probably not impressed that his big fare just shrunk significantly, but that's not my problem. At least it means he keeps conversation to a minimum as we pass under the huge trees, the house behind us disappearing in the dense foliage before we pull out into the light of the campus.

And isn't that some kind of metaphor?

Down a dark, dark driveway there's a large, large house. In the large, large house seven Devils live.

It only takes a few minutes for us to leave the campus completely, pulling out onto the main road as I gesture for him to pull over. I pay him for the fare he expected, and, as the car lights flash from the opposite side of the road, he checks I'm okay before leaving me high and dry.

Good job I am, isn't it?

I was in more danger in that house than out here, not that he'd ever understand that.

The sleek black car pulls forward slightly as I cross the road, climbing into the back without a word. The locks engage as we pull away, the soft leather as familiar as the cigar smoke that curls from the front.

"You good?" he asks.

Just two words, but they hold more meaning, and more questions than you could ever imagine. My head pushes back into the seat, the engine roaring beneath us practically a picture of his unhinged response to my lack of reply.

"Yeah."

The engine eases, my thighs clenching as I stutter out a breath that I know he can't hear. I don't know if it's from being out here, free-ish, or being around those girls, but I'm all kinds of pent-up.

They're beautiful and talented, and they take whatever they want without thought or question. It's as infuriating as it is admirable because they don't intend any negative outcome, and yet, someone else always pays the price for privilege.

There's no first class without economy, and I'm as economy as it comes. Not that anyone there treated me that way. Still, it's all just a role I need to play, a small piece in a big picture.

He doesn't attempt to make any conversation, not that I expect him to, and the combination of the alcohol I've had and the engine purring has me at least a little drowsy before we eventually make it back to my place, because, of course, that's where I belong.

Not with Ivy and her friends, and certainly not with him.

The two-bed terrace is dilapidated, at best, surrounded by other shitty houses, all of which are probably worth less than the striking car I'm sitting in, not that anyone around here would ever dare comment on it.

"Is it done?" he asks, turning off the engine and catching my gaze in his mirror.

Delicious darkness swirls there, something that I know deep in the core of me only promises pain, but like the moth to the flame, I can't help but be drawn to him. He holds my gaze until I nod, the only confirmation he needs from me tonight.

He climbs out, his over six-foot tall, broad frame blocking everything as he opens the door for me, the boot opening at the same time. That same gaze focuses as I slide one leg out, finally placing my heeled foot on the ground before swinging the other to join it and standing.

Just his presence has me weak at the knees, add in the heels, the drive, the alcohol, and the drop in adrenaline and unsteady is potentially not even the word. Heat sizzles as his gaze tracks up my legs, skimming over my stomach before admiring my pushed-up tits for longer than is polite, not that he cares.

His teeth grind together as he gestures to the back of the car for my things, his restraint impeccable. I walk, stumbling as I round the car and land on the edge of the boot, luckily not finding myself in an embarrassed heap on the floor.

Sadly, he doesn't jump to my aid, catching me before I fall like Wyatt would, or rush to check I'm okay like some of the others might. He just watches and waits. Silently, patiently. The boy I knew hides in the depths of that gaze, somewhere, and as I shake out my wrist, the bones already smarting from where I landed, I finally get a hint of him.

He reaches out, a fission of electricity that coils deep in my stomach as his fingers trace the bones, rotating my hand to check I've not done anything permanent. With a nod, he releases me, clearly happy it's okay, although, I could have told him that, but the touch and the half-second of vulnerability was worth keeping my mouth shut for. *It's not my forte.*

"Is there anything you need, anything you want before I go in?" I ask, much bolder than usual, the words coming out husky.

His body is barely inches from mine, blocking out the world that spins slightly, but he doesn't move. He's solid and stable, always has been. His gaze flickers down the length of me, appreciation shining through before his thumb and forefinger hook my chin, dragging my face to his.

He leans in, my breath held as my heart flutters in

my chest, his lips so close to my own before he runs his cheek against mine. His rough stubble sends electric sparks through me, with need that coils deep in my stomach. Fuck, does he even know what that does to me?

"Careful what you wish for." With my chin held firmly in his grasp, the words come out scratchy, his breath fanning down my neck. "Now go to bed, baby girl."

Like the fool I am, I sigh, my held breath seeming to come out forever as I sink back down into myself. I'm not stupid, he feels exactly the way I do, so why we're doing this idiotic song and dance, I have no idea.

Stringing someone along is mean and unfair, but with a fortifying breath in, his cologne and the rich cigar smoke that curls around him like an old coat seeping into my lungs, I put the walls back up.

He's just doing a job. So am I.

Puppets on a string.

"Good night," I say, my hand finding the bag behind me without turning.

I feel the sting of the tiny squeeze on my chin before he steps back, letting me go and gesturing to the house with his head. I know he can taste my disappointment on his tongue, but I'll not give him the satisfaction of seeing it.

Instead, I push my shoulders back, step up on my heels, and do my best to saunter down the short path before opening the door and going in.

I lock it behind me, knowing my mother is already home, but it isn't until the light goes on in my room that I hear the engine rumble, him pulling away into the night.

I don't doubt he spent his night sitting outside that

campus, waiting and wondering. Does he even care about sending me into the Devil's lair? Does he care about me at all?

# SIXTEEN

"**H**ow do you shower with this damn thing?" Tamsin complains, rubbing a nail beneath the edge of the leather band.

"The same way you would with any jewellery," I offer, looking up from my laptop.

"Well, I'd normally take mine off…"

"Ah, that might be a problem."

She adjusts the towel around her, sliding her top on whilst I turn the page looking for my next piece of quotable material. *There's got to be something useful in here.*

"Well, just slide it down a bit and you should be fine," I say absentmindedly.

"Can't," she says, thrusting her wrist in my face. "There's not enough slack in it to shuffle it, and I'm going to end up disgusting if I can't clean and dry it properly. Can you imagine? Gross." She shudders.

Sticking my pen in the book, I turn and open one of the vanity drawers, rifling through the bags and boxes stashed in their depths until I find the pads I'm looking for. The soft cotton is almost paper thin but layered together so it doesn't just fall apart. Grabbing two out, I add a little micellar water to one, sliding the edge under the leather and running it around her wrist.

"Ooh, that's cold," she comments.

"I'm sure your shower gel is working just fine, but if you're concerned, any cleanser will work, I'm sure." I pull it out, replacing it with the dry one to soak up any excess moisture.

She snatches the rest of the packet off the desk with a smile and a wink, heading to the bathroom to stash them wherever she needs them, I suppose.

"They're nothing special," I call. "You should be able to order more pretty easily."

"Perfect. You're fucking amazing." She grins. "How's the work coming along?"

"Slowly," I complain, eyeing the workbooks before giving them my back and slumping down in the chair. "I've got that reading to do before we get on our Zoom training later on too."

"I've done it. Let me summarise it for you… drugs are bad, just say no." She nods.

"Really?"

"Yeah, really. I did the work, is that so hard to imagine?" She flops onto her bed, textbook and highlighter in hand. "I'm not a complete flake, you know?"

"Of course not. It's just that you've been a little preoccupied recently."

"You say this like it's a bad thing," she admonishes. "This year is about more than just getting through the work, Ivy. It's about finding out who you are, and what you want from life."

"It's not about what The Sect want from you then, no?"

"The only thing we've been *requested* to do is the Little Sister programme, and Ruby and the other girls are great. Spending time with them, getting to know them, and supporting them in achieving their goals is not a hardship, it's a blessing. Just lean into it and enjoy."

"There's more to this than picking a boy and mentoring, Tamsin." I sigh, the breath huffing out like defeat personified. Even after linking herself with Taylor, she doesn't get it and doesn't see the danger around every corner. "Masks, robes, secret identities. That's not normal."

"So they're a little extra about it all." She shrugs. "So what? I think it's kind of fun. Oh, and think of all the things we'll be able to do once we're through this… whatever it is. We can become whatever we want to be."

"We could do that before," I grumble, swinging the chair left and right. "We've always been able to do and be whatever we wanted."

I hadn't realised that she'd been feeling so stuck when we came, but I suppose it makes sense. She'd been off the rails, more than usual. The parties were getting more extreme, and the way she dove into the mixer straight off… well, she's always been free with her affection, but that was something else.

"Maybe you could," she says, pointing her pen in my direction, "Some of us have been lined up as nothing more than trophy wife material for a very long time."

The one thing I've been fighting against since the second we turned up in this place.

We might have joked about it over the years, but there's no way she'd ever settle for that, no way I'd allow her to. She's too creative, and too thoughtful—it would be a complete waste.

"That's not going to happen."

"No, it's not. Now, I have Taylor by my side, and he's going on to do great things, and so am I." She nods.

It hurts my heart to hear that she doesn't feel like she could do this on her own, or with me. That she thinks I'd really leave her tied to someone she doesn't care about, just going through the motions of life. *She can't really think that, surely?*

"You always were," I reply, sadness creeping into my tone. "As long as you're happy, that's all I want."

"Same," she replies, catching my gaze and holding it before changing the subject. "You and Nick looked cosy the other night at the party… are things going better?"

My gaze flicks to my phone, his last message sitting unread.

"Yeah, they're good."

Our conversation disappears with the nod of her head, Tamsin going back to her books as I turn back around, attempting to find the information I need for this next piece, but my mind wanders…

It's not a complete lie, just a minor manipulation of the truth. *Isn't that happening more at the moment?* Things are, as always, complicated, and I'm finding myself leaning on Wyatt for explanations and understanding, for friendship. It doesn't hurt that I know for certain all my messages to Wyatt wind Nick up even further than he already is.

Any time Nick and I are together, either in class or when we're around other people, is charged and electrified. I know more than well that he wants to stop me, to dictate who and when I talk to other people, the rest of the Devils especially, but I also know he's holding back from doing so. I guess there's only so long before it all comes to a head.

I know exactly how crazy a little jealousy can make you feel, just the thought of Penelope alone in a room with them makes more anger surge through my veins than I thought possible, and the strangest thing about it is, I don't get that way over Jacob being with Leo.

They've become more open with their affections since they lost Emmerson. I don't know if somehow it's becoming more *real* to them both, or if something happened whilst they were in their challenge, neither of them is open to talking about it, but the two of them hover wherever the other is.

The longing looks have been replaced with gentle touches, and the secret touches with kisses hot enough to make your toes curl. It's interesting and exciting, and if it weren't for the magnetism with Nick and the way I feel about Wyatt, it's something I'd consider.

Well, now, anyway.

Tamsin has kept no secrets about how fucking hot it was with both Jasper and Taylor, and I have to admit, part of me is interested in what that might be like. A very small part, shoved somewhere deep down in the pit of my stomach, because it is not happening...

I don't think.

You get one band. One choice.

And yeah, Nick chose me, it would make sense to pick him back, but, then, what about Wyatt? Leo and Jacob have a thing, they could totally secure each other, but I know that Wyatt is my friend, and more. He's going to end up alone in this game. He won't make it alone. Would Nick?

I can't even entertain the thought of him being linked with someone else, anyone else. The very idea makes my stomach turn and lava run through my veins.

So, that should be it, shouldn't it?

It's just that simple.

I can't imagine him with anyone else, so he's the one for me, but what about Wyatt?

"Ten minutes," Aimee calls, tapping on the door twice. "I'm making coffee and then we should be ready, okay?"

"Sure," Tamsin replies.

Where the fuck did all that time go?

I've spent way too long not working on my project, day dreaming about three ways with the guys I like, and one that I can't walk away from. And still, I have no answer about the wristband… or any work done.

Throwing the pen down in irritation gets me no further, but I do it all the same, shutting down the laptop and trying to will the heat that courses through me down. *That was way too much time thinking about the Devils. Hot. Wet. Sexy. Naked.*

"Are you okay?" Tamsin asks from behind me as I pop my laptop away, shoving it in the bag with more force than necessary, clearly caught out with the daydreaming, again.

"I'm good. Sorry. I thought I'd get further on this than I have, that's all."

"Oh, I've been there." She closes her books up, stacking them all neatly on the bedside table. "I swear I was writing like a maniac, all the words were flowing and I knew exactly where I was going. I was in the zone, you know?"

I nod.

"Then I checked my word count... I'd barely added anything. So disappointing."

I don't think finding myself distracted all this time is exactly the same thing, but I appreciate the thought.

"I can imagine," I reply, grabbing the stuff I need for the Big Sister training session we're about to be late for, despite it being in our living room. "So, drugs are bad, don't do that. That's the line, yeah?"

"Exactly." She nods, throwing me a pen as we head out into the living room.

Luckily, Aimee has everything set up. The TV is prepped for the meeting, the coffee cups are on the table with steam rising as we grab a spot on the sofa, joining Stephanie who's texting on her phone.

"I can't believe he's even thinking about it," she mutters under her breath. "A fucking beard, in your twenties? No way."

"Who, Oliver?" Tamsin asks, her interest piqued as I attempt to scan through the text I should have already read.

"Ooh, he'd look kinda cute with a goatee," Charlotte comments from the floor. "That would suit his face shape, don't you think?"

"Maybe," Stephanie admits. "But a beard? Like a full-on, itchy on your face, fluffy beard?"

"That's a pass from me," I agree, giving her a high five

across Tamsin.

"I think it would be nice," Penelope says, dropping into one of the chairs and grabbing her mug. "They're perfect for sitting on too." She winks.

"What, and have his beard hair all over my… tickling your legs and everything? Nope. No. I don't think so. It's not happening."

"Don't knock it until you've tried it," Penelope continues. "I told him as much the other night."

"I'm sorry, what?" Stephanie asks, tension rippling from her as we all still.

"I told him beards were great for oral." Penelope shrugs, looking from one of us to another, hoping for someone to back her up, but we're all silent. "It's no big deal."

It is.

"So, let me get this straight, you talking to my boyfriend about oral sex is not a big deal, not in the slightest bit inappropriate at all?"

"It's not like you're together-together, like Tamsin and Taylor," Penelope clarifies.

No, Oliver just bludgeoned someone half to death with his bare fists for Stephanie. No, it's not the same thing at all.

"I'm going to tell you this once," Stephanie hisses, pointing her finger towards Penelope. "Stay the fuck away from him. If I see or hear you anywhere in his general vicinity, you're dead."

"Really?" Penelope rolls her eyes dismissively. "You're completely overreacting here. It was one little conversation."

Because the way she rallied around Oliver and made the guy who frightened her pay was not an overcorrection in the slightest. She's proven to be a bit of a loose cannon. This was a mistake.

"You fucking heard me," Stephanie continues. "I swear to God, I'll cut your beloved hair off in your sleep. Stay the hell away from him."

The silence that spears the room is uncomfortable as Stephanie glares at Penelope, and I'm sure if she could physically harm her with just one look, she would, but Penelope looks anywhere but back at her, shrugging like it's no big deal before pulling her book out and ignoring us completely.

I get Stephanie's feeling, how ragingly jealous I was just minutes ago only thinking about someone else getting near Nick or Wyatt. So, to have someone throw that kind of comment in your face, well, I get it.

Stephanie goes back to texting furiously on her phone as Tamsin nudges my elbow, gesturing to the text I'm supposed to be reading. Aimee looks at Charlotte and shrugs, just as the meeting on the TV blares to life, our tutor finally arriving, ready to start.

There's an air of awkwardness that simmers through the whole meeting, our group not quite the single unit we've become on the back of Stephanie's outburst, and it goes on way too long. The meeting too. The second it's over, Stephanie is slamming her books closed and storming out the door, no doubt going to tell Oliver exactly what she thinks about him discussing oral sex with another woman.

"I don't know what her problem was, it was just a conversation," Penelope says with a disbelieving shrug of her shoulders. "It's not like we did anything."

"That's the line is it?" Tamsin asks. "You don't entertain men wearing these matching bands, and you don't fuck them, but flirting is fine, even if they're with someone else?"

"I'm not responsible for his actions."

"No, but you're responsible for your part in it," I argue. "Just because *all* you did was talk about sex with someone else's boyfriend, that does not make it okay. What if it was someone less captivated by their partner? Is sleeping with them okay? Just because you're single and not responsible for someone else's actions? That's a fucking cop out and you know it."

Red nails on his white shirt flash before my eyes, my blood heating even further.

"Oh, and whilst we're on it, you can stay the hell away from Nick, and Wyatt too."

"So, who exactly does that leave for the rest of us, Ivy?"

Somehow, we've both stood, facing off against each other across the coffee table as my anger surges.

"What's that supposed to mean?"

"George is gone. Emmerson is gone." She counts them off on her fingers. "Oliver is with Stephanie, Taylor is with Tamsin, Jacob and Leo are so obviously fucking it's not even funny, and now you're saying to stay away from Wyatt and Nick, so that leaves us with who? Jasper."

I sink back into the chair, realisation hitting like a sledgehammer.

"Liselle keeps telling us how important it is to pair up with one of these amazing guys, and then they fucking disappear. Charlotte, Aimee and I… what chance do we actually have here?"

Silence swallows the room.

Aimee collects the coffee mugs and disappears to the kitchen, no doubt washing up and prepping food for everyone. That's her go-to, her calm in the storm, it's something for her hands to do whilst her brain processes, or at least that's the idea of what she explained.

"Look I'm not trying to be a bitch," Penelope says. "And I really wasn't trying to mess with her relationship, but you've got to see the position the rest of us are in here, right?"

I nod, refusing to acknowledge it out loud.

Tamsin stands, and the two of us disappear back into our room, but not before she throws out, "You should still apologise to Stephanie when she gets back. Not cool."

"She was flirting with Nick on Saturday night," I admit, once we're back in the safety of our room. "Just seeing that drove me insane, so I can only imagine how pissed off Stephanie is knowing what they've been talking about."

"I get that, and I get her not thinking it's a big deal. But also, they're in a tricky position here." She grabs an eyebrow pencil, adjusting hers in the mirror. "You do you, that's all that matters."

"Thanks, Tamsin."

"Worry about your happiness and forget about everyone else. If you want both of them, have both of them." She shrugs like it's the simplest solution in the world.

If I want to keep Wyatt safe and keep people away from Nick, then I need to have both of them. Leo and Jacob can look after each other, even if I would be interested in something with them.

# SEVENTEEN

## Leo

Spencer's gaze flicks to my side, briefly. The longing there is as clear as if he'd written *'lovesick'* on his forehead. *Fucking pathetic piece of shit.*

You'll never guess his excuse for being in Ivy's space and ignoring her completely when she said no. Apparently, she doesn't know what she wants.

Well, maybe not, but when a woman says no, you fucking listen to them. I might not have many morals, but at least that's one of them.

And who the hell is he to say that about her anyway? He doesn't know her. Not really.

She puts on this cold, confident front and pretends that it doesn't bother her that everyone here knows who she is, and what she's linked to. That she's been raised and put on a pedestal by The Sect.

She doesn't see it, the target that's placed on her back. She doesn't hear the whispers from the other women here, or the jealous looks they send her way. And then some look at her like she's hung the sun and moon, like she's got the ticket they didn't know they wanted; The Devils.

What a joke.

*Prove your worth.*

*Show us what you're made of.*

*The final three will have the world at their feet.*

What they don't tell you is what it'll cost you.

And the Angels? They get even less information than we do. It's been more than clear that Ivy has no idea the game she's been dropped into. I guess she has a better clue about that now though.

She flicks her hair over her shoulder, a waft of her shampoo breaking me from my reverie as I watch Spencer scuttle away and head out of the door. *Spineless.*

Throwing my books in the bag at my feet takes less time than it ought to. I'll never find my notes now, but I know she's got a class after this one and we need to move quickly, otherwise she's going to be late.

"How are things at the house?" she asks as I take her bag from the table, carrying it as we cross the room.

"Yeah, they're okay," I admit. "It's been a little tense, since, you know."

"Yeah."

"I guess this is what we signed up for though." Not that anyone actually *signed up* for anything. "Nobody said it would be easy."

"But getting to know people only for… that's messed up." She shakes her head in disbelief.

I can read the undercurrent of fear in her words. Who next? How? When? All things every single one of us has thought about, but there aren't answers.

"It could be better, I'll give you that," I admit, my phone

vibrating in my pocket. "Are you good from here, or do you need me to walk you over?"

"Nick's outside," she says with a smile, sliding her phone back into her pocket, mine growing more insistent by the second. "He's just dropped Taylor off so we can walk together, but thank you for the offer."

The external doors loom as my phone goes quiet, finally. It's his shoulders that catch my eye, his gaze focused on something in the opposite direction. He's broad and strong, but so willing to hand all that strength over, yet, as he moves, the energy is off, and I suddenly realise it's Nick and not Jacob, not that my dick seems to care much.

With Ivy's gentle softness on one side of me, and his overbearing presence ahead of us, I could be a happy man. I'll take his brother's subservience, no matter how much of a brat he likes to be, but to break the straight one would be truly delicious.

I know, I know, it's cliché as fuck wanting the straight brother and his girl as well. I should be happy with the man I've got. And I am.

Ivy and I have a connection, an understanding, something more than just the desire that simmers between us whenever we're nearby. And Nick? Well, he looks exactly like his hotter-than-sin twin brother, only he won't bend for me.

What can I say? I like a challenge.

"Thanks," he grumbles, his attention focused solely on Ivy and the smile she's got for him, despite the words being for me.

"I'll chat to you later?" she confirms, looking at me.

"Of course." I smile, leaning in to kiss her cheeks, her hand coming to my arm briefly before I step back, leaving the two of them to go to their class.

My hand is in my pocket, dragging the stupid vibrating thing out even as I watch them walk away, but as I take in the name flashing on the screen, my heart sinks like a stone.

Shit.

"Hey," I say, answering the call and turning away from them, unable to look at the light and the future whilst taking this call.

"Don't 'hey' me, boy," he clips. "Do you know how many times I've called you?"

*Nope. I didn't check. I just took this call before you tried to murder me down the phone, or worse.*

"Sorry, I've just come out of class," I reply, shoving down the caustic response I'd like to give him.

"Yes, a very nice bit of skirt you were entertaining there too," he says smugly. "It's a shame that's not your colour on her wrist though, isn't it?"

Double shit.

"Yeah, about that…"

"Don't bother with your fucking excuses, boy."

Moving away from the main building and the people milling around there, I head towards the driveway and back to the house, glad I didn't drive today. This is not a conversation I need echoing around an enclosed space, even if I would be alone.

"Did you know about the exercise at the weekend?" I ask, choosing my words carefully as I navigate down the driveway.

"Parents don't get updates on the inductions until after," he says, and I'm not sure whether he means until after we're out, or until after it's over. "But you're still there."

"Obviously."

The lack of belief would be insulting, especially considering the amount of pressure he's put on the point, but it's not surprising. The bar is set high, always has been.

"Have you seen anything of your boys recently?" he asks, that deep throaty chuckle a warning I've come to heed.

I suddenly realise the sarcastic remark that slipped from my tongue, the warning clear.

"No," I reply, my hackles raised as I look around. There's nothing but trees on either side, dark, dense and alone.

"Interesting."

"I thought you were sending them on a new job or something?" Not that he'd give me any details about it. No, they were intentionally removed from me and anything to do with me.

"I have."

*Insightful.*

"And they're okay?"

The tension that wraps around my insides is like a vice, and I can barely breathe until he answers, my steps nothing but automatic at this point.

"For now."

Tipping the microphone away from my head, I close my eyes, releasing the held breath as quietly as I can manage.

"We're down to seven," I say by way of a reply.

"Four more to go."

*As if I can't count.*

"Almost half way," he continues.

*As if half way would be good enough. It's all or nothing for this man. Always has been.*

"Don't let me down."

*As if that would be an option.*

If The Sect didn't bury me, he would.

"The bands," I rush out before I can rethink the question. Not that it comes out as a question, but still. "Can you request more than one? Can you receive more than one?"

I'm not sure why I'm even asking him, he wouldn't know, he hasn't cared about anyone or anything for his entire life. I'm sure his Angel was nothing more than a means to an end.

"Interesting." The word curls from him like smoke. "You can't request more than one, from what I remember. Or if you did, it would likely be rejected, but I can't see why you wouldn't be able to receive more than one. Although, that would make it tricky if one of you were to *fail.*"

Fail.

The word is a stone in my stomach as I stop, pushing my way back into the trees, into the darkness. Where I can see better, and think better. Remove the softness that's crept into me just by being here.

"It would be a chain reaction," I ponder, thinking of the logistics of such a situation.

"Yes, that's like the way it would be approached."

"Good to know. Thank you."

It's not quite what I was hoping for, but there'd be a way to make it work if needed. I can honestly say I wasn't expecting a helpful answer from him, but this, I can work with.

"Is this for that girl?" he asks.

"Maybe."

He saw us together today, and has, no doubt, had report after report sent back showing how much time we spend together, both as part of a larger group and alone. But it's good to have his spies confirmed, I suppose.

"Or is it for the boy you've been spending all your time with?"

There's no inflexion in his tone, and warning prickles at the back of my neck.

"Maybe," I hedge, the house finally coming in to view as I hide in the darkness, a beacon for something I shouldn't want.

He sighs, the sound echoing down the phone so familiar I might as well be standing in front of him reporting these cagey answers. I know exactly how that would go, and it wouldn't be with me leaving in one piece. Family or not, the rules still apply.

"We lost George based on his performance, or lack thereof, and Emmerson went at the challenge last week. I don't know what else is coming, but they keep turning up in the house," I say, falling back into line. "They're moving things quickly."

"I bet they are," he muses, taking a sip of his drink.

I can almost picture the look on his face, the smell of the expensive scotch he drinks, and see the leather coaster it lives on.

I hadn't realised just how much I'd relaxed being here,

how much his influence had pushed me into a corner, until I was out—until now. I wouldn't have even considered not giving him a straight answer and a detailed explanation before this, before them.

And I know, deep in my soul, any one of the men in that house would have my back without question, we all did when someone threatened Stephanie, but they're not the only ones at play here.

"I think I've identified the right players," I admit, the words like sandpaper on my tongue because they're more than that. More than just pieces on a board to be moved and adjusted at will.

"Good, keep them close," he says.

I wait at the edge of the driveway, hidden in the trees as Oliver's car barrels past me, pulling around the house to the garage.

"Watch those Angels, pick your partner carefully, and keep your fucking nose clean."

"Yes, sir."

"Lives are depending on this, and not just the ones in that house, do you understand?"

Dex. Blaise.

"I understand," I clip, attempting to hold back the threats I'd like to give instead.

"Good."

He ends the call, the single word clipped out through gritted teeth and I release a breath. Navigating the line between both worlds is trickier than it used to be.

I'm here for a reason. To do a job.

There isn't time to play around with indecision. It's

time to make a move.

# EIGHTEEN

*Ivy*

"**H**onestly," I say, rifling through the back of the kitchen cupboard. "I thought there'd at least be a stash of cookies back here or something."

"I can't believe we don't even have ice cream, just sorbet," Tamsin replies, her disgust real. "What kind of ridiculous healthy shit is this?"

"Right, we're going out to find cake," I decide, climbing down from the chair.

"And we need a serious conversation with whoever is ordering the food in this place, because this just will not do," she continues. "Sometimes you need ice cream and chocolate, and damn, just some kind of cake."

"That coffee shop had tasty treats," I offer. *Finally, a glimmer of hope.*

"Let's do it," Tamsin agrees. "Does anyone else want to come?"

"I'm good." Aimee waves us off, engrossed in some crime thriller drama show.

"I'm going to see Olly in a bit," Stephanie says. "He

offere to help me with this paper. Hopefully, he'll have a clue."

The door closes as we grab our purses, but it's not Charlotte coming in, instead, Liselle strides down the corridor, turning the two of us around as her security follows behind.

"We've been requested. Get your masks." Gone is the silly smiling face she's usually wearing, instead, a seriousness that has concern swarming in my gut. "And get Charlotte and Penelope's too, please. They'll be meeting us there."

"What masks?" Aimee asks, her confusion clear.

"The ones from the masquerade party. Hurry now, there's no time to lose," she says as we all step-to.

"Is there something wrong?" I ask, hovering in the doorway, Aimee and Stephanie paused on their way to the stairs.

"Not at all," Liselle replies, her smile way too easy for me to feel comfortable with her reply. *Something's amiss.*

"We're meeting The Devils there, so put your best foot forward, please."

Wonderful.

I'm sure she can hear my eye roll as we walk away, digging out the delicate masks from the masquerade party.

It's just as beautiful now as it was all those weeks ago, a lifetime, or at least that's how it feels. Tamsin smiles, adjusting hers as she slides it on. And then, the four of us are ready, gathered and loaded up.

Liselle takes her own car as the four of us pile into the G-Wagon, and nobody dares to comment or question as we drive, keeping conversation to the minimum as the nerves eat away at us. Well, I'll be damned if I show any weakness here, either to her or the men trying to use us like prizes in some fucked up game.

Liselle said to put our best foot forward, and that's what I'm going to do. Head up, shoulders back, smile, but take no shit. *The game plan is ready.* Charlotte and Penelope are waiting nervously as we arrive at the old church building, their driver-slash-security already masked up and waiting disconcertingly by the car.

Our driver slides out too, hovering nearby like we might be a flight risk.

"Game face on, ladies," I comment quietly, handing their masks over. "We're together here, right?"

It's been tense over the last few days, the fallout from Stephanie's actions and the words that followed being felt by everyone, or at least that's how it's felt for me. But right now, we need to be unified. We don't know what awaits us here, but historically, it's not been anything in *our* best interests.

They nod, sliding the masks on, clearly as aware as we are that something isn't right this afternoon. The cloud coverage is thick as we get ourselves together, not raining but cold, that winter chill imminent.

"Ladies," Liselle calls, gathering us together at the entrance. She waits until we're all there before continuing. "The Devils are already here, keep your masks on at all times, and remember, this is a privilege, please approach it as such."

Great.

The main doors draw back, the security behind us pressing forward as Liselle strides up the stairs, waiting for the rest of us to catch up before entering the old hall. There's nothing more than a handful of masked men standing around, with who I assume to be our Devils gathered together in the centre.

The last time we were all brought here together we were dressed to the nines for our official introduction—we're a long way from that right now. That night, the room was full to bursting, with an energy that I couldn't explain, and now, it's sombre, quiet, concerning.

"Thank you for joining us," the man standing by the Devils says, drawing all attention to him.

The Devils watch us as we meander down what used to be the aisle, everyone else focusing on him as Liselle joins him, gesturing for us to stand at her side.

"So, it looks like our first official pair has been created," he continues. "Can you come forward, please?"

Nervously, Tamsin steps forward, twining her fingers with Taylor as he joins her, the two of them standing before everyone.

"Your fates are now mirrored, your achievements and weaknesses linked," he declares.

"There are some practical things to address," Liselle says a touch lighter, keeping the tone more familiar. "There are suites on the second floor if you'd like to stay together. You can use them permanently, or whenever you need to, should you decide to stay with your respective roommates for the time being."

A honeymoon suite, great.

Well, at least that answers the question about what happens to the roommate. Not that I'd given much thought about it since she mentioned it after Nick *claimed* me, and to be perfectly honest, I'd completely forgotten.

The two of them nod their understanding, and whilst I get wanting to be with your other half, I'd prefer to keep hold of my best friend.

"There are some other benefits," the man continues. "At any point during a challenge you can call in your Angel to assist, or we can request you work together for it."

Not necessarily a benefit…

"You two are a unit now," Liselle says, looking between them. "You're a mirrored pair, and around here that means something. So, treat each other with care and respect."

They both nod, and I can't help but feel like this explanation is more for us than for them. They're together, *in love*, of course, they're a pair and they're going to look out for each other, but Nick and I aren't, not properly, so that makes the explanation all that more poignant.

The silver line on Taylor's mask glints as he turns to Tamsin, and as my gaze flicks to the men behind them, I can't help but wonder how useful would a second person be to them in their moment of confusion, or would it be more of a distraction than an asset?

The leather burns at my wrist, a promise was given but not returned, not like the one Leo and I made to each other, the vengeance we would hand out if anyone fucked with the other, but am I really willing to risk Wyatt alone in this?

The stupid circle of thoughts keeps rotating, going around and around and getting me nowhere but back at the beginning. Frustrating.

"Well, congratulations to our first power couple of the challenge," the man says with a nod. "We'll be watching you all closely."

"If we could have a moment alone with the new couple, please?" Liselle asks.

I catch Tamsin's gaze as we file out, her excited smile twinkling in her eyes before we leave, the boys striding as we meander our way back to the cars. *Well, that was weird.*

Wyatt's hand finds my lower back, briefly, his signature bead bracelets giving him away as a comfort I didn't realise I needed until his warmth begins to heal the concern swarming around my stomach.

Everything has been so carefully structured, so regimented, with every move having a purpose, so what on earth were those people for? The ceremony was witnessed by two of the Devils already, is there more that comes afterwards? Something I've not been privy to yet because I haven't chosen him back, haven't claimed him too.

But I'm not the only one that feels like something is off, that reads the undercurrent of tension, as Nick declares, "Ivy rides with me."

"Angels and Devils travel separately," one of the security or drivers or whatever they are says, only raising further alarm bells as I look at the girls.

I don't want to leave them too, but something isn't right.

"She's his Angel," Leo says, striding my way and holding up my wrist.

"Fine," the guy agrees as Wyatt ushers me into a car behind Nick, Oliver already taking the back seat.

Aimee sends a small smile my way, waving, but it doesn't reach her eyes, and I know she's feeling the divide being drawn in the sand. *Aren't we all?*

It's not that I want to go with the guys over them, but I also don't feel safe right now and they're the better option here. Sad, but true. And as strange as it sounds, they've become one of my safe places.

If you'd told me that a month ago, I'd have laughed in your face. But they have.

I somehow find myself stuffed awkwardly between Nick and Wyatt, tension rolling off them both. Wyatt slides his arm along my shoulders, drawing me into his comforting embrace, and far from the chest-banging caveman display I expect from Nick, he just takes my hand.

Now, this isn't the threesome experience I'd been imagining recently, never expecting Nick to be so calm about someone else reassuring me, and I can only imagine what Oliver is thinking in the back seat, but it feels good. Wyatt's calming warmth at one side, and Nick's determined strength at the other.

Oliver and Wyatt talk about something for one of their classes as we head back, Nick's thumb rubbing back and forth against the back of my hand silently, and by the time we make it back to the house, I've almost forgotten about the weird meeting we've just come from.

We are all out of the car and climbing the stairs to their front door when that awkward avoiding of the obvious finally breaks, Oliver asking the question first.

"Did it seem strange to any of you that they pulled us from class for that?" Oliver asks, opening the door.

"Totally," I agree.

"Well, we're all home safely, so let's just get a drink and wait for everyone else," Wyatt says as we strip off our masks.

Nick hands his to Wyatt before stalking off to the kitchen, his long strides carrying him away quickly. *Strange.* With a shrug, Oliver and I follow, Wyatt heading upstairs with their masks to put them away properly. He's fidgeting around in the cupboards when we get there, stacking up drink after drink on the counter.

"I wasn't sure what you all wanted," Nick mumbles, refusing to make eye contact.

"Cheers, dude," Oliver says, either not picking up on the strange way he's acting or not caring. "I'm gonna load up if you guys want a game?"

Wyatt comes back in, picking up on the tension immediately and sending me a concerned look. "Sure," he agrees, grabbing a drink and leaving the two of us alone. "Will you message Stephanie too, get the girls here instead of at their place and give Ivy some company?"

"Can do."

Their conversation dies down as they move around the house, heading further away and into the den.

"They're taking a long time," Nick says, his gaze flicking to the clock on the wall. "They should be back by now."

And suddenly, it all makes sense. We aren't all back safely, yet. I might be here with him, but Jacob is still out there.

"We were the first ones out of there, I'm sure he'll be

back any minute."

He nods, pressing his lips together as his gaze finally comes to mine, his vulnerability a gift I wasn't expecting to receive today. I stand awkwardly on the other side of the island, wanting to go to him, to comfort him, but I'm not sure what I'm soothing, if anything.

But I feel it still, that apprehension.

Until the door sounds, Stephanie's voice carrying through. It's not the sound either of us was expecting as we both train our ears to find out who's back.

"Ooh, nice flowers," Charlotte comments as I move towards the doorway automatically.

Maybe the girls came first, chivalry and all that.

"And they're for Leo," Aimee continues, plucking a card from the fresh bunch we walked straight past.

"What's for me?" he asks, stepping through the doorway, Jacob behind him deep in conversation with Jasper.

I feel the sigh of relief puff from Nick, his heat on my back as we wait for everyone else to come back.

"Lily, Rose, and Hedera." Charlotte nods. "An interesting combination. Personally, I prefer Calla Lilies, but I guess it works. Who are they from?"

Leo takes the card from her, his dark gaze flicking over one side and then the other before sliding it back into the holder. "No idea." He shrugs.

"Well, they're not from me," Jacob says, placing a kiss on his cheek before heading our way with a smile and a wink. "If you've got some kind of secret admirer, we're gonna have a problem."

"As if." Leo rolls his eyes, following him into the

kitchen.

As does just about everyone else, and it looks like we're all back apart from the happy couple. Nick squeezes my shoulder, my head resting back against his chest before we move, going back into the kitchen with everyone else.

"Wyatt and Oliver are playing something in the den," I say, plucking a couple of bottles of water from the side and handing one over to Nick. "If anyone else wants to join them."

"How about we put the rest of that series on?" Aimee asks, looking at Jasper.

"Sure." He shrugs, completely missing the interest in her eyes.

Eventually, we all grab drinks, most of us settling in the movie room to watch some magical romance thing with heart whatever and people who control metal or wind or something… no idea.

The lights dim, Jacob and Leo taking one sofa whilst Nick and I take another, settling in for God knows how long of this stuff.

When the second episode begins, somewhere around a million hours later and it looks like everyone is settling in for the duration, I decide to head back. To see if Tamsin and Taylor went to ours instead.

I'm not sure how good an idea that is, or what I might be walking into. *Maybe I should send Jasper instead.* No, she's my best friend, I'm sure they're just decompressing or whatever, but I need to see it with my own two eyes.

"I'll walk you back," Nick says, standing.

"I'm good. It's literally across the pool. I think I can

manage."

"I'm sure you said that about turning the sauna on," he replies with a smirk.

I flip him the bird before grabbing my phone and mask and heading out, thanking everyone else for their company, but, of course, he follows.

Silently, we make our way through the kitchen and to the sliding glass doors.

"I'm more than capable of getting myself home, you know?"

"Oh, I know," he says, wrapping his arms around my waist. "I just wanted a minute with you, that's all."

"That's all, huh?" I huff out a laugh, the stress of earlier on finally tempered, a tired contentedness seeping in at the edges as he pulls me back against his chest. *I guess that's what spending way too long in a darkened room doing your best to avoid the sexual tension wrapping around you will do.*

He rests his chin against the top of my head, his fingers interlocking beneath my breasts, and where I thought it might be cloying and suffocating, it's protective and reassuring.

"I don't want to fight you. I just want to make sure you're okay."

"I'm fine," I admit with a contented sigh. "Are you?"

"You're good, Jacob's good, so I'm good." But still, he doesn't let go, the two of us soaking in the moment before he places a kiss on my head and releases me. "Go, before I whisk you upstairs and have my wicked way with you."

The words are a delicious promise, one I know he'd

happily follow through with, but right now I just want to decompress. And check on Tamsin.

"I'll see you later on," I say by way of a reply.

"Let me know you get back, and that they're at your place, okay?" he says, releasing me to catch my gaze, turning me in the process. "Your safety is important to me too, yeah."

His fingers burn against my chin as he grabs it and tilts, all the sexual tension that's been sizzling away focusing on that single point of contact, his gaze penetrating.

"I understand."

"Now be a good girl and go check on your friend." He winks.

Amusement sparkles through the brown in his eyes, and his mouth tips up in a smile as heat pools low in my belly. *That phrase.* Never in my life have I considered a praise kink, but the words *'good girl'* coming from those sinful lips do it for me in a big way.

He releases my chin, eventually, and I step back on wobbly legs, heading out of the glass doors and down the steps. These gardens are extensive and lined by the woods that head down the driveway, but the patio, pool, and path to our house are well-kept and quiet, and before I realise it, I'm sliding open the glass door leading into our living room.

I love sitting in here on an evening, watching the sun sink behind the trees, the orange, pink, or red hues cascading across the canopy before turning dark and the evening drawing in, but I'm suddenly conscious of how exposing it also is.

With a shudder, I close the door, calling, "Honey, I'm

home." The last thing I need is to walk in to the two of them at it, but maybe they're not here yet. The house is quiet.

I cross the room and knock on our door twice, covering my eyes before pushing down on the handle.

"I can't see anything," I say, entering, but no one answers.

The silence that echoes around the room is unnerving. *She should be here.* Placing my mask on the vanity, my heel catches on the box and I uncover my eyes, picking the stupid thing up and placing it on the table. But something isn't right.

She's not here with Taylor, or at the desk working. She's not laid out on the bed with her headphones on, and the room feels empty. Vapid.

Her throw no longer lays haphazardly across the end of the bed, and as I look at her vanity, it's clear. The panic sets in quickly as I rush to the wardrobe, flinging back the doors to the empty space as a chill creeps over my skin.

My heartbeat thunders in my ears as my stomach twists, heat rushing over me. *She's gone.*

Grabbing my phone from the side, I pull her up and press dial.

**Beep. Beep. Beep. Call ended.**

*What the fuck?*

Panic courses through my veins, a reality that I couldn't possibly fathom stretching out in front of me. She's not gone. She can't be.

She changed her mind. Decided to move into one of the suites with Taylor after all…. That's all.

I pull her parents number up, her mum first and then her

dad, but all have the same answer.

**Beep. Beep. Beed. Call ended.**

I can't get hold of any of them. Blocked.

But why, if she isn't gone?

The panic I was pushing down, twists, and heaves, and I turn, grabbing the nearest bin and emptying the contents of my stomach into it, acid creeping up the back of my throat as I heave everything away, a cold sweat settling across my shoulders and down my spine.

Leaving it, I open every drawer, pulling them out and abandoning them in a heap on the floor. Empty. Empty. Empty.

I'm as empty as the drawers that lay around my feet once I'm finished. The light that's been such a central part of my life, blinked out in an instant.

The emptiness that stamps its way around my insides is consuming and joined by a wave of anger so strong I couldn't control it if I tried. In an instant, I'm out, leaving the sliding doors wide open as I stalk my way back down the path, around the pool and to the glass back doors of the main house, and as I hammer the door, it takes everything I never realised I had not to scream.

She's gone.

An unmarked grave was her likely destination.

And we sat here watching TV while they did it.

My stomach twists again, the thought so disturbing my body can't even control its reaction to it.

While we were here worrying about what was going to happen to us, the unconsolidated group of men and women, the ones that aren't paired up and *safe,* the two that declared themselves each others are done, gone, lost.

*And why the hell isn't anyone answering this door?*

Eventually, Leo appears, flicking the lock and sliding it back as the anger tumbles from me in a rush, collapsing into a heap in his arms, tears tracking down my face.

"Woah, angel," he placates, catching me and pulling me in against his chest, wrapping his arms around me as we lower to the floor and I sob uncontrollably.

"She's gone. It's all gone."

He stills around me, anger rippling out in waves.

This is what we promised each other.

Vengeance when the other was hurt.

And I'm hurt. Incapacitated. Bleeding my pain into the arms of the man that promised me blood. Pain. Retribution.

I don't even realise he's contacted anyone until Jacob arrives, his presence a balm not just for me, but also Leo as his rage simmers around us, a palpable force.

"Taylor's stuff is all gone." He confirms the one thing I was hoping wasn't real, and any tiny amount of hope I was desperately clinging onto tumbles from me in waves that I couldn't control even if I wanted to, but they said it earlier on, didn't they?

*"Your fates are now mirrored, your achievements and weaknesses linked."*

# NINETEEN

*Nick*

**Me: You didn't message me...**

**Me: Did you make it back okay?**

**Me: I'll be coming to find you if you don't reply...**

I fling the final message through to her and drop my phone on the sofa, unable to settle until she replies to me. I've got no idea what's happening on the screen, but both Jacob and Leo have disappeared somewhere. *So much for popcorn, I guess that's code for something else.* They could have just said.

*Oh, hey, the tension in this programme is so high you could boil water with it, we need half an hour alone so we'll see you later...* that's all it would have taken. But no, they make this all about the fucking popcorn and never come back with it, and Ivy hasn't replied to me either.

Checking the phone again gets me nowhere, still no reply, so I shove it in my pocket, giving Aimee and Jasper the room as I go in search of this damn food I was promised, only, the doorbell rings.

That feeling I had as we left the church comes back in force, and dread sinks in my stomach as I open the door. The Sect are here.

"Good afternoon. Can we have everyone gathered in the movie room, please? Masks on." He strides straight past me, two security guards following gaze to the ground as the other locks the door behind them, waiting for me to move.

Watching them gets me nowhere as I stand there stunned and silent. The security guard coughs beside me, forcing me into action, banging on the den door twice and calling out, "Masks on, movie room."

"What?" Oliver asks, pausing the game and looking my way.

"The Sect are here. Masks on, we're needed in the movie room. Now."

Stephanie, Charlotte and Penelope look suitably confused, placing whatever it is they're doing down on the coffee table in the circle of cushions and shit they've gathered. It's cute, if that's your thing.

Wyatt pushes past me, heading to grab ours from upstairs.

"Can you get Leo and Jacob too? I think they're upstairs," I admit.

My gaze flicks back to the girls, the sparkles in their masks catching my attention as they're slid back on. The colours and lace are a complete dichotomy to the black of ours, and where ours are solid, theirs are fluid, the feathers giving it movement, like two sides of the same thing, linked together.

The girls push past, heading to the movie room unphased. They don't huddle together and wait for us to protect them against anything. They've never had The Sect walk into their house like this. They don't know what's coming.

And neither do I, but whatever it is won't be good.

"They're not upstairs," Wyatt says, handing me my mask and heading into the den with Oliver.

"Then where the fuck are they?" I grumble under my breath, sliding the black plastic over my face, settling the fabric against the back of my neck and falling into character.

This is the Nick Barrett that will do whatever needs doing to get to the end; he'll take the woman he wants to keep her safe.

The dread that sits in my stomach like a stone churns as I pace through the dining room, not finding them, and a quick look in the kitchen has alarm ringing in my ears, until I hear them, well, her… the sob that has goosebumps prickling against the back of my neck.

"What the fuck?"

I'm stalking across the room, red creeping in the edges of my vision as I find Ivy curled up in a ball in Leo's arms, Jacob beside them.

"The Sect are here," I state, knowing whatever the hell this is about links to what's going on right here.

I left her all of five minutes ago and she was fine, on her way home to find Tamsin and Taylor, and now she's here… sobbing.

Leo won't meet my gaze, his jaw clenched but his arms loose, free, comforting, rubbing soothing circles on her back as the other one bands around her protectively.

There's only one thing that would upset her this much.

Tamsin and Taylor are gone.

As is reading my mind Jacob nods. Fuck.

"Get your masks."

Bending down, I pull Ivy from his arms, standing her up as they slide out from around us, hopefully heading to get their masks and buy me five minutes whilst I get her under control.

"She's… they're…" She hiccups, unable to say the words.

"I know," I reply quietly. "And I think we're about to get an explanation."

She shudders, tears still falling as she crumples in on herself again, her footing unsteady.

"Ivy, I need you to take a breath. Just one. Deep in, deep out." She tries, shuddering air in and out of her lungs unsteadily. "Again," I say gently. "Good girl, you've got this." Her next ones come out easier, and her legs finally feel stable beneath us, her weight drawing back from my arms. "Deep breath in, deep breath out," I continue.

She nods, wiping the back of her hand across each cheek.

She's a mess, but she's beautiful.

"They're here," she repeats.

"I'm assuming your mask isn't?" I ask, drawing her to the task at hand.

She shakes her head, clearly remembering something about going home, her eyes watering once again.

"Hey, hey," I say, trying to catch her before she breaks down again. "You're linked with me regardless. Just stay with me whilst we get through this, okay, can you do that?"

She nods, shuddering a breath in and squaring her shoulders. There aren't words to explain how proud of her

I am at this moment, especially as Jacob sticks his head around the kitchen doorway, gesturing behind him.

We've stalled long enough. It's time.

Wrapping her fingers in mine, I take a step back and she follows with a nod.

"Sorry about the delay," I explain, opening the door but keeping Ivy behind me. *There's a reason they asked us for the masks.* "My partner doesn't have her mask with her. I can go and retrieve it on her behalf, but that will delay us further."

"Turn around," he clips out, the security lining the room turning around instantly to face away from us. "Problem solved. Please close the door behind you."

"Thank you," I reply, pulling her in with me and tucking her under my arm.

I can't be much protection against what she's about to be bombarded with, but I'll always do what I can.

Whoever they sent sits in the middle of the sofa, the rest of us lined up against the screen once again. Only this time, instead of it being the early hours of the morning and us heading out into the campus to complete a challenge, this is at the end of something, and the Angels are here for the first time. *This is getting real, quickly.*

Tucking Ivy into my side and wrapping my arm around her waist, we wait, the door closing behind us.

"Please remember that The Sect sees all and knows all. There isn't anything that will stay hidden from us," he begins from the comfort of his seat, all attention on him. "There aren't a lot of rules for being here, but there are consequences when they aren't followed. Consequences that are mirrored when you're linked."

Ivy stiffens in my arms. She knows what's coming. We both do. But that doesn't soften the blow of the words, and no amount of soothing circles I can paint with my skin on hers will help.

"Complete the challenges." *Taylor skipped out on part of the clean-up the last time we stood right here. He watched George get beaten because he and Taylor carried on drinking instead of coming back with us, and then, by the end, he was too tired, had put too much shit up his nose, and his mouth ran. His leg took the brunt of the response from The Sect on that one.*

"Support the rest of the team." *Jasper and Taylor both went to Tamsin instead of finishing off the flyers whilst we were supporting Oliver and his retribution.*

"Two drinks. Now, that one is for the Devils, rather than the Angels, but the sentiment is the same. You represent The Sect; the elite and the best of the best aren't rolling around wasted at the end of the night." *Taylor was smashed at the end of the party, the one we held to celebrate them tying their lives together, their fate.*

Shit.

"Taylor and Tamsin have been removed from the competition." Ivy whimpers beside me, her knees buckling for a second as I squeeze her waist, but I've got her.

There's a hushed intake of breath in the room. This is the first one of the Angels that's left, and I'm not sure how much the girls are aware of, Ivy clearly more than the rest.

"Choose your partners carefully. We'll be in touch soon."

He gets up but nobody moves, everyone is stuck in a stunned silence.

We were just celebrating them getting together, officially. They were showing it off to the rest of the campus, and now to The Sect, and just like that, they're gone. Done. Out. Because of something stupid that he did to get her in the first place, the corners he's cut.

Ivy manages to hold it together until the front door slams, all three of the security going with him before she crumbles. Luckily, I'm there to catch her, and Wyatt isn't far behind.

"Can someone go get her a bottle of water, please?" he says, helping me get her to the nearest sofa.

She slumps into the soft fabric, curling in on herself as the entirety of this situation sinks in. Everyone else removes their masks, chatting amongst themselves.

"Well, I guess that explains the flowers," Charlotte says, catching my attention. "Lilies are usually given during the period of mourning, roses are thrown on coffins, and the common name for Hedera is Ivy."

My gaze flicks to Leo, he bought the flowers or someone bought them for him, but they knew.

Aimee returns with a handful of water bottles, passing them out to everyone and loitering closer to Jasper, clearly as shaken up as everyone else, except for Ivy…

Stephanie slides the black and silver mask off her face, flicking her hair over her shoulder before declaring, "Well, I've requested one of those for you," and pinning Oliver with a serious look. "Do better."

"Sorry, but that's my girl." His gaze follows her as she

storms out of the room, one step away from slamming the door before he chases after.

Ivy sniffles beside me, Charlotte's sad gaze coming our way before suggesting they give us some space and the rest of them filter out, the silence all-encompassing.

"Why don't we get out of here?" Jacob suggests. "We could just get in the car and drive, go somewhere else, anywhere you want."

Leo's hand goes to his calf as he drops to the ground at Ivy's feet, catching her dropped gaze. "I think it might be better to just take a minute," he suggests. "Although I understand the desire to outrun the news, sometimes it helps to sit with it, you know?"

Jacob nods.

We've done that, sat in the moment, we've run from it too. Losing someone you call family is a pain like no other. Blindsiding. And in circumstances like this, indescribable.

"Well, let's get out of this room for a start," Jacob decides. "Leo, come and give me a hand with something, will you? I've got an idea." He looks at me, thoughts playing behind his eyes like a movie only the two of us can watch. "See you upstairs in five?"

"Sure," I agree.

The two of them disappear, the door slamming, making Ivy jump. *What a fucking shit show.* I managed to get her to pull it together enough for The Sect, but watching someone I care about fall apart isn't really my area of expertise.

Wyatt draws her in against his body, whispering quiet words of consolation as I hold her hand, counting down the seconds until we can leave, until I can do something helpful.

"Why don't you grab some drinks and snacks?" I ask Wyatt when the moment comes, gathering Ivy into my arms and standing.

I'm pretty sure she's cried out, nothing left but a sadness that cascades from her like a tidal wave that I can't stop, but holding her in my arms feels good, useful, and as Wyatt disappears and I head up the stairs, the sound of everyone else talking and laughing filling the house, I get it.

Build her a safe space from everyone else, from the empty bed her friend should be in, from the room she had it confirmed in, from the people who don't get it, who don't want to. We can't take this pain from her, it's hers to bear as she chooses to, but we can give her space to process, accept what's happened, and support her when she's ready to move forward.

Opening the door is a task, and I'm grateful I made the right choice by heading to mine and Wyatt's room when I take in what the boys have done. The lights are off, the side lamps on to make the room dimmed and intimate. The beds are pushed together, covered in twenty billion pillows and blankets with the laptop propped up on the desk they've moved.

Wyatt almost walks into me as he comes through the door behind us, his arms and pockets loaded up with stuff as he takes in the solution to mine and Jacob's childhood woes. Placing Ivy down on the ground takes more than I thought it would, kicking off my trainers before climbing over the bed and adjusting the pillows so there's space for both of us.

I'd love to pull her into my arms and gather her in a million blankets and let her snuggle her sadness away, pour it into cushions that we can remove, but finding her space in here has to be her choice.

Leo perches on the end of the bed, an action I wasn't expecting as I look at the four pillows laid out against the headboard. *This could get cosy.* Jacob sighs, turning him to lay his legs out properly before sliding between them, a contented sigh tumbling from him that heals my heart just a little.

Wyatt doesn't waste any time, dropping everything on the end of the bed and taking her by the hand. He settles on a pillow between Leo and me, the perfect buffer before he grabs one of the huge cushions and places it between us, Ivy sinking into it before reaching over to grab Jacob's hand.

And that's where we spend the next few hours. Nobody from downstairs interrupts us, and we go from one film to the next with as little conversation as we can manage. Nobody talks about the friends that aren't here, or the challenges, or the rules. We just sit and watch, and ignore it all.

At one point, someone gets up to use the bathroom, and someone else restocks the snacks, but no one goes down for dinner, instead leaving the rest of them to it. The five of us hide in our pillow fort bubble, ignorant of the world.

Everything we need is right here in this room, for now.

# TWENTY

y eyes are gritty as I finally wake, the last twenty-four hours feeling like a lifetime, and yet no time at all. Still, the overwhelming feeling that cascades through me is numbness and a heat that doesn't make sense until I take in where I am. Nick's huge arm is wrapped over my side, his leg hitched up and resting against mine as his gentle breaths puff over the top of my head; still sleeping.

His steady heartbeat pumps rhythmically against my back in the darkened silence of the room, and just for a minute, I try and forget. Forget that this is all just a game, forget that we're all pawns being moved in and out of play at will and that my best friend is now gone.

My breathing stutters, but nobody stirs, at least not Nick or Wyatt, who's fast asleep in front of me, but Leo looks my way, turning down the lamp at his side.

"Sorry, I didn't mean to wake you," he whispers.

"Not at all," I reply, my eyes adjusting as I shuffle an arm, wiping them.

Jacob moves in his lap, adjusting the pillow he's on, Leo's shirt rucking up before he continues to sleep soundly.

His hair is beautifully mussed, much like I imagine Nick's is, and I can't help the smile that slips free, no matter how much it probably doesn't meet my eyes.

Everyone else forwent their shirts in favour of sleeping topless, and I learnt way more things about their sleeping habits than I needed before we got settled down. Nick thrust his shirt over my head before I even had the opportunity to get my top off, Wyatt handing me a pair of his shorts.

How the hell we all managed to fall asleep in here, I have no idea, and how we got through the night without someone ending up on the floor, even less, but the proof is in the three sleeping men surrounding me.

They're all here, present, willing, and giving me the support and space to process what happened, and what's still happening. To deal with the fact that the one person that's always had my back is gone, and I didn't even get the opportunity to have hers. It wasn't her fault, she's done nothing wrong. It was his. Theirs.

Wyatt stirs, shuffling his shoulders, a deep sigh releasing from him before he stretches.

I can't think about that right now, pushing the sadness back. I need to be here, present, even if it is hiding, just for a little longer.

"What are you reading?" I ask, attempting to get my mind on something else.

"No idea." He shrugs. "Some shit off lover boy's bedside cabinet. It's rubbish, but my options are pretty limited right now."

"Good point."

"I don't generally sleep very well," he admits. "Even

without this one draped all over me." Smiling, stroking the tip of a finger down Jacob's cheek, fondness glints in his eyes. "I didn't have Nick down as a cuddler, though. You learn something new every day."

I huff out a laugh, the arm around me tightening briefly. Even in his sleep, he doesn't want to let me go. Possessive to the very end.

"We've requested them, Jacob and I," he says. "The wristbands."

Like I didn't know what he was talking about.

"Good. That's good."

They'll be okay together. They've got each other's back.

"Hmhmm," Wyatt grumbles, shuffling again, his hand dropping down to adjust his very obvious morning wood. "Shit, sorry," he apologises.

"You don't have anything there to apologise for," Leo says, one eyebrow raised as he peeks over his shoulder.

"Perv," Wyatt replies sleepily.

Their banter is so straightforward, so easy, and it holds none of the tension I'd expect from one guy's erection next to another.

"Did you sleep okay?" he asks, covering his dick as his gaze connects with mine.

"Yeah," I reply, a blush creeping over my cheeks.

It's not like I'm some blushing virgin who's never woken up with a man before, but this is different. I'm not sleeping with any of them, well, not right now, and even the passing thought of my conversation about menage moments with Tamsin hurts. And they see it.

"How can we help?" Wyatt asks gently, his hand coming

to my cheek.

"I need to forget," I admit. "Help me to forget it all."

His fingers slide in my hair, electricity zapping across my skin before he brings his lips to mine, his tongue tangling a lazy pattern that's all Wyatt. Instinctively, my hands go to his chest, tracing the smooth planes with my fingers, even as Nick holds me captive in his arms.

It's relief, freedom, something of my own, something I can give or receive, and it's more than just care and attention, friendship and support, it's a connection, and it's just ours, but even as he languidly kisses me, it takes me away from it all, from the pain, and it sucks me into a different kind of heat. The kind that burns when Nick's dick presses against my ass, someone else with something to say about what's going on.

"You're free to want whatever you want, whoever you want," Leo says, pushing out the thoughts of how mad Nick might actually be about this. "There are no rules within these walls."

Nick stirs again, grinding against me in a delicious tease, his arm moving, fingers grazing against my nipple. If Wyatt notices the movement or hears Leo's words properly, I don't know, but he doesn't stop, his fingers in my hair, his stubble grazing my face as he worships me, savours me, enjoys every last stroke of his tongue and press of his lips like it might be the last, but it isn't.

And then Nick is back, his arm firm beneath my head, the other one sliding beneath the shirt that covers me; his shirt. Goosebumps raise as my skin is exposed to the air in the room. And then, he's there, his large hand wrapping around my breast, lifting, holding, squeezing, tugging at my nipple, and all I can think of is the feelings, the sensations cascading over me.

"Oh, God," I pant, pulling back from Wyatt and drowning in the moment.

"Don't think, just feel it," Leo coaches, catching my gaze as Wyatt moves, shuffling down between Jacob and me.

Jacob moves, straddling Leo's thighs and giving Wyatt more space just as his tongue swipes across my nipple, the same one Nick squeezes to the point of pain, and the need that coils through me is indescribable.

I want him. Them. And I need them, *now.*

"Fuck, please," I whimper.

I'm barely above begging, my thighs pressed together, Nick's huge cock rubbing and grinding against my ass as they torture me slowly. Leo's hand grasps my chin, dragging my hazy gaze to his steady one, even as Jacob trails bites and kisses down his neck, their very hard cocks ready for more.

"Do you want this?" he asks.

"Yes," I agree, trying to nod. "Yes, I want this."

"Nick, get those shorts off," he demands.

And despite any arguments they've had in the past, he does it.

His hand leaves my tortured breasts, only to be replaced by Wyatt's as my shorts and underwear disappear. It's awkward, and a little tricky, but we manage it, Wyatt sliding the top off at the same time.

Then, I'm naked, completely exposed, and I've never

felt safer in my life.

Wyatt doesn't hesitate, tracing a pattern down my stomach with his tongue as Nick slides his hand along the inside of my thigh, opening me up as he rests my leg over his. The cold air hits my over-sensitive skin and a shudder ripples over me, tightening the buds of my already aching nipples even further.

"Fuck, these are amazing," Nick rumbles behind me, getting another handful of my tits as Wyatt finally reaches my pussy.

He's not lazy or languid anymore though, meeting me with the hunger of a starved man seeing his final meal. He plunges his tongue in deep, parting me fully before sliding up to my clit and pulling, nipping, and sucking until I'm a hot, sweaty, writhing mess, barely conscious of anything outside the two men showering me with affection.

That is until drawers are banging and swear words are hissed.

"There's lube in the bottom drawer," Nick says from behind me, my head turning enough to see what Jacob and Leo are doing, barely aware they were even here.

Clearly finding what they need, Leo drags Jacob's dick from his underwear and slicks the sticky liquid along both their shafts. I've never seen two men together, not in real life, not even in porn, but there's something so fucking hot about the moan that tumbles from Jacob, the way his head tips back and his hips jut forward chasing the exact same thing I am; ecstasy.

Their hard dicks rub and glide, hands everywhere.

"More," I whisper, getting hotter by the second. "I need

more."

Wyatt could tumble me over the cliff any second, and he knows it, pulling back as I writhe against the two of them desperately.

"Please," I beg, my eyes closed.

"We've got you," Nick whispers in my ear, his hand finally releasing his cock, the hard flesh silky against my ass.

He moves, my head jiggling with the action as the head of his cock glides carefully through my slickness. I have no idea about the practicalities, and I don't even care, all I want, all I need, all I can feel, imagine and contemplate is the fullness I'll feel when he finally, eventually, gets there.

I'm wound as tight as a piano string as Wyatt holds my leg, teasing a pattern up the inside of my thigh to match the dance his tongue does against my most sensitive flesh, Nick sliding up and down, so close and yet so far.

"Now," Leo growls, and I'm not sure if he's talking to us or Jacob but  Nick sinks in deep, one thrust without any warning and I cry out, the fullness exactly what I was looking for, even as Wyatt pulls back, the orgasm that was so close ebbing away again.

My head bumps against Nick's arm in frustration, the oblivion I'm seeking so near and yet so far, even as the sound of skin slapping against skin rings out, the smell of sex permeating the air, because it's not just me, Nick and Wyatt, Leo and Jacob are here. Even whilst they're dragging my pleasure out as far as they can manage, someone else is getting theirs.

Nick pulls out as I drag my eyes open to take it all in.

Jacob bounces and grinds against Leo as Wyatt licks and lathes at my pussy, the sensations overwhelming, even as Nick thrusts back in, hard and deep as his pace picks up, clearly as close as the rest of us are.

Wyatt's hand disappears from my thigh, taking his own dick in hand against my leg as I watch Jacob take Leo, the two of them pushing, pulling, grinding, and bouncing. A sexual dance I've never seen before, but one that excites me more than I ever anticipated.

Nick's fingers wrap around my neck, his palm against my throat as he fucks me from behind, Wyatt stroking his dick whilst continuing to tease me to the edge.

"Do you like what you see?" he asks, the words panted.

"Yes."

"Fuck you feel good," he admits on a rumble. "Are you gonna come for us?"

"Yes."

I can feel it building and have been able to for far too long, but every time I'm almost there, ready to crest that hill and tumble into oblivion, someone moves, something stops or changes, and it ebbs, intentional or not.

"That's it," he purrs in my ear, his dirty words only encouraging me on, pushing me further, higher. "Come on my dick, Ivy. Show them how beautiful you are."

His hand squeezes, my airways constricting as Wyatt pumps harder, sucking fervently as Nick hits the spot that has stars flashing behind my eyes. My orgasm crashes over me like a tsunami, wave after wave wracking my body as Wyatt continues, Nick holding me open for him until I'm a spent, twitching, sated mess between them.

"Oh, it's not over yet," Nick promises in my ear, releasing my leg and pulling me, twisting so he's on his back, me above him but facing away.

Wyatt moves, standing at the foot of the bed as I attempt to adjust to the new position, Nick feeling bigger and deeper than he did just a moment ago as he continues to thrust, to fuck, to take and give pleasure that ripples over my body. Never have I had this, whatever this is, but I don't have time to dissect it, to think.

All I have is this feeling, this moment of bliss.

"Suck his cock, angel," Leo rasps out. "Make him feel good."

My languid gaze flicks to Wyatt, slowly stroking his cock just there, close enough for me to reach, just. Leaning over, I'm close enough to taste the salt at the tip as I continue to grind against Nick. He swats my ass, the sting nothing more than a warning before Wyatt slides the tip into my mouth.

The groan that tumbles from him is glorious, and as we fall into a rhythm, I'm swept away by sensation. Filling. Stretching. The bite of Nick's hand as it comes down harder on my already reddened skin. The gentle touch of Wyatt's fingers in my hair. The heavy breathing and grunting from beside me.

I can't even turn to take it in, pinned between the two of them and wrapped up in feeling as another orgasm twists and builds.

"That's it," Nick encourages, shifting his hips and fucking me harder.

My hand goes to Nick's thigh for balance, the other

precariously holding me up against Wyatt's leg.

"Fuck," Wyatt growls, his hips stuttering as he cums in my mouth, hot jets that I swallow down instinctively, my mouth stretched around him before Nick's fingers find my clit, working me expertly.

I cling to Wyatt for dear life, my eyes closed as my head tips back, my body rocking as I climb higher and higher, falling off the edge with a cry, my body bucking and bowing, but Nick doesn't relent, holding me in place and fucking me until he cums deep inside me, the three of us a hot sweaty, sated pile of limbs.

And then Jacob throws a towel in our direction, and an embarrassed blush creeps over my chest, rushing over my neck and cheeks. I just did that, and they just witnessed that, and they just did that too.

Fuck.

"Don't look so horrified," Leo says with a sated smile, resting back against the headboard, Jacob comfortably nestled against his chest. "That was so fucking hot."

The two of them look way too composed as Nick stuffs the shirt back over my head, covering me instantly.

"I'll run you a bath," Wyatt says, bending down to kiss me.

Kissing him back feels as natural as breathing, and nobody has a growl, a grumble, or a comment about it as I watch him hitch up his shorts and cross the room.

"That ass," Jacob comments biting his lower lip as he watches him leave.

Leo tweaks his nipple in response, both now shirtless as Nick attempts to make some sense of the tangle of sheets, blankets and pillows strewn across the bed.

"His baths are really good," Nick comments, throwing a pillow at the headboard. "You should make the most of every last moment in it."

"You don't even like baths," Jacob comments.

"When someone sets half a dozen guys on you one after another when you've literally just finished your workout, you need all the help you can get," he quips back.

"Hang on, wasn't that weird for you guys?" I ask, looking from Nick to Jacob and back again, their casual familiarity suddenly dawning on me. "I don't even know where to begin unpacking the whole thing that just happened, but surely seeing your brother... you know, doing that, is awkward or whatever."

"Nah, it's fine." Nick shrugs.

"Water's almost ready," Wyatt interrupts, steam billowing from the bathroom, along with a lush smell I could be quite happy sinking into forever.

"It's nothing new," Jacob confirms with a wave of his hand. "His dick isn't that special."

I'd kind of like to argue with him, but I'm really not ready for that conversation.

"I'll go and grab some clothes from your place," Nick says, effectively ignoring his brother's sideways comment. "Buy you a little breathing room."

My brain momentarily flicks to the world outside, the one that's continuing on without us like a piece of me hasn't just been ripped from my chest.

"Shit, I've got classes today," I say on an exhale.

The thought hits me like a ton of bricks, reality crashing

down on my shoulders.

"Don't worry about any of that," Leo says, attempting to snap me back out of it. "Send me your schedule over and I'll sort it."

"Sort it, how?" I ask, looking around for my phone and not finding it. "I left it with the mask on my bedroom floor."

When I went back to my room to find Tamsin, only…

"I'm on it," Nick says, slinging a shirt over his unbelievably sexy muscles and sliding his trainers on. "Go get in the bath, we've got this."

He kisses me, no doubt tasting Wyatt on my tongue, but instead of seeing disgust on his face, he smiles and winks before heading out the door. I must have walked into some other reality. *What the hell is going on here?*

I'm still attempting to piece it all together as Leo tidies the bed up, ushering Jacob out to shower in his room and giving me five minutes of peace.

"Don't overthink it. We've got you." He winks as Wyatt opens the door behind me, drawing me into the candlelit bathroom.

Under other circumstances, it would be sexy, romantic. Hell, it's both of those things right now. He's got soft music playing on a speaker, and something that smells amazing rising in the steam from the bath, water still dripping from his hair and a towel wrapped low around his waist showing off every dip and curve of the abs I didn't realise he was hiding.

"So, you're not getting in with me then?" I joke.

"Jumped in the shower," he admits. "But I can stay if you want some company?"

"That would be nice," I reply.

The T-shirt hits me mid-thigh, and considering everything we've just done, there's really no need to be shy about it, but for some reason, this feels different, more intimate.

"I'll give you two minutes," he says, picking up on my nervousness and being the gentleman he is. "There are some new toothbrushes on the counter if you want one."

"Thank you."

The door closes quietly behind him as I quickly relieve myself, brush my teeth, and sink into the perfect water with a contented sigh. The bathroom is huge, bigger than ours, that's for sure. Or mine, now. I shrug the thought off, going back to taking everything in as I look over the double shower, the his-and-his sinks and the black marble tiles that make up the bath. This place really was made for lots of people.

Because two adults are supposed to be here, not together, just individually. Pawns in a game we don't know the rules for. But before I have time to spiral much further, Wyatt comes back in, a steaming mug of tea in his hands.

"Are you good?" he checks before entering.

At my nod, he joins me, handing over a mug of tea and taking a seat on the lid of the toilet. How many times have Tamsin and I done this exact thing? A smile almost hits my face before I realise we'll never do that again, because she's gone, maybe dead.

Maybe she's another one of those nameless, faceless people that ended up in an unmarked grave in a churchyard that nobody attends.

"Woah, woah, woah," Wyatt says, catching my gaze immediately and rushing over, his hands coming to my shoulder. "Whatever you're thinking right now, let it go. We're in the bubble, okay?"

"The bubble?"

"What happens in the bubble, stays in the bubble." He nods. "And nothing from outside can penetrate."

"Like what we just did," I say, swallowing thickly.

I'm not sure whether I want to do that all again or leave it in the bubble. A one-off amazing memory where they drove me wild and gave me exactly what I needed; a respite from my own thoughts.

"Maybe, or maybe that follows us out into the light, but none of that needs to be decided just this second. All you need to do is recover from what we just did and breathe these oils in."

"Okay." I smile. It's small, and it barely meets my eyes. It's forced, but not fake, and it feels weird on my face. Something just a few hours ago I never thought I'd do again.

He drops onto the floor at the foot of the tub, in my eye line but somewhere different, clearly picking up on what set my brain spinning.

"One step at a time," he says.

"Baby steps."

"One baby step at a time."

# TWENTY-ONE

Nick

"Tell me you've got a plan," I say, placing the bag of Ivy's stuff on my desk. But no one is here.

Voices carry from the bathroom, and as I stick my head around the door, I find Wyatt and Ivy laughing, him sat uncomfortably on the floor.

"They've gone to Leo's room to get cleaned up," Ivy explains, tipping her head back and giving me the perfect view down her chest. "They should be back soon."

"Good idea," I reply. "There are clothes and stuff out here when you're ready."

She thanks me and I sneak out, heading across to Leo's room and knocking before entering. I don't need to walk in on them enjoying round two.

"All okay?" Jacob asks, picking up on my tension as I walk through the door.

Leo slides his jeans on, paying absolutely no attention to the fact I'm here as Jacob finishes getting dressed, Leo disposing of the towels.

"We need to talk," I say, following his movements. "About the—" he cuts me off, his hand coming to my arm before I can finish.

"Let's go get Ivy some coffee from that place she likes," he says instead. "Jacob can stay with Ivy and Wyatt if you're worried."

"You just want to get me alone," I fire back.

"Yes, because you're so irresistible." He rolls his eyes, kissing Jacob. "Get over yourself. I'll be in the garage."

The door closes behind him and I raise my eyebrows Jacob's way. The truce between Leo and I has been tentative at best, but if he trusts him, I'll go with it—this is his opportunity to get out though, if he wants to.

"Go and get her some coffee," he says, pushing us out the door. "And if you come back without the almond croissants I like, you're dead to me."

"Who needs enemies when you've got a family like this, huh?" I joke, shoving him. "I've brought her laptop and the workbooks that were on her desk, but I'm assuming Leo has a plan for the classes."

"Yeah, I'll ask her to send the schedule over when she's ready," he says, loitering by the door. "Just go and talk to my man. We've got her."

"This is so fucking weird," I grumble, leaving him and heading to the stairs.

I'm not going to say it was expected to wake up to her rubbing my dick and kissing someone else, because it wasn't. And I don't think she was even doing it consciously, but it took some serious control not to pull her into my arms and remind her exactly who she belongs to.

And then there was that little puff of contentment that fell from her. It was almost a moan, barely a whimper. How could I deny her that?

How could I deny her anything?

Luckily, the house is quiet as I head downstairs, making my way to where Leo waits, fucking great. I can hear the rumble of the GT engine before I even open the door, its sound echoing against the ancient stone.

"You're going to end us early with all the carbon monoxide if you carry that shit on," I comment, climbing in the passenger seat.

"You shouldn't have taken so long then." He shrugs, reversing out and heading towards the driveway.

"Right, you've got me alone. What couldn't be said in front of Jacob? You know, my brother, the one I'm going to tell all this to—in fact, the one your with who you should have probably explained whatever this is to first…"

"I've already spoken with Jacob," he says, sliding his hand along the leather. "But we can't talk in the house, it's bugged."

"Bugged?"

"They've seen and heard way too much that goes on in there for it to not be riddled with cameras."

"Great."

"I found this when I was tidying up the other day," he says, pulling over and opening up his phone. He brings up a picture, zooming in on a small camera above his bookshelf.

"Did you leave it where it was?"

"Yeah, I didn't want to risk alerting whoever is watching, but I haven't seen any others around."

"It seems a little obvious, don't you think?" I ask, handing it back over as he starts the engine again, rolling us towards the main road. "Did you find any when you moved our room around yesterday?"

"No."

"I'd be tempted to say that's been placed by someone else. If there are cameras elsewhere in the house, then they're seriously discreet and well hidden, and *that* is neither of those things."

"Good point," he ponders. "So, what do you know about The Sect?" he asks, pulling out onto the main road and leaving the campus behind.

"They apparently put cameras in your house and are generally pretty scary and unpredictable."

"Yes, but there's more to it than that. The Sect is an elite secret society and membership is passed through bloodlines from father to son."

"But our dad passed away earlier this year."

"Hence you didn't get the full details before being dropped in the thick of it," he explains.

"But you did?" I ask, cocking my head and adjusting the climate control.

"More than you did. They made it sound like it's a level playing field at the initiation, but it isn't, there are only three bloodlines in each intake, the twist this year is that one of them includes twins."

"So everyone else is what, filler? Cannon fodder? Those are real fucking people's lives they're messing around with."

"Messing around. Yeah, that's what they're doing. Fucking about with their futures."

"Huh?"

"Don't you remember what you signed in blood? *I*

*understand there is no way out from here, except by death or excommunication."*

"So, they've been excommunicated. What does that even mean?"

"They're fucking dead, Nick. Don't be so damned naïve."

Fuck.

"Are you telling me we're guaranteed to get through though, with us being the bloodline members?" I clarify.

"If only it was that simple." He sighs. "If we fuck up, we're still out. There's no guarantee in The Sect, but there's also no way the non-bloodline initiates will ever make it to the end. Tamsin was fucked the second she picked Taylor as her partner."

"Let's not mention that to Ivy."

"Wasn't planning on."

We fall silent, me processing what he's said and him waiting.

"None of that explains the flowers."

"No, it doesn't." He pulls down to the coffee shop car park, parking the car as he works out what he's going to tell me about it.

"It's not a coincidence that on the day Ivy's best friend is *removed* from the competition, you get death flowers wrapped in Ivy. You also found that code breaking book ahead of the escape rooms, and the handkerchief before Oliver's tirade that night."

"I think someone on the outside is trying to send me warnings."

No fucking shit.

"The same person that was watching us at the pool by any chance? Yeah, don't think I've forgotten about your sketchy answers."

"My father is a very powerful man—"

"Common theme here," I say, cutting him off.

"In the underworld," he finishes between gritted teeth. "I have two brothers, not by blood, that work for him, and he's holding their lives over my head. Now, I'm not telling you this to get you on my side or for any sympathy, I can handle all that on my own, but I also know that parents don't get updates or details on the initiates until the end. So, he's not sending them, or the clues, but I think they've managed to get them anyway."

"And how would they do that?" I scoff.

This is ridiculous.

Friends sending help from outside, or trying, even though they work for his father who gets no information as to how it's going. Yeah, that makes perfect sense.

"Our connection runs deep, our contacts further. It's entirely possible it's them. If not, I have no idea."

"Does it even matter who's sending them as long as we can figure it out in time? So far we're doing all right, we just have to make it through the next four cuts."

"And the third bloodline is Wyatt," Leo adds.

Shit.

"At some point, they're going to cut one of us."

My stomach sinks.

Ivy is attached to us all.

Jacob is too.

I could even learn to live with them, but who could be

taken from our group without decimating the rest? No-one.

"Jacob and I have our bands, we want to do the swap when we get back and have you and Wyatt witness. I want him tied with me, safe, but I don't know what that does for you and Wyatt," he admits.

"That decision still lays with Ivy, as it should. This thing has taken more than enough from her, I'm not going to influence her choice."

"It would break Jacob to lose you," he says quietly.

"And it will break Ivy further without the supportive guiding hand from Wyatt. We all knew what we had in that room wouldn't last. It was all just a dream wrapped up in a nightmare.

"There's got to be another way," he says resolutely.

Sure.

But if there is, I can't see it.

"I'm going to get the coffee," I reply.

With no answer to this conundrum and no good way to work it out, the best thing to do is to put it to one side and ignore it. To walk away and see if a resolution presents itself at a later date. Sometimes they do.

We manage to get the drinks and get back without any more talk of The Sect or what's going to come in the next few days and weeks.

"Just be careful what you're saying inside the house," he reminds me as we pull back down the driveway. "They've already admitted to  hearing and seeing everything."

"Do you have a way to contact these brothers on the outside?"

"Not safely."

At some point that's not going to matter.

"Let's just try and keep each other in the loop if anything else turns up, yeah?"

"Sure," he agrees.

Jasper's car is back as we pull in, his usual music pumping through the house as we climb out and head straight upstairs, avoiding as many questions as we can manage. I have no answers to anything they might ask, so what's the point?

The three of them are laid out on the bed when we eventually get there, laughing at some joke they don't feel like sharing as I drop Jacob's croissant on his chest and Ivy's cake beside her.

"Sorry it took us so long, I know he's like a bear with a sore head before he gets any food," I apologise, gesturing to my brother.

"I am not," Jacob argues, horrified.

"I'm sorry to agree with him, but you totally are," Leo agrees, placing a quick kiss on his lips before dodging the playful swipe coming his way.

"Did you get my message?" Ivy asks, diverting the conversation. "With the schedule."

"Yep. Classes for the rest of this week are sorted. You'll have comprehensive notes in your inbox within two hours of the lecture. If you don't, let me know."

"You didn't need to do that, just today would have been more than enough," she replies.

"Well, this way you can go back when you're ready," I say, taking a sip of the now-cooled dark roast. "This just gives you wiggle room, that's all."

"Are you two really agreeing on something?" she asks, looking from Leo to me and back again. "That's weird."

"There's nothing I can do about your Zoom training later this week I'm afraid," Leo says, ignoring her jab with a playful smile.

"Yeah, I didn't think even you could work your magic on Timeless Inc." She scoffs out a laugh, but Wyatt's head cocks, some small amount of recognition flaring.

"Something you'd like to share?" I ask.

"It rings a bell," he says. "But I can't place it."

"Well, when you figure it out, let us know, but until then, can we get on with this film? I'm sure I missed the last twenty minutes, at least, and we've still got another one to go," Ivy interrupts.

"Well, before we do that," Jacob says. "I was hoping we could do something else."

Her eyes widen as he takes out the black leather band from his pocket, looking at Leo. Wyatt produces the clippers as Jacob wraps the band around Leo's wrist, securing the two ends with a snap.

"No last-minute option to get out of this one then?" I ask light-heartedly.

"Hell no. He's stuck with me now," Jacob replies with a resplendent smile.

"Same goes," Leo says, producing the band from his pocket, but before they get a chance to finish it, the door bangs.

"Nick, bro, I need you!" Oliver calls, banging on the door again.

"Can you give me five?" I ask.

"I'm sorry to interrupt but it's urgent."

"Fuck. Well, I've seen enough, consider it witnessed," I say, leaving them to finish off before heading out the door to a panicked Oliver.

"Quick, she's down here," he says, taking the stairs two at a time.

The blood in the hallway is the first indication that something went seriously fucking wrong, and as I take in the carnage that used to be the light, bright and airy changing room, I begin to question if I was the right person for this.

"What the hell?"

# TWENTY-TWO

"We can't really finish this without him, can we?" Wyatt asks, taking in the disappointment on Jacob's face.

"No," he grumbles by way of a reply, dropping his hand.

"Well, he saw most of it," I attempt, hoping they'll just finish the thing so we can celebrate together.

"Not enough," Leo says sadly, sliding the band away. "Next time, baby, and until then, I'm still yours." He pulls Jacob in by his waistband, searing him with a kiss that has the heat in the room skyrocketing.

"I think even I need a smoke after that one, jeez," Wyatt comments light-heartedly as he pulls the laptop back out, flicking through, looking for the film we were watching.

"Obviously there's no rush for you to leave, but do you need anything else picking up?" Wyatt asks as the four of us settle in the blanket fort, once again safe and sound in our bubble.

"Probably," I reply. "What Nick picked up is great, but I'm going to need something that isn't loungewear for meeting up with Ruby, and the Zoom class and stuff," I reply, thinking of the empty drawers strewn across the floor. The hangers without dresses. The vanity with no make-up. *What did they do with all her lashes?*

"The five of us are not going to fit in here for very long," Leo comments.

"But I'd rather not go back to your room," Jacob says. "It's got an awful draft, and I swear that spider is going to pop back up and kill me in my sleep."

"There are suites upstairs," I say, not expecting the words to tumble out of my mouth. "Now Nick and I are tied together, and I guess the same for you guys, we could go and find bigger rooms up there…"

The four of us look at the ceiling, the film completely forgotten.

"Upstairs? Where the hell is there an upstairs and how did we not know about this before?" Leo asks.

"We've not exactly had time to explore Narnia," Wyatt replies, throwing a cushion at him. "And the door must be somewhere by your room, so *we* at least have an excuse…"

"Let's go," Jacob says.

We are all up and clambering across the bed at the same time, tripping over blankets, the film completely forgotten as they push and shove to get to the door.

"Ladies first," Jacob says, holding the door open for me, then shoving Leo through with a giggle.

The warning look Leo sends him suggests he'll pay for that later, and I could totally be here for that. They guide me the right way down the corridor, passing what's apparently Leo's room before coming to the end of the corridor, only, instead of the side of Leo's room, there's a corner and a staircase.

Lights flicker on as Leo takes the first step, drawing us further and further up until we come to a corridor. But where everyone's rooms downstairs are labelled with their names, these are blank.

The Pendleton Prep logo sits proudly on each one, surrounded by a marble circle, The Devil's logo, and as I peek in the first one, excitement tumbles over me.

These are more than the basic twin suites the guys have downstairs. The huge bed sits to one side of the room, a comfortable range of sofas taking up the majority of the space in the middle of the room. Wyatt draws back the heavy curtains, flooding the room with light as he peeks out.

"We could stay in your room," Leo offers. "And then you guys could come up here."

"Let's keep looking," I offer, turning my back.

It's not him.

It's the thought of having them elsewhere.

I can't even face the thought of walking back into that house, that room. It's not just my best friend that's been stolen, it's my peace. Your home is supposed to be a haven, somewhere you can go to get away from the dangers hidden around every corner, and now, that place isn't safe either.

We step out, Leo checking out one room as Jacob tries another one, until Wyatt calls, "Guys, I think I've got the solution right here."

"We could just move the beds around if you want us all together," Jacob says, coming to my side. "But is having Leo and I on the other side of a wall really that much of an issue?"

Yes.

Nick was twisted up enough when he had to wait for Jacob to get back after the last challenge, there's no way I want to put him through that again.

Interestingly enough, the solution is the other side of the door that Wyatt guards with a grin. "You're going to love this," he says, opening the door and stepping back.

He's already pulled back the two sets of floor-length double curtains, a fully stocked reading bench set into one, but it's the massive bed that draws everyone's attention.

"That has got to be two beds together," Leo says, heading straight over and looking around the edge.

"No, I've seen these on social media. It's like a family bed or something," Jacob says as we all follow him over.

"It's massive," I say in awe. Six pillows lay across the headboard, jacquard bedding with silver, red, and gold threaded throughout. Like marble.

"All the girls say that," Jacob replies with a wink, nudging my arm before kicking off his shoes and climbing on the bed. "Come on."

He holds his hands out for me, pulling me on and standing me up as he starts to bounce, dragging me and my laughter along with him. Before I even realise it, the four of us are jumping on the bed like a bunch of children, laughing and giggling. Someone starts a pillow fight and I duck out, carefully jumping down and heading further into the suite to explore.

There are two double bathrooms, marble inlaid everywhere, a shower with more heads than even the five of us would need, and a free-standing tub that must be wide enough for even Nick and Jacob's shoulders to fit comfortably, the thing might as well be a jacuzzi for eight it's that big, and I can only imagine how long it would take to fill.

Oh, and how quickly it would empty with us all in, hot, wet skin…

"That looks like fun," Wyatt comments from behind me, making me jump. "But did you see the wardrobes?"

He takes my hand, dragging me away from the thoughts of us all sliding in the bubbles and bringing me back to reality.

The two triple walk-ins are amazing, there are no other words for it. This suite is something else. Well, they're all pretty awesome, expensive and luxurious, but this, this was made for us. It had to be.

"You could stay in the bubble as long as you want to if we were here," Wyatt says, his hands resting on my hips.

He's right.

I wouldn't have to sleep alone in that room. I wouldn't have to face the emptiness that consumes me ninety per cent of the time. The limb I'm missing.

Leo and Jacob are busy logging in to the apps of the TV, sprawled out on the U-shaped sofa sharing a bean bag footstool, and something akin to hope blossoms. We could do this, share a space, support, friendship, and more.

"Is it weird?" I ask, dropping onto the sofa beside Leo, the heat from his leg pressing against mine as I turn to face him. "If we're like… staying together like this."

"Only if you let it be," he replies with a shrug. "I'm not

here to put a label on anything, ever. I can be your friend, I can be your lover, and so can anyone else. Nick might not like it, but he was certainly on board with everything while he had his dick buried—"

"Yep, thank you," I cut him off, waving my hand in the air.

"He's only saying what we're all thinking, Ivy," Wyatt continues. "This isn't us vying for scraps of your attention and us waiting for any small amount of time you have for us. This is us all, you included, saying that we need each other, and we work well together, and we're willing to care and support each other through whatever else is coming our way."

"Of course, you're welcome to stay in the makeshift bubble downstairs," Jacob says, interrupting the thoughtful silence that follows Wyatt's declaration. "But the wardrobe space is fucking horrendous, and I'm assuming returning to the pool house is probably a no-go."

"Thanks for the positivity," Wyatt says with a roll of his eyes.

Fuck, this is a lot.

Yesterday morning I was complaining to Tamsin about the mascara I brought with me, and trying to find out why hers are so much better than mine, and now she's gone and I'm talking about moving into a suite with four guys. Four. Not just the controlling one, or the friend I have complicated feelings for, or the one I like but shouldn't. No, all of them. Awkward.

Except that it isn't at all.

It's as far from awkward as I can envisage.

"Well, I'm in," Jacob declares. "Oliver snores, Leo's room has the spider of doom, and I'm not spending another night where I can't even attempt to turn over. There's more than enough room to do that in there."

"How very practical of you," Wyatt says.

"And how else would you like me to approach this?" he says. "My brother seems to have picked you two and I've got my own Devil, oh, and he seems to want you too," he says, his gaze flicking to mine. "I'm not going to try and dictate or control anyone here, and if it means I get to keep both of them happy and finally have somewhere big enough for my trainer collection, then I'm all for it."

"You sure?" Leo asks, twinning their fingers together, the moment becoming suddenly serious once again.

"Absolutely," Jacob replies with a smile.

"You two are very cute," Wyatt says, interrupting. "But I'm not gay, or interested in either of you… like that, just to clarify, but other than that, I've got your back."

All three of them look at me, waiting.

This answers all the questions we've had for weeks, months. There would be no more going around in circles about who I'm drawn to more, no more choosing between heated friendship, caring protection, and a chemistry that's completely undeniable. No leaving anyone out.

"I can't go back to that house, to that empty room." My stomach twists just at the thought of it. "I'm in."

"Now we just have to show this all to Nick, and move everything up here," Leo says.

"Give me ten minutes and I'll sort it," Wyatt says. "Get the film going."

Leo pulls up the film we abandoned downstairs, a million times better on the huge TV that perches on a dark wood unit rather than the laptop screen.

This is a big bubble, and I'd kind of like to stay in it.

The opening credits for the next film are just rolling when a knock rings out on the door. Confused, I head across the room and open it up, Charlotte, Aimee, Penelope and Stephanie standing there with their arms full of my stuff.

"What the hell?"

"Someone said you had a new room and you needed help moving," Aimee says, barging in.

"And rather than having weird moving men going through your things, we figured it might be better if we did it," Charlotte says with a small smile.

"Well, I'm just nosey," Penelope says with a wink as she walks through. "But I get it. I'd be the same," she calls, heading through the room.

Each of us came with our bestie; Penelope and Aimee, Charlotte and Stephanie, me and… well, it's just me now.

"Are we doing this now?" Leo asks, his head popping up from behind the sofa and dragging me out of my melancholy moment.

"Looks like it."

"Amazing," Jacob says, excitedly jumping up, pulling Leo with him and heading out the door.

"Which one of these are they going in?" Aimee asks, standing by the entrance to the walk-ins.

Between us, we pick a wardrobe and find space for all my clothes, stocking up the vanity and stashing the rest of my study materials in the office I hadn't even noticed.

Apparently, they take the work portion of this seriously now we're together, there are work desks and empty bookcases, places for us to concentrate.

"I just want to say, we don't hate you," Charlotte says, plopping into one of the bean bags.

"Speak for yourself," Stephanie counters, winking my way.

"We totally get why you don't want to come back to the house, but you're still an Angel, still part of us, even if you're living it large in a suite bigger than our entire house," Aimee continues.

"And you have no more cooking," Stephanie says. "I'm looking forward to making use of the chefs here when Olly and I are official, the dinner last night was amazing, no offence Aimee."

"None taken, you're exactly right," Aimee replies with a nod.

"We might have to Zoom from here though. This set-up is perfect, and it means we get to come and visit," Penelope says with a smile, adjusting the cushion behind her as Jacob drapes yet another blanket over the back of the sofa.

"I won't have far to come shortly, anyway," Stephanie says. "Oliver and I will be doing the bands thing soon too. So, we'll just be down the hall."

"You're all leaving us," Charlotte complains, sticking her bottom lip out. "No fair."

"Trust me, you're better off where you are," I counter. "At least that way you won't end up like…" I trail off, unable to even joke about it.

"I'm sure she's okay, wherever she is," Penelope says,

reaching out to squeeze my hand.

Little do they know.

"Just, look after yourselves, okay?" I say, refusing to acknowledge it.

She's gone. They could be too, at some point.

For now, I've got to preserve my sanity as much as I can.

Luckily, Stephanie changes the direction of the conversation and we all start talking about her plans for swapping bands with Oliver. They're not nearly as cute and romantic as Tamsin had been, but it is what it is.

"What's this, a slumber party?" Oliver asks as the door opens, Nick and him finally turning up.

Jasper had been around earlier on, helping the girls and Wyatt to bring stuff over from the house, and I was beginning to wonder what the hell had happened to them.

"Not quite, baby," Stephanie says, jumping up. "But we can have our own one soon. I've seen the perfect suite with gorgeous red drapes just down there. Let me show you." She grabs his hand and pulls him away without another word or a backwards look.

"I wouldn't recommend anyone going in there after this," Penelope says, wrinkling her nose.

"So, you guys picked a room then, huh?" Nick asks, looking around.

Smiling, I nod, going over to take his hand and show him around. It's small, the smile, and it just about meets my eyes, but we can do this, together.

"So, the girls set all my stuff up in here, and we've left space in both wardrobes so you can choose where you want to put your things."

"Cool," he says, looking around, but it's like he's not really here, he's unfocused, his mind somewhere else.

"Is everything okay?"

"Fine. I just had to help Oliver with a thing… I could have done without it, that's all."

"Are you sure?" I ask, turning and wrapping my arms around his neck.

He missed all the touching declarations earlier on, and it must be hard seeing this now we've already started making it our own space. He kisses me by way of a reply, deeply and wholly, waking up the ache in my core that I'd only just forgotten about.

"I'm still yours," I promise, not sure why I feel like it needs saying. "But now, you get to keep Jacob too."

Sure, it's a touch more complicated than that, but Leo's right, we could make this a lot harder than it needs to be, so let's just go with the flow.

"Sounds good."

# TWENTY-THREE

## Nick

It sounds too good to be true.

And if something sounds too good to be true, it usually is.

We all know that, don't we?

"It looks like you've managed to get everything set up beautifully, and if you're ready for people, dinner should be about ready," I offer, doing my best to get out of here.

"With a little help," she agrees, pulling back, her eyes narrowing. "Are you sure it's okay? Is this not what you wanted?"

"Of course it is. We've got a few people tagging along for the ride, but I guess that's okay."

Jacob has Leo, Ivy has Wyatt, and they have each other. They'll keep her safe, look after her in the ways I can't. *I'm not needed here.*

"Let's get some food in you," I say, stroking my hands up and down her arms as I ignore the twist in my stomach. "Then maybe a girls night up here would help?"

"Are you sick of us already?" she asks, but finally a smile graces her face.

"Never," I reply, kissing her quickly. "But you need

to remember you have friends around you, as well as us. You're not alone."

"Thank you," she replies, her fingers still tracing patterns along the back of my neck. "Did you manage to get Oliver sorted out?"

"I did, but that's not a story for before dinner. Come on, let's get some food in you."

She shrugs, accepting that as an answer for now whilst we gather everyone up and head down to dinner, and it's not nearly as awkward as I expect it to be.

Oliver laughs with Stephanie, and Aimee and Charlotte talk together as we enter en masse, but nobody stops and makes a fuss, smiling and waving at Ivy, but otherwise unphased. It's not quite the reception I was expecting, but it's appreciated nonetheless.

The chefs somehow manage to cook for everyone without any prior warning, and damn is the food good. They even agree to put some snack palates together for the girls and their movie night—clearly they've been charmed by the gorgeous women milling around just as much as we have, and I guess it's no surprise.

"So, as marvellous as you all are, who's up for some sparring?" I ask as we finish up.

There's been a lot going on, a lot of shit changing, and fighting helps me focus, it always has. It's the reason our older brother started taking us boxing in the first place, not that Jacob ever really appreciated that, but I did the shit he liked to do too.

"Absolutely," Jacob replies, cracking his knuckles.

"Fine," Leo says with a roll of his eyes, even though I

know he loves the opportunity to get a hit or two in.

"After this afternoon, you damn well better be joining us," I say, pointing at Oliver.

"Sorry, babe, it looks like you're with the girls tonight," he says, kissing Stephanie's head and standing.

Wyatt and Jasper opt to join us but not spar, and after bringing us all together, we split into the Devils and the Angels, just for the night.

"So, what was more important than your brother and his band-swapping thing?" Jacob asks, throwing his shirt on the floor as I fasten the gloves securely. No holding back then, eh?

"Do you want to ask me that now, or when you can hit me?"

Leo smirks, pulling the straps on my brother's gloves before holding the ropes for him to climb through to the ring where I wait, bouncing on the balls of my feet.

"Oliver, do you want to explain this?" I call.

"Nah, you're good," he replies from the rowing machine.

"Enough stalling," Jacob says, feigning a shot to the left before catching me with a right kick. "Just spit it out."

"Someone *saved* a bird from the back garden this afternoon."

"A bird?" Leo asks. "His emergency was a fucking bird? A flapping around bird, with wings…"

"Yep. I guess a cat got hold of it or something. There was a lot of blood, to be fair," I say, my fist glancing off his chest as he moves at the last second. "And feathers."

"So, he found a bird and the two of you magically fixed

it, took it to a bird vet, or what?" Jacob asks.

"Neither of the above. It was pretty fucked up by the time it had finished attempting to flap its way out of the changing room."

"Well, at least you cleaned it," Leo grumbles, watching Jacob land a clean hit against my jaw, following it up by getting in close against my chest. *The shithead.*

Our conversation falls to the wayside as I pummel his ribs, attempting to make space to parry. We go at each other a little longer, the entire thing forgotten as we knock the shit out of each other, that is, until we finish up.

"So, what did happen to the bird?" Leo asks as we climb out, handing us both towels.

"Oh, it was fucked. We put it out of its misery and buried it in the garden."

"I should have totally hit you harder," Jacob says, rubbing the blossoming bruise on his cheekbone.

"You could have tried." I chuckle, snatching back as he half-heartedly swings my way.

"Maybe it should be my turn," Leo suggests, advancing.

"Sure," I agree. "Oliver, you're up."

I throw the gloves in his direction, slinging the towel around my neck as I quickly manoeuvre my way around the machine and away from Leo. It's not that I can't or won't jump in the ring with him, it's just that I have plans for tonight, and they include being able to breathe properly and not needing stitches.

Jacob and I might go at it pretty hard, but we know each other's limits and tend to not pass them. Leo doesn't know them or doesn't care. Circling back around, I join Jacob at the side of the ring as Oliver and Leo spar, testing each other out, not really doing any damage, yet.

"So, what do you have in mind for your mirroring?" I ask Oliver. "You and Stephanie have requested bands, right?"

"Yep," Oliver replies. "I'm thinking about taking a leaf out of your book and kidnapping her after class or something."

"Really?"

"She'd fucking eat that shit up," he agrees before Leo connects with the side of his face, knocking him sideways. "Not here for that, bro?" he asks, connecting with Leo's irritated stare.

"Your girl, your decision," Leo replies with a shrug.

If he thinks he's fooling anyone with the indifferent words coming out of his mouth, he's completely delusional. Even I can see the irritation rippling from him.

"Jasper, you down for helping me out with it?" Oliver calls.

"Sure."

And just like that, neither of them is holding anything back.

Oliver sends a vicious kick into the side of Leo's knee, and Leo connects more than once with Oliver's face, and eventually the two of them limp from the ring—after Jacob intervenes.

I've seen first-hand how devious Oliver can be with his fists, but neither of them comes out unscathed.

"Wyatt, will you be the other Devil for my mirroring thing?" Oliver asks, catching the towel I throw his way.

"I'm not interested in kidnapping the girl, but I'll witness for you," Wyatt replies from the climbing wall, looking down from his elevated position.

"Sounds good."

Leo and I head for the weights, Jacob going to the treadmill as Jasper adjusts the playlist and we all fall quiet, concentrating on the workouts at hand until we're all done, hot, sweaty, and ready to get out of here.

I take the shower in our room, or our old room as I suppose it is now, whilst Wyatt, Jacob and Leo go up to the suite—three of them can use the two bathrooms without issue, but the room feels weird as I enter.

The beds are still shoved together, the pillows haphazardly abandoned, but all of Wyatt's things are gone, and I get my first taste of how Ivy felt when she got back to her empty room. The big difference is that I've known Wyatt for nothing more than a few months, not years, not most of my life. I can't even begin to imagine how she felt.

Turning away from the half-empty room, I flick on the shower, leaving it to warm up before chucking my things in the washing basket and pulling some clean things out. My workbooks glare at me from the shelves, a threat that I should be taking more seriously, because whilst Leo has organised cover for Ivy's classes, the rest of us are on our own.

If we're going to continue to gather around her like this then we'll need to sort out some kind of schedule that means we can still get work done. And so, with thoughts of classes and schedules, I jump in the shower, wash up quickly and throw on a pair of joggers and a shirt, heading out to go up to the suite.

"You know walking around in those pants will get you in trouble, don't you?" Stephanie asks the second I get out of the door, Ivy beside her. "Sweatpants season is totally a thing."

"What kind of thing?"

"It's like man lingerie or something," Oliver says from his doorway. "Don't ask me why, but it works." He grabs Stephanie by the back of her neck and drags her into the room, pulling the door closed behind him.

"I can totally see the outline of your... in those," Ivy says, looking at my crotch.

"Nooo," I argue, leaning over to look. "You guys are having me on, they're just pants."

"Sexy boyfriend pants that you should not be walking around the house in," she replies with a little chuckle, linking her arm through mine. "What are you doing down here anyway?"

"Oh, I needed a shower," I reply. "It just seemed easier to leave the other guys to it, with all my stuff being down here anyway."

"You could change that, you know?"

"I will."

"No pressure."

She says it, but I'm not sure she feels it, probably still too raw from losing her best friend and wanting to cling to everyone she can. Even us.

"What did you watch?" I ask, changing the subject as we head up the stairs together and back to the suite.

"Dirty dancing."

"Well, at least you didn't carry on our film festival without us," I reply, attempting to be light-hearted, despite the stone in the pit of my stomach.

"Well, if you're all back, we could carry it on now?" she offers.

"Sounds good to me."

And as we get in, the guys are already joking about on the sofas, but they light up the second she walks in, and I know exactly what has to be done.

# TWENTY-FOUR

*Leo*

"He's been acting strange, don't you think?" Jacob asks, taking a huge bite from his avocado on toast.

"It's a big change, just give him the opportunity to adjust properly, he's perfectly fine."

"It's not that," he argues. "Something feels off with him."

"Is this a twin thing?" Ivy asks, coming into the kitchen and filling up her travel mug, the silk shorts that barely cover her sumptuous ass a complete crime.

She leans against the counter as he ponders the question.

"Yes and no. He hasn't moved his things into the suite, he's been working away on something in the office that he won't talk about, and he hasn't suggested a gym session, a run, or anything weights-related in like four days."

"And that's unusual?"

"Yes," we both reply.

I hate to admit it, but Nick and I have more than one thing in common. Not least our need to work out daily, our inability to deal with other people's crap, and our care for Jacob, Ivy and Wyatt. It's not much on paper, but we've been getting on better, and it shows.

"I think he's feeling left out."

"I've requested a band," Ivy admits. "It was a spur-of-the-moment thing while I was still in the blur of losing Tamsin, but it arrived yesterday. Charlotte brought it over for me."

"Well, that's not what I thought you were going to say," I admit.

"I'm not going to tell you who to pick, that's down to you, but Penelope has been trying it on with Nick again, and it would be great if we could make it clear to everyone that he's with us and to leave him alone."

"Again?"

"Yes, she's been told categorically that you guys are off-limits, and I thought Jasper had a thing for her anyway?" she says, mug halfway to her mouth, her eyes narrowed in irritation.

"Jasper and Aimee have been spending a lot of time together recently, and she's probably feeling the pressure now Oliver and Stephanie are Sect official."

"If you tell everyone to meet us outside the main administration building in the morning, I'll make a statement that he's off limits, but I'm not going to be pushed into picking one or the other because of the other Angels."

"Thank you, thank you, thank you," Jacob says, and I can practically see the relief on his face. "And then hopefully everything will go back to normal."

"Sure," Ivy says, a sadness still lingering in her eyes.

This isn't normal for her, not normal for any of us, and that's not really what he meant, he wants Nick to be back to his usual self.

"I think I'm going to have an early night," she says, mug in hand as she heads upstairs.

Jacob gets up, rinses his plate and loads it in the dishwasher.

"You watch her like you want a piece," he comments with his back to me.

"I do."

I've never denied how I feel about Ivy, not with Jacob.

"More than you want a piece of me?" The vulnerability in the question takes me by surprise. I thought we were good, stable.

"It's different, not more, not less," I say, abandoning my tea and tipping it down the sink. I add the mug to the dishwasher, claiming his lips in a kiss. "You've never wanted two people at the same time?"

"I'm a serial monogamist," he admits. "And as much as Nick and I have shared and whatever for one night, this is a weird situation for me too."

"I think we're all just working it out as we go," I agree. "But there's one thing you can be sure of, and that's how I feel about you. That will never change."

"It fucking better not," he grumbles, pulling me in against him. "How would you feel about me checking someone else out?"

"You mean like you were doing last night? Don't think I missed it." I chuckle darkly, only imagining the depraved things he had in mind.

Not that Jacob would ever act on them if the guy wasn't interested, but it was more than clear to me Wyatt was drawn, open, and curious. It wasn't just the feel of Ivy's lips wrapped around his dick that got him off.

"Will you two get a room," Jasper says with a wink, grabbing a bottle of water from the fridge. "I am not cleaning jizz off the counter."

"As if you clean it regardless."

"Good point."

"Oh, Jasper, Ivy wants to say something tomorrow, would you let everyone know to meet first thing outside the administration building?"

"Sure thing," he says, waving us off as he leaves. "And not on the counter, guys, that's just gross."

"You look like a snack," I argue. "I should totally eat you here."

"I think you do that in the dining room," Jacob argues. "And don't we have people waiting for us upstairs? Maybe they're already making the most of Ivy and her early night?"

"Hmm," I agree. "We could work with that."

It takes forever to get up the two flights of stairs, the anticipation building, only for us to find Nick working away on his laptop and Wyatt watching the TV, Ivy wrapped up in the middle of the bed looking absolutely tiny. *Well, that's not what we had in mind.*

She still has the shorts on as I draw the sheet back, climbing in beside her, not that she's asleep, her hazy gaze coming to mine.

"Do you mind if we join you for your early night?" I ask, running my hands up her thigh.

Ivy and I have always lived along the edge. I'd do anything for her, without question, and aside from that almost kiss, neither of us has made a move, but that's about to change.

Her skin is so soft it's practically unreal, and she's warm and cosy, until my meaning sinks in. If I'm wrong and she's not into this, or me, that would be fine, albeit a touch awkward, but I'd deal.

"I thought you guys were… together?" she whispers, looking at Jacob who's snuggled up behind me, the big spoon so to speak.

"Oh, we are," Jacob replies lazily. "But it looks like you are too."

"Oh." The surprise on her face is cute, the blush even more so.

"So, you wouldn't be upset if Leo and I…"

"Nope."

His breath skitters along my shoulders, making a shiver ripple down my body, and he notices, they both do. She shuffles forward, her breasts pushing against my chest, her legs tangling with mine before her beautiful green eyes come to mine, her softness at my front and his hardness at my back, and a peace washes over me that I didn't realise I was missing.

The danger of the situation we're in disappears into nothing but background noise when I can feel their breath on my skin, their heat on my body. It's a heady combination, especially when Jacob reaches over, taking hold of her hand and placing it against my already swelling cock.

Her eyelids flutter, and I really can't wait, pushing into their hands as he squeezes her smaller fingers around me, my lips coming against hers as I close the distance between us. Her tits press into my chest, and Jacob thickens against my back as I rock against the two of them.

The others haven't noticed anything yet, certainly not the three of us grinding against each other fully clothed in the bed just a few feet away, but when Ivy breaks away, pushing my pants down, I have a feeling they're about to.

"Can you show me what he likes?" she asks, a tentative vulnerability in her gaze as she looks at Jacob over my shoulder.

He must agree, the two of them shuffling before he pulls my sleep shorts off completely. There's no hiding anything now, my seriously hard dick stood proud and leaking as the two of them lay right there.

"He's going to enjoy anything you do," Jacob starts, swiping up the sticky precum and sucking the tip in his mouth before releasing me.

He wraps his fist around the base, offering me up like a dick lollipop, but I miss everything else he suggests as the two of them take turns in winding me up until I'm more than ready to sink into someone or blow my load on the spot like a horny fucking teenager.

"Jacob, get your fucking ass up here," I growl. If the other two still haven't noticed yet, they're about to. "And get those pants off. I want your dick in my mouth, and I want it now."

"So bossy," he whispers to Ivy, the two of them sharing a secret smirk that is certainly not a secret.

Eventually, Jacob gets his damn pants off and positions himself above me, Ivy getting herself comfortable between my thighs. I suck his balls into my mouth as he leans down, lapping along my length at the same time as Ivy whilst I buck up between the two of them. Absolute fucking heaven.

Wyatt and Nick join us, the two of them finally getting a clue about what's happening in the room around them, their obliviousness astounding. Parting Jacob's cheeks, I drag my tongue down to his greedy hole, lapping around as he moans before teasing back up and moving him so I can finally get him where I want him. In. My. Mouth.

Jacob's commentary is minimal and panted out through hissed breaths, but Wyatt does something that has Ivy shivering and stumbling, pressing her forearms into my thighs, Nick seemingly just enjoying the view… for now.

Ivy cums hard, swallowing my dick like a pro, intentionally, or otherwise, and it drags me over the edge with her, her hot mouth more than I can take while Jacob fucks into my face, pinned between the two of them like the greedy bitch I am right now.

Jacob pulls back, stoking his dick hard before cumming across my chest possessively, until Ivy runs her fingers through it, dipping one in her mouth, and the other in mine. But it's not just his taste on her, it's hers too, and I wonder what else I fucking missed, lost in the heat of the three of us.

The moment is broken as Nick flips her over, pulling her thighs apart and pushing straight in. It's a dominant display by anyone's standards, but it doesn't last. Grabbing the first thing I can find, I wipe my chest clean, Wyatt and I taking a nipple each before Jacob lifts her head, sliding behind her as he pulls her into his lap.

Nick's eyes flare, the angle changing as he pumps harder, Ivy's spent body giving everything and more as he holds her hips in place, chasing the high. He cums on a roar, his body shaking and shivering as he slumps over the bunch of us, a tangle of sated limbs.

"Fuck," Ivy says on an exhale of breath, Nick pulling out.

He returns with a pair of warm cloths, doing his best to clean her up on his shaky legs whilst I wipe down my chest.

"You lot are going to be the death of me," he mumbles, taking the cloths and discarded clothes and dumping them in the washing basket.

The five of us slump under the sheets, no words left to be said as the sleep Ivy had been chasing finally catches up with her. Wyatt and Nick aren't far behind, and as Jacob and I lay there, tangled together, I finally ask, "Do you think that was enough to make him feel part of the group?"

"Not really," he admits in the silence of the night.

"Nudge Wyatt, I have an idea."

****

"Are you sure you want to do this?" I ask, the rest of the Devils and Angels standing behind us as conspicuous as a black sheep in a field of white.

"Absolutely." She nods. "You guys have made your statements, and now it's my turn."

It takes five minutes, but soon enough there's a crowd gathered around, the majority of those supposed to be in lectures in nothing but ten minutes, I'm sure, but still no sign of Nick or Jacob.

Carefully, I check my phone again, hoping for some kind of message, notification, or explanation, but there's nothing, until the gathered crowd silences, a car door slamming behind them.

"You're all more than aware that the Angels of Pendleton Prep are off-limits. I'm here to make it clear that the Devils are too," she says calmly.

The assembled people move as he carves a determined path through them, his sights set on one person. *Her*.

Ivy stands tall and proud beside me, Wyatt on the other side of her as we bolster her courage and backup our Angel. But she's not only *our* Angel, she's his too, and as he strides towards us, his commanding steps bringing him closer and closer, you can cut the tension with a knife.

She doesn't fidget as his gaze locks with hers, doesn't cower beneath the weight of his stare as the silence stretches around the courtyard. There's not so much as a whisper that scatters through the masses as they all wait for this moment, the moment he claims what's his. Ours.

Except, as he climbs the three steps towards us, his gaze flicks to mine, the briefest second of concern swirling through the familiar green tint. *It's not him*. My jaw clenches, and my fists match the movement, but nobody else sees, nobody else understands.

He stops just short of Ivy, looking at Wyatt and then me before holding his hand out for her, letting her come to him. There's an apology written on the tip of his tongue, but I don't hear it, nobody does, because the words never tumble from his lips.

"The Devils are ours," Ivy says, as she steps into his embrace, one hand sliding around her waist, the other threading through her hair as he drags her to him, their lips meeting in a clash of tongue and teeth, animalistic in their brutality.

Looking away, I scan the crowd, those that came to watch, to see, waiting for something or someone to catch my eye. Someone that's not supposed to be there, or something that just doesn't feel right, because it'll happen, it has to.

But… the noises.

He growls, the sound drawing my attention firmly back to Ivy and Nick, only it's not Nick, it's Jacob. She pushes and he pulls, and I can't help the jealousy that swarms in the pit of my stomach, fury that nobody else even sees.

Except, Ivy does, she has to.

She pulls back, removing his arm from her waist and threading her fingers through his and waiting, his forehead pressed against hers as their chests bound against each other like they've run a marathon.

His hand slides from her hair as he squares his shoulders, drawing himself to his full height before looking at me and nodding. It's a small movement, one barely noticeable by the people that surround us, but it's an acknowledgement all the same. As much as that pained me to endure, to watch, it wasn't easy for him either.

He turns, guiding her to his side as Wyatt and I box them in. Closer. Together. A unit.

"We are The Devils of Pendleton Prep, and this is our Angel."

The whispers begin then, a ripple that cascades through the crowd. They know of The Devils, and they know of The Angels, now they can put faces to some of them.

"She's ours, and we're hers. Anyone who thinks they can take what's mine, what is ours, I welcome you to try."

I can't see it, too busy scanning the crown for the face that shouldn't be there, the brother I haven't seen in too long, or someone else, but I can imagine the dark grin that spreads over his face, the devilish twinkle that Nick is famous around here for.

"I wouldn't bother attempting anything with The Devils either," Ivy clips. "Nobody here plays nice."

And with that, we walk. The four of us. United. Together. And the rest follow; Stephanie and Oliver, Jasper and Aimee, Charlotte and Penelope.

The sea parts as we march towards the parked cars, nobody daring to so much as breathe in our direction.

The doors on the X5 close silently as we pile in, Jacob and Wyatt in the front, Ivy and me in the back.

"What the hell is going on?" I ask, deadly serious as we pull away.

"We've got a problem," Jacob replies. "It's Nick."

*To be continued*

***

Thank you for reading His Angel, I hope you enjoyed it.
Get ready for more in Their Hell:
www.goodreads.com/book/show/194928475-their-hell
Can't wait for more? Keep in touch with me here
https://authorhlpacker.com/keep-in-touch/

# ACKNOWLEDGEMENTS

So, keeping on with the theme from Her Devil, I'm going to start this section with the so-named 'stars of the show'.

Nick – So, I'd like to start

Leo – I'm sure you would *grabs mic* but you're not the only one around here. *Chuckles* So, I didn't get chance to say much in the last book, but I'm hoping you're all finally coming around to see the truth; he's just a dick and I'm the main man, am I right? Anyway, I wanted to just say thanks for being here, for seeing our journey play out. I'm not really sure what the hell this author thinks about portraying me this way, but hopefully she's gonna sort it out next time, yeah?

Ivy – And that's enough of that, thank you very much. *rolls eyes* I just want to thank you all for still being here, it's been something, that's for sure. I know things are getting a little hairy right now, but trust the process. The author, she's got this, and if she doesn't then we sure do.

Well, that was fun!

So, for me, the author, I have to start with thanking my husband. I've been deep in book world for so many weeks at this point that he's had to pick up just about everything and that's no mean feat around his own stuff. Thank you listening to me ramble about characters and the weird and wonderful things they're getting up to, the corners that I've written myself into and the ways I can get them back out.

Thanks, babe. You rock!

A big thank you to the team; Angela, Karen, Fay, Aliana, Christina, LeeAnn, Donna, Adina. Thank you all for the multitudinous things you do and the feedback you provide. You're an essential part of the process and I appreciate everything you're here for, you're all amazing!

And, of course, a massive thank you to anyone who picked this book up and read it; whether you're a blogger, a reader, a reviewer, and it doesn't matter if you got this as part of the book tour, if you're in the street team, or if you purchased it at your retailer of choice, thank you for taking the chance on this book and the insane characters that live inside it, they're driving me a little crazier each day LOL

# About the Author

HL Packer is quite frankly, a busy bee.

When she's not running around after her free-spirited three children, and husband. You can find her tending to the dogs, bearded dragons, and snakes that also reside with them.

When she finished her office job for maternity leave, her husband purchased a Kindle E-Reader to give her something to do, and oh what a journey that has been. From reading to reviewing, then blogging and creating Romance Readers Book Box UK. And now, her own words being put out into the world.

When she is not coordinating her worlds, you can find her soaking in a bubbly bath or enjoying a glass of wine, often still with a book in her hand.

Newsletter: https://bit.ly/3rdYAny

_Also by H.L. Packer_

**Fated Series**

Home

Within Reach

Within Hope

The Shadow

Amore

La Familglia

The Ties that Bind

The Bonds That Break

Broken Lies

Fractured Truth

**Pendleton Prep**

The Sect

Her Devil

His Angel

PENDLETON